THE LAST SUNRISE

MARTIN SHANNON

PRAISE FOR THE LAST SUNRISE

"This is vampires done right."

DOUGLAS W. LUMSDEN - AUTHOR OF
TROLL WALKS INTO A BAR AND
OTHERS.

"Classic vampire stuff, cranked up to eleven and with a modern twist. Every step of her undead life is engrossing…"

5 - STAR AMAZON REVIEWER

"Mr. Shannon does not spare us from his talent for writing violence and I like it that way."

4 - STAR AMAZON REVIEWER

"I loved this novel to pieces! Marvelous story, fresh ideas… Brilliant."

5 - STAR GOOD READS REVIEWER

For my fellow bloodsuckers.

CHAPTER 1
IDLE HANDS

I LEFT my brother in the car. Okay, before you give me a look, he's twenty-two, it's not like I left some kid in the back seat with a bottle of water and a cell phone. Come to think of it, I did leave him in the car with a burner, but it had snakes on it, so at least he had something to do.

Not that it mattered.

He would forget just about everything by the time the sun came up, and when it did, both of us would have to go to ground. It wasn't like we had a hole in the earth we crawled into. This was Florida, any hole in the dirt would just end up filled with water.

Still, we couldn't risk the sunlight.

Neither of us.

Not anymore.

My name is Mallory Evers, and I'm a vampire.

Wow. That feels really good to get off my chest. I mean, I'd been thinking about it for a long time, ever since everything in my life went to absolute shit, but I never really got it out like that before.

Yeah, that feels better.

I leaned against the car door while Nate sat inside and raced his thumbs over the phone's glowing buttons.

Yes, it has buttons. I bought a burner phone at the quickie mart. We were just lucky it worked and had a game he could play.

We needed to conserve our cash.

I put a hand on the back pocket of my jeans and let my fingers trace the wad. Girl jeans sucked, but they would have sucked more if we'd had anything in the way of cash.

We didn't.

So those tiny pockets were just fine to hold the equally tiny stack of barely sufficient bills.

It was hard to get cash when you couldn't really hold down a job, or weren't interested in murdering people for it.

This is the point where you are asking yourself if I'm a vampire, why don't I just kill people and take their money?

Well, if you're asking yourself that, then maybe you should be asking yourself if you are volunteering? If so, then step right up while I peel my face apart.

Yeah, there's that too.

Before you get started, I didn't ask for any of this. I didn't get some special deal, some offer to live forever in exchange for a little non-ritualized bloodletting. This was done to me, and to Nate.

Nate.

Nate was the twenty-two-year-old sitting in the car playing snakes on the phone. He was a good kid. Hell, he was only a few years younger than me, and a little better looking too, if I was being honest, but he wasn't much for applying himself. Even worse, the one time he'd thought he was making something of his life, he'd ended up in the wrong place at the wrong time.

Of all the drug dealers he could have hooked up with…

I let that thought go and turned away from the flickering screen, and the glow in my brother's eyes.

I could still keep it together.

He couldn't.

Sadly, that realization had taken me a while to come around to, and because of that, people had died, good people. People that had only been trying to help us. Now I had to keep him close. I couldn't trust Nate on his own, not in the shitty old shack we stayed in during the day, and not at night when we came out.

The phone was keeping him busy for now, but he'd need to feed soon. When his face unfolded it didn't come back together until he was full of blood.

Nate was a big eater.

I pushed all that away and focused my attention on the bar. My brother might not remember those drug-dealing bastards or the thing they brought to our apartment, but I did.

It had taken me months to track them down. It was hard to do when you couldn't go out during the day. Thankfully, the vermin I needed to lean on spent most of their time prowling at night.

Still, it wasn't like I could just walk up to them.

They thought I was dead, and being dead, like being undead, had its advantages. I wasn't about to pull that band-aid off until the last possible second, when I knew I had them cornered and ready to give up the asshole who'd done this to Nate and me, even though I had no hard proof. I was convinced whatever it was they'd done could be undone.

If not for me, then for Nate.

The kid should have a life.

I'd had my chances and screwed the pooch, but he still had a shot at making something of himself.

He just needed to have the IQ of a normal person and *not* be a blood-thirsty face-eater.

I glanced at my watch, and then at the door. They had to be inside. The shit bar was pretty far off the highway. Far enough that I was a little concerned at how long it would take for us to get back to the concrete cave before sunrise should things go sideways.

Things always seemed to go sideways.

Even now the edge of the distant horizon had put on a pinkish hue.

That was something I'd never really appreciated. Working nights and weekends, spending my life slinging booze and fending off the drunken advances from men twice my age, I'd missed seeing the sun rise.

I knew it happened, but I'd never really bothered to appreciate it before. I promised myself when Nate was safe, cured, and functional, then I'd see the sun rise one last time, and it would be fucking glorious.

I glanced at my watch again. There was no waiting anymore. If I was going to confront those assholes and figure out what they knew, then I was going to have to do it now.

I turned back just long enough to get a good look at my brother. I waved. He never looked up. It was just me, waving at myself, all five foot nothing with mangy auburn hair, and a cliche metal concert shirt tied off so that I wasn't swimming in it.

On the surface there was nothing about me to be afraid of.

My lips rippled in the glass like an angry dog and I had to put a hand up to make them stop.

It was what lay beneath that gave people nightmares, me included.

I pulled a ratty trucker cap out of the back of my jeans and shoved it over that mess of ragged hair. This was my Clark Kent disguise. All I needed was some glasses, but I hadn't found any yet. I was just lucky I'd found the hat on the floor of our borrowed hovel.

I took one last glance at Nate to remember who I was doing this for. His almost feral face lighting up in the phone's faded glow.

Just sit tight, bro. I got this.

I left him in the lot and pushed my way inside. This part of the bar wasn't much more impressive than the outside. It was one of those post-western swamp style cajun bottle jockey places. I'd done a few beer girl stints in places like these during my illustrious younger years. Given the clientele and decor, this was just the sort of place I would have excelled at.

Show a little skin, get a tip.

Then again, after a few seconds panning the walls and counting the number of rebel flags, snake heads, and the pair of gator skulls mounted above the bar, I wasn't quite so sure. A tip here might be the front edge of a knife against your neck and a recommendation to get those clothes off faster.

A quick scan of the rest of the bar didn't make me any happier.

They weren't here.

I checked my watch again. Everything I'd been told pointed to this being the place and right before closing being the time, but they weren't here. There was nothing that resembled the assholes or their South American freak of nature.

Shit.

Given the proximity of sunrise, I had no choice but to call it. I'd lean on my contact tomorrow night. I'd lean on him hard.

I wasn't halfway to the door when a warm and decidedly blood-rich hand grabbed my arm.

"Hey, sugar tits, how about you come sit with me?"

He fit the mental image of exactly the sort of guy who uses the term "sugar-tits," right down to the dinner plate belt buckle, snakeskin vest, and copious chest hair.

He wasn't my type, at least not yet.

I liked them bleeding.

"Really?" I pretended to pout. I was terrible at most of that shit, but it's amazing what you can fake.

As a woman, I'd learned to fake a lot of shit.

"What, you don't want to sit with me?"

I put a hand on his. "Oh, no. I was just thinking we could take this outside? Like, to my car or something? It would be a lot more private."

I could tell by the way his sunburned cheeks flushed with tasty blood that this was not the response he had been expecting.

"Yeah."

"Good," I ran my finger up his hairy arm. "And don't worry. I don't bite… much."

CHAPTER 2
NO BATTERY

HE WASN'T FOR ME.

He was for Nate.

Yeah, I know. Those are questionable morals. Well, I never said I was human. I just said I preferred not to murder people and take their money.

Besides, taking one more user of the phrase "sugar-tits" off the board might actually be considered doing a public service.

Still, we never reached the parking lot. No sooner had we moved toward the door, than my real prey wandered inside. Long and stringy, with muscles honed through years of questionable activities and coated in a thick sheen of sweat and tattoos, Nate's former drug bosses were pretty easy to spot.

Thankfully, I was not.

The trucker hat and my stinky arm-candy gave me the anonymity I wanted. They sauntered right by and made tracks for the bar.

"Which one's your car?" the road grit asked, his face a vomit-inducing picture of desperation and sleaze.

I contemplated sending him to Nate, but then I remembered how messy my brother had become. The car would be ruined, and getting a new one would be next to impossible for a few days. By then the stench would be eye-watering and attract attention we didn't need.

Instead, I dragged him just outside the door, and pointed toward the distant edge of the darkened gravel lot. "It's right over there."

"Wher—"

Sugar-tits dropped like a stone, my fist landing in that soft spot beneath his ears and just under his jaw.

The Magic Button.

There were a lot of shitty things about subsisting on human blood. You had to brush your teeth—a lot—and it ruined any clothes that weren't black, but it did come with some benefits.

I was a damn bit stronger than I looked.

I grabbed his feet and dragged that guy's sorry ass around the side of the bar. He'd wake up eventually, and when he did, he might consider using different terms for the next lovely lady he met.

Lovely lady? You're pushing it, Mal.

I was pushing it, but I was also pushing something else —hunger.

It had been a while since I'd fed. I didn't know the rules, because the nearest I could tell I wasn't supposed to be alive. When you aren't supposed to survive, I imagine no one bothers to worry about telling you how life is going to be when you get up.

My lips twitched. Like a flag caught in the breeze, they rippled just enough to remind me what was on the other side.

Just a taste.

I clamped a hand over my mouth.

There was no such thing as 'just a taste' and I knew it.

I took a second to stop myself, then shoved a hand in his normal sized pockets.

Bingo!

His cash wad was bigger than mine. Not a lot bigger, but that was gas money, and if we needed it, something more.

See? Just like I said. I don't kill people and take their money. I just take their money, especially when they call me sugar-tits.

I pushed the wad into my small pockets and promised myself I'd get boyfriend jeans just as soon as I found a boyfriend, but cash and the additional utility of fat pockets weren't my priority tonight.

My mission was inside the bar, and the sun was coming up soon. I needed to find out what they knew about the South American man-mountain who did this to us. Where was he? What had he done? And what would it take to get him to undo it?

That last part was critical, if not so much for me, for Nate. Speaking of my brother, I found him exactly where I left him, still playing with the phone quietly in the car.

I had no idea how much battery was left on that thing, but with any luck I wouldn't have to find out. I paused at the dark glass of the bar's only door and waited for my lips to stop dancing. They did, but they didn't like it.

We compromised.

After I got what I needed, they, and the snake-like stinger behind them, could enjoy all the drug-dealer blood they wanted.

My face returned to normal, or what passed for normal anymore.

It was time to get some answers.

I slipped back into the bar to find it largely unchanged in the ten minutes or so I'd been gone. The few remaining patrons didn't appear to be in a hurry to move on, and their drinks weren't showing any signs of flagging.

Still, as tasty as they looked, those blood-rich truckers and their hearty American cuisine-infused arteries weren't what I was here for.

The guys I'd come for were just behind the bar, talking it up with a girl whose eyeshadow game made raccoons blush. They didn't linger long, a slap on the ass and a hand through the hair and they were gone, leaving through a door behind the wide, wooden counter.

Oh no, I'm not losing you that easily.

Thankfully, it didn't take long for raccoon-girl to get caught up with someone or something else and give me a chance to slip by. Her tiny body and sprayed-on top reminded me of myself in the early years. I would have taken a job like this, and I would have gotten pushed around for it. I'd have pushed back too, which was probably why she slathered on the eyeshadow.

I added that to the list.

Once I had what I needed, I'd tear their fucking faces off.

That made me smile.

I pushed the door open quietly and slipped inside.

There wasn't much to write home about: beer case boxes, some wire-shelving, and a handful of kids hog-tied on the dirty tile.

The smell of sweat, urine, and something else equally vile hit me front and center. I'd been expecting to find those assholes, and maybe a bunch of drugs, but this was not on my list of potential scenarios.

Neither was the knife to my gut.

The taller of the two skinny jerks I'd followed back here hadn't wasted a second. I'd been far too focused on the bus-load of rugrats they had on the floor to notice him spring out of the boxes, blade in hand.

What got me even more was how much it *hurt*.

See, I've been stabbed before, and shot at, and run over. Shit, there were plenty of ways I'd had the crap kicked out of me, but they never really hurt.

This was pain, real pain, and I crumpled as he rode me to the ground. Somewhere along the way I lost my trucker hat, and with the one and only piece of my Clark Kent disguise gone, it didn't take him long to figure out who I was. I didn't know who was more surprised.

"It's that kid from Ybor's sister."

"I thought she was dead." The knife-wielding asshole's partner-in-stupid appeared next to his buddy, their faces already long since burned into my memory.

"Yeah, I did too. She must have found a way to change. Well, look at you. Maybe you're worth keeping around after all." He dug the knife deeper into my side, and I swore it nicked at my spine. "She doesn't look feral at all."

His partner nodded. He had that look that said: "I have two brain cells and I rub them together for warmth whenever I can."

Our peanut gallery of tiny witnesses stayed quiet. No doubt they knew just how dangerous these two jerks were, but they didn't know how dangerous I was.

Even *I* didn't really know that.

I let my lips go. I wanted them to peel apart and free the stinger trapped beneath.

I was a monster now, and I was hungry.

Nothing happened.

I must have looked pretty damn confused, because that got a laugh from the two of them. "Somebody's never taken silver to the gut. Fucks with you pretty good, doesn't it?"

Silver.

What the hell was this, some sort of old school joke?

Next they were going to tell me I needed to avoid garlic and holy water. I tried to pull the stupid blade out, but no sooner did I get my fingers around it than it started to burn.

"Son of a bitch!"

That outburst solicited a few laughs from the lanky twins.

"Yeah, hurts like a bastard. At least that's what they tell us. Here's the deal. You aren't supposed to be here, and you sure as shit weren't supposed to change. So, here's what I'm gonna do. I'm gonna enjoy myself, and then I'm gonna shove that silver into your skull. I tell you what, I'll even let you pick the hole. How's that for being generous?"

He dropped to one knee and ran a finger over my face. I wanted to bite that thing off, but nothing I would have used to do that worked.

That was right about the same time someone screamed from the bar.

It sounded like raccoon girl.

There was only one person I knew who had that effect on people, and I'd thought I left him in the car.

Batteries must have run out.

CHAPTER 3
BULLETS FOR BREAKFAST

"WHAT THE HELL IS THAT?"

Hell? Yep, that's pretty much exactly what that was. You see, I could control myself.

Nate was another story entirely.

My brother lacked the part of his head that said: "Maybe I shouldn't tear this person's face off and suck the flavorful innards out?"

I got the impression, based on the shouting, slurping, and general sense of hysteria on the other side of the door, that the batteries had run out on my convenience store burner phone.

"How the hell should I know?" The asshole who'd stabbed me with the fiery hot knife of silvery suckitude removed a gun from his waistband.

That was good. Nate could eat bullets for breakfast.

Breakfast…

The sun was coming, and when it got here I'd be stuck. Or worse, they'd drag me out into the front parking lot to welcome the last day of my life.

I *was* going to get my last sunrise, but I wasn't doing it until Nate could watch it with me and sweep up my charred remains.

"What about—"

Mr. Knife, who I guessed was Julio based on what limited information my brother had been able to provide before his brain turned to gelatin, chambered a round. "She's not going anywhere. That's silver. She's screwed until I take it out. Come on."

And with that, they left me to languish on the dirty tile.

It wasn't long before the gunshots started, and they were followed by more screaming.

Yeah, that was Nate.

Damn it!

If he killed them we'd be right back in the same dead end spot we'd spent the last few months in.

As much as I loved sleeping huddled in the corner of an old concrete one-room shack off the highway, and hoping to hell the roof didn't blow off and vaporize us on a hot, sunny day, I'd been really looking forward to finding the monster who'd done this to us in the first place.

One, because I was tired of watching my brother erode, and two, because after I fixed him, I was ready to see the sun again.

All of these grand aspirations hinged on not killing the only two guys who could help me find the person responsible for this mess.

To do that, they needed to be alive, and not spending the rest of their days on a ventilator either.

I tried to move the knife, but Julio was right. I couldn't touch the damn thing without wanting to scream.

Shit.

Judging by the sounds outside, someone was still in the bullet stage, and that was when it dawned on me. These guys weren't complete idiots, even if I was. They knew to stab me with a silver knife. What if they had silver bullets?

What if that was what they were shooting at Nate?

That was a visual I didn't need, and judging by the sounds in the bar, it might be accurate.

I wasn't getting the distinct sound of Nate tearing someone apart with his bare hands.

Come on, Mal, move!

I pushed myself to a seated position, but that was about the extent of my range of motion. The damn silver was doing a number on me.

The kids!

"Hey, kids."

I'd never been a babysitter, or had any desire to own dolls, let alone play with them. The fascination with kids was completely lost on me, so it was no surprise the combination of shouting, guns, and my lack of anything resembling a comforting tone, did little to improve the working situation.

They cried—a lot.

"No, guys. Don't cry. I'm here to save you."

I mean, I guess I was. In a roundabout sort of way.

Aside from being tied-up, they were also blindfolded, because that must have been one of the rules of shithead human trafficking.

All it meant was it made things so much harder for me.

Great.

"Listen, guys. I'm sort of running into a problem here. I've got this big knife stuck in my belly, blood's everywhere. Wow, does it smell good. You guys picking up on that? I mean, damn, top shelf. It's like premium vodka. You know? Not the cheap stuff, either."

Mallory, they're kids.

Right, they've probably only seen the cheap stuff.

One little boy raised his head. Of course he couldn't see me, but he appeared to be decent at tracking my voice.

Way to go, Daredevil.

"Yeah, what do you want us to do about it?"

That was not the response I was expecting. Still, this one

wasn't crying, and that alone made me appreciate him all the more.

"I want you to scoot your butt over here and pull it out."

More gunshots in the front of the house set my already frayed nerves on edge. Nate could have eviscerated the entire bar by now, but someone was still firing.

The kid tilted his head like he was weighing his options, which seemed odd because he really didn't have any. "What's in it for me?"

"I set you free."

He frowned. "You're lying."

"I am not—Second thought, I let you keep the knife."

"Deal."

That little shit flopped on his back and wormed his way over the tile. I had to give him a lot of credit. It was hard to wiggle around all tied up like that. Now, how I knew that was decidedly not PG rated, but still, from first hand experience, I was impressed.

I did the kid a favor and pulled up his blindfold when he arrived. Turned out he was a good bit older than I expected.

His little blue eyes gave me a once-over. "Damn, you're hot."

Eww…

"And you are like, what, ten?"

"I'll be thirteen next month."

"That's great. I'm not showing you my boobs. Get the damn knife out."

The little man deflated like a spent party balloon, but twisted his body around enough to pull the damn silver blade out of my gut.

The effect was immediate, and I suddenly had a genuine appreciation for how the lion felt when the mouse pulled out his splinter.

I was only mildly tempted to drain the mouse where he lay.

My rippling face was majorly tempted.

"What the hell?" The kid's eyes told me my evil was showing.

"Yeah. Hell is right, kid." I reached out and snapped the plastic tie-wraps holding his hands together. "You need to get your little buddies and get out of here before the bigger one shows up."

"Bigger one?"

A crash from the bar couldn't have been timed better. All the color drained from my savior's face. I couldn't help but imagine how tasty it would have been had I done that and not the fear.

I shook that thought away even as my lips peeled apart like the skin of an overly ripe banana. "Go. Now!"

The preteen knew his way around a knife and had his own feet free in seconds. From there, it wasn't long before he set to work on the rest of the sob brigade.

I didn't have time to watch the industrious little soldier do his thing. I had to feed.

I faced the door and let it go. All of it. I often wondered what it would be like to live like Nate, to just be. I kept it under wraps as much as I could, but the monster was there. The flailing folds of my face were just the beginning. Buried beneath them were fangs and razor-sharp teeth, hungry to tear through flesh and bone.

But all of that was just a precursor to the real star of the show, the stinger.

A second tongue that coiled deep in my throat.

It was there, waiting, and primed to siphon up blood by the gallon.

Precious blood that would keep me alive.

I wasn't afraid of the monster I'd become, and that was what worried me.

I pushed through the door and into a blood-splatter scene from the best of slasher movies. Julio was there, but his partner had long since vacated his mortal coil. They had used silver bullets. The smoking holes on my brother's chest proved as much, but somehow he was still standing, and more than that, he had his fang filled lips wrapped around Julio's neck.

There was a gurgle and a pop, and that was the end of our best lead.

"Nate!"

My brother's eyes had gone full red. He wasn't processing anything. He was the full definition of living 'in the moment.'

Nate was blood and Zen.

An idiot kid poked their head out behind me just in time to get my brother's full and unadulterated attention.

"Nate, wait, stop, don't—"

My brother was bigger, faster, and full-up on go-juice. It was nothing for Nate to plow through me like a cheap piñata. He crashed through the door and into the back of the house, newly freed kids screaming in a more than justified panic.

I am my brother's keeper.

I didn't like kids, but that didn't mean I wanted them dead.

CHAPTER 4
LIKE ME

I SCRAMBLED AFTER NATE, but even without a silver blade dangling from my gut, I wasn't able to match his speed.

Whereas I was built for attitude, bad-manners, and passive aggressive violence, my brother had all the aesthetics of a mack truck on the run-away vehicle lane. He tore through the door and left little more than splinters to hint at his passing.

I ran in behind him, only to find the back of the bar in a panic. My little knife-wielding hero had freed about half the kids, but they'd all removed their blindfolds.

I was pretty sure there was nothing quite as terrifying as seeing Nate in full blossom.

His face was like mine, flappy and loaded with sharp fangs. The difference was, my brother reveled in it. He had his stinger up and out, and swinging back and forth like a snake on the prowl.

This was how it always went with Nate, but even I had to admit he was getting worse. Normalcy and my brother were not accepting each other's calls at the moment.

Still, it wasn't like I was the bastion of stability and grace, but I wasn't a goddamn movie monster on steroids.

The hero kid swung Julio's silver knife back and forth in front of him like it would do shit against my brother. I didn't have the heart to break it to him that Nate had taken silver bullets to the chest, and not the ones that come in a pop-top can from Colorado.

The kids screamed, and that only got Nate's blood pumping faster. My brother's already split-face swelled like the wings of a falcon.

Shit!

I let my own jaws go as far as they could, then did the only thing a little sister knows how to do.

I jumped on his back.

Nate had a lot of pounds on me, but even he couldn't out-muscle physics. Having a pissed-off Mallory land on your shoulders made it hard to stay upright.

Nate tumbled forward, but not before wrapping his stinger around a young girl's leg. The serrated edges of my brother's rope-like tongue sliced through her jeans effortlessly.

She cried and the sound only drove my brother into a foamy lather.

Damn it, Nate!

I hooked my legs around his shoulders and grabbed the stinger. The same sharp edges that had torn her pants did a number on my hands. Blood dripped from my fingers and coated an already red and pulsing tongue.

"No, Nate!"

He didn't listen. He couldn't listen, not when he was like this, and he was rapidly becoming just like this all the time. I'd had to hammer in a damn chain in our concrete safe-house to keep from waking up with him ready to snack on my face.

And that moron just killed our two best chances of finding a way to save him. With a flash of silver, my little hero man detached the tip of my brother's stinger. He'd saved that little girl's leg and sent my brother into hysterics in the process.

An angry Nate wrapped his strong hands around my head.

He was going to chuck me off. So I did what any other vampiric sister would do. I latched onto his neck with the strongest thing I had, my jaws.

Blood, glorious and unceasing blood, flooded over my jaws and down an unquenchable throat. It came with power, rage, and smoothed out the sharp edges.

Everything came into focus, and as it did, the world slowed down.

Each beating heart rang out like some holy chorus-line of life.

Then there was the smell, a visceral wash of life, sweat, blood, salt, and God knows what else. All of it blended into a perfect concoction of heavenly bliss.

It was life in its purest form.

To live on the blood of others had put me at the top of the food chain. I was the apex predator, surrounded by prey—tasty prey.

I dropped Nate out of my hands, his tired body slumping on the red-streaked tile. He would recover, and quickly. He always did. My brother might be stupid now, but he was strong, and that strength made him deadly.

He would be back.

I turned my attention to the tiny morsels scurrying like a school of confused fish around the storeroom.

I would enjoy them one at a time.

A flash of silver gave me pause. Something in the back of my head said that was dangerous and should be avoided.

I shook off that worry and let my stinger drop out.

The knife-carrying kid cut the last captive free, while one of them discovered the back door.

In an instant, my dinner had gone from front and center to streaming into the purplish light of pre-dawn.

I raced for the open door, only to have my path blocked by

an indignant appetizer. He rattled off words, but they came out bent and twisted. Whatever he said, it couldn't get past the blood.

The blood was running the show, and I did what it wanted.

My stinger shot out and caught his wrist. The flesh-slicing edges of that perfect weapon cut grooves in his pink skin.

He yelped and the silver blade hit the ground.

Whatever my muffled mind had been worried about, it vanished like smoke in the wind.

Still, even trapped, my dinner had fight in him. The kid twisted and turned, fighting the stinger's pull.

I let him. It was fun.

I had a fish on the line and enjoyed toying with him. He pulled me out into the dimly lit parking lot behind the bar.

I laughed at his futility and yanked him back, reeling the kid in like the catch that he was.

He swung his tiny fists, but they did nothing. I'd felt worse at the hands of violent men, men that maybe he would have grown up to be.

I snapped a hand out and wrapped it around his neck, then slammed the scrawny snack against the pavement.

My hips pinned him down, while my jaws swelled like the wings of a great bird. I would feast on his blood, and revel in the joy of being for another night.

The kid cried and shouted something, but again the words didn't make any sense. I lost them to the beating of a blood-rich heart.

My stinger pulled back for the final strike, when something caught my eye, something I'd forgotten.

Bright and glorious, with a fiery light all its own, the sun broke over the horizon. Those first orange and yellow rays sliced through the parking lot, past the sitting cars, and across the young man's face.

There, reflected in his eyes, I found the monster I'd become, the monster I'd always been.

Being changed hadn't made me this way. That ship had sailed many years ago. Becoming this thing hadn't turned me into something else, it had only brought out what I really was.

Maybe that's what it had done to Nate, too. Maybe he was a brainless thing, because he was never meant to be anything else.

I hesitated, my lips sealing up slowly in the painful light.

My last sunrise…

I'd promised myself I would see it eventually, but that wouldn't be today.

Golden rays burned my stinger, and it went to ground. It dove deep into my throat to lick its wounds.

I pushed the kid away and scrambled for the door, my legs suddenly churning like they were caught in quicksand.

For his part, my tiny victim didn't run. He stood tall, ringed by the light of a star that rejected me.

This was his time, and his world. If I stayed any longer, I would become dust and ash.

I dragged myself to the back door. Blisters bubbled up on my arms and across my neck. They swelled and then popped in the fiery light.

I slammed the door shut behind me, smoke drifting off burnt flesh, my numb fingers struggling with the lock. I found Nate on the floor and rolled him over. My brother's body had already ejected the silver bullets like skin pushes out deep splinters.

He would heal.

I would too.

But, deep down, I knew it didn't matter. I was just prolonging the inevitable. We had no leads. The only people who had known anything were dead on the floor in the other room.

I dragged Nate into the corner and pulled some broken-down boxes over top of us. We just had to rest, survive the day, and then we'd be fine.

Rest.

Survive.

Those were the only thoughts in my head as a small face appeared in the empty space that had once been occupied by the door to the bar.

I tried to move when the kid snuck in, but the day was too strong.

Heavy eyelids closed slowly, unable to hold back the morning. My last visual was his face, the silver knife, and a look of pure clarity of purpose.

He reminded me of myself, even as he dragged the sharp edge across my arm, and placed his lips on the blood that flowed.

So much like me.

CHAPTER 5
FREEZER BURNT

MOVEMENT.

They say when you sleep in a strange place, your brain doesn't let you rest completely. Your mind stays half awake, keeping tabs on your surroundings, the unusual sounds, and the movement.

It was that last part that made me functional again.

I opened my eyes and took in the back of the bar. It was just as ruined as I left it, with Nate next to me, and the faint smell of a kid who I owed my life to.

The boy was gone, but Nate and I weren't alone.

Two heartbeats echoed softly from the front of the house. One of them was moving fast, *too* fast. I was no doctor, but that was an overworked ticker if ever there was one, the other heart moved at a snail's pace in comparison.

There were more smells, caustic ones. The sharp scent of gasoline, followed by the acrid odor of melting plastic.

Yellow light slipped in around the edges of the door, followed swiftly by smoke. It didn't take a degree in rocket science to realize what was going on.

Someone was burning the evidence, and us with it.

"Nate, get up." I pushed the cardboard blanket off and

struggled to rouse my sleeping giant. I was tired, too tired. It didn't take long to realize there was still daylight making its way through the opening where the back door should have been.

"Nate!"

The heartbeats were gone. They'd left not long after the fire started. It was just Nate and me now, trapped in a blood-soaked prison and about to be roasted to perfection.

My brother stirred. His lazy eyes opened just enough to take me in, then closed again.

"Okay, if you want to die, then fine. Me? I'd rather not be char-broiled."

I scrambled to the rear exit. Light flooded in, and it was Nate that kept me from running out into the fading day. My brother wasn't much for talking, but it appeared he wasn't much for boiling alive either.

"Damn it, Nate. We have to get out of here." I pointed to the smoke, and now flames slipping through the seam from the front of the bar.

It was fire or sun.

What a way to go out.

There had been a time I'd worked in a bar like this one. When I'd had regulars, a reasonably steady paycheck, and a life. All of that was gone now. Mallory Evers might be undead, but her life was very much dead and buried. I made a motion for the outside again, but Nate put a stop to that. Even with the considerable strength not-living provided, there was no way I could overpower my brother, not if he got angry, or hungry.

I'd learned that lesson the hard way.

The big man's jaws rippled. Those two fleshy sides, like the wings of an angry raptor, flared just enough to remind me who the strong one was in this relationship.

He might be tougher, but the change had cooked most of his noodle.

Before all of this, my brother had been a pretty smart cookie. Smart enough to get into college, but sufficiently emotionally stunted as to drop out before graduation and go into drug selling as a career.

It was his fault we were here, at least partially, but it was also mine for not keeping him from going off the rails.

Mom hadn't left me much in the way of directives, but she had said take care of your little brother, which I figured included not letting him turn into a face-eating monster.

Sorry, Mom.

Nate raised a hand to block the heat spilling out from the bar, his lips fluttering in frustration.

"Right. Like I told you. That's fire. You remember the campgrounds with Mom as a kid, don't you? Fires. They were, like, the only part you enjoyed, that and stealing moon pies from the rich kids."

My brother banged on the wall and left a hole in the concrete.

"Right. It sucks. It would suck a lot more if we were breathing right now, but we aren't. So hey, small wins. We need to get the hell out of here before not breathing is the least of our concerns."

Nate frowned at the door, and at the sunlight slipping through the seams.

"I know. The sun is bad, very bad, but pretty soon that fire is going to make it back here, and then we'll be screwed either way. We just have to find the first place to hide as soon as we get outside."

A brief flash of panic lit up Nate's face.

"I know there's not much. It's a parking lot. Maybe there is a car we can hide under, or maybe we can make the tree line."

Nate shook his strong neck.

"Yeah, the trees are thin, I know, but it's something. We

find some wide palmettos. We get under them, and we hang on."

My monster-sized brother's hand shook. He didn't like the sun. I couldn't blame him, I didn't either, not anymore. But it was that, or burn up in the oncoming fireball. I put a hand over his.

"Nate, look at me."

I waited until the big man made eye contact. It was immensely hard for him to do that anymore, but he would do it for me.

That was all I needed.

"I'm not going to let anything happen to you, do you understand me?"

There was hesitation in his eyes.

"I'm serious. I got us this far. I'm going to get us the rest of the way. I promise. We're going to find the guy that did this to us, and I'm going to squeeze his balls until he undoes it. I told you that, and I meant it, but in the meantime I need you to listen to me, and do what I say. You got it?"

He slowly removed his hand from the concrete and let those wide shoulders slump.

"Good. We have one shot at this. Follow me and do exactly what I say." He nodded.

"Okay then." I put a hand on the door frame and closed my eyes.

What the hell are you doing?

I'm saving my brother and surviving. Mom always said I was the survivor in the family.

'You're like a cockroach, Mallory.'

Thanks, Mom.

I grabbed Nate's hand and raced into the light.

The sun was low in the sky, but that only meant it had an easier time hitting us. My skin burned in seconds, that fiery star doing its worst faster than I could hope to stop it. Nate screamed something, but I lost it in the haze of pain.

The lot was empty.

There were no cars.

Shit.

I pulled Nate onto the sidewalk, but my brother yanked me back toward the dark of the bar.

"No! It's a death trap. Come on!"

The sidewalk burned and the sun flayed the skin from my arms. I'd picked the wrong night to wear an old concert tank-top. It had looked cute when I found it, and now I'd look cute melting in it.

I dragged Nate away from the bar, searching furiously for some place to hide. The trees were too far away, and too sparse. This part of the state wasn't much more than scrub palmetto and slender pines. We'd boil away to nothing out there in no time.

Freezer!

A big metal cooler lay pressed up against the concrete. It wasn't much, in fact it didn't look very big, but maybe if we tried we could both fit inside. We didn't need long, just a few hours and the sun would be down.

I dragged Nate to the metal doors and pried them open. The thing wasn't cold, in fact it was hot as an oven, but it would be dark, and that was all that mattered.

"Help me!"

My brother grabbed the back of my jeans and tossed me into the sweat box. I scrambled to make room, but there was little to be had.

"Nate! Get in. We'll find a way. Get inside, now!"

His face bright red and peeling, my brother hesitated. Even in his state, he could tell there was no making that work. The box was only big enough for one, and just that.

I tried to claw my way back out and give the big man my spot, but Nate's strong hand pushed me down.

"No, you get inside. I can make the tree line. I'm faster. I'm smaller. I can hide, you get inside and I'll—"

He slid the metal door shut.

"Nate!"

I tried to pry it back open, but he'd jammed the lock. My arms were too burnt and tired to fight it.

He was out there. My brother was in the sun and panicked.

I had one job, to keep him safe, and I'd failed. And now I had hours to lay in the dark and think about only that.

Just stay alive, Nate.

Please just stay alive.

I'll find you.

I hope.

CHAPTER 6
SCOUT'S HONOR

THE TIME TICKED BY SLOWLY, each agonizing minute passing like an hour in that metal death box. If I could have sweat to death, I would have, but I didn't sweat anymore.

There were a lot of things I didn't do anymore, but worrying about my brother wasn't one of them.

Nate was all I had.

And he was out there, in the sun.

I banged my fist against the side of the metal a few dozen times, then stopped the instant the sirens arrived.

Fire Fighters…

There were at least half a dozen of them, judging by the muffled heartbeats. They moved about the gravel like a well-oiled machine, dragging what sounded like hoses and heavy equipment.

Like an idiot, I reached up to slide the heavy lid a crack. It budged, but just enough to send a scalding beam of sunlight slicing across my cheek.

I hissed and pushed it shut.

That was stupid, Mal.

It was stupid, but it was also desperate. Hunger had a way of making stupid ideas look smart.

How long has it been?

Muffled heartbeats, pounding like kick-drums in that gravely parking lot, were busy letting me know just how long I'd gone without feeding.

Too long.

You open that lid and you die.

I had my fingers back on the hot metal before I realized it, and it took even more strength to yank them back the second time. There was blood out there, glorious blood. Even through the metal I could smell it. The scent drifted through the seams like a cool breeze after a heavy rain.

I wanted it. I needed it.

You will die.

So what?

I raised a fist to bang it against the walls of my makeshift prison, but stopped just short.

What about Nate?

Nate's dead.

Two words, they were only two words, but they burned worse than the stupid sun boiling overhead. Was he gone?

My fingers returned to the blisters sprung up along my cheek. They were the result of a couple seconds in the sun, how long had Nate been in it? Minutes?Hours?

I tried to imagine a scenario where he'd gotten away, where he made it to the tree line, or found some hollowed-out trunk to crawl into. But deep down I wondered if he was still that smart, that resourceful, that capable.

I huddled against the oven-hot sides of my metal prison, lusting after the blood and heartbeats moving about only a tantalizing distance away. They might as well have been on the moon for all the chance I had at reaching them.

More minutes ticked by, my thoughts turning from food to guilt.

I should never have brought Nate. I should have left him in that concrete cave. I should have charged up his phone. I should have—

His phone! It took me a second to pull my scuffed-up unit out of a woefully undersized pocket, and even longer to mash the button down until it came on.

I'd made it to the late afternoon, but the sun wouldn't set for a few more hours. I ignored all that and focused on the buttons, firing off a text to my brother and hoping he'd have the wherewithal to see it, and maybe the smarts to fire off a response.

Nate, you okay?

Sent.

That might have been the first message, but it wasn't the last. I spent the next few hours in that steel cell sending messages, chewing through battery and willing myself to stay hopeful. He was out there, somewhere, and when night fell I'd find him.

I told him as much in yet another string of texts.

At some point I drifted off. My fingers were tired and my eyes blurry. I didn't know how much time had gone by, but the sound of a door slamming shut startled me from my slumber.

Heavy steps on the gravel outside let me know it was a man, and a big one at that.

Loud and proud, his heart beat like a dinner bell just beyond the walls of my cage.

"Yeah, honey. I'll be home soon."

He paced quietly, those thick boots moving in ever-narrowing circles. "I know you made steak. You told me you were going to do that this morning. Yes. Yes, it sounds lovely. No. No, I'm not doing this on purpose. Well, I mean, I am, but only because it's my job. Steaks don't grow on trees."

But maybe they do show up on doorsteps…

No messages from Nate. I tucked the phone in my pocket, then put both hands on the sliding top.

It was cold.

"Five minutes, maybe ten. The guys said it burned like there was an accelerant. I just need to check a few things."

I pulled softly, turning my face away the instant the lid opened expecting to get yet another searing blast to the face, but that didn't happen.

Stars… There was still a faint pink hue to the sky, but the sun had long since dropped below the tree shrouded horizon.

"Just a few things. Damn it, woman. I promise you I'll be home in a few. I don't know. Put them in the oven on low."

I slid the lid open a little further, listening to him pace and following the sound of those feet. It was the heart beating in his chest I couldn't ignore. That, and the blood. It drifted on the smoke and ash, a rich blend, a meat-eating medley of strength and vitality.

I needed it if I was going to find Nate. I needed all of it.

"Honey, honestly. The longer you keep me talking the more dried out it's going to get."

I found him not far from his car. Both the vehicle and its owner appeared to have believed in the motto 'bigger is better.' The monstrous SUV blocked most of him, but from what I could see there would be plenty of blood, plenty and to spare.

My lips rippled and I didn't bother to stop them.

It was blood, then Nate, in that order.

Arms tired, cramped and sore from being stuffed in that box, it took me a lot more effort than I expected to drag my body over the lip.

Clang!

I hit the narrow strip of concrete with a thud, but it was the trailing elbow against the metal that made the real noise.

"Hang on, honey." His feet moved fast on the soft gravel. "I think I heard something."

I scrambled under the car, sliding my tired and hungry body beneath those massive tires.

"Yeah, listen. I should call you back."

They were right there, two cowboy boots, dusty and speckled in ash, but it wasn't the leather that called to me. It was blood. This close he smelled like fast-food, burnt wood, and tobacco.

It was an oasis to a woman dying of thirst.

"Okay." he turned, his back to me and to my swelling jaws. "Yes, I love you too. I'll see you shortly. Scout's Honor."

He wouldn't be seeing anyone tonight, or ever again.

I shot out from under the monster car, propelled by hunger and need for blood. He didn't turn around before I hit his feet. The big man crashed into the gravel, a hungry woman on top of him in seconds. I didn't hesitate. I didn't debate the morality of my actions. I let my jaws unfold like the menu of some cheap roadside diner and wrapped them around his neck. The skin broke easily, burned by the sun and coated in a salty layer of sweat. It was not unlike jerky, but it was the blood on the other side that mattered.

It was all that mattered.

I gulped it down, losing myself in a sea of red. I was deep in it, too deep to notice him twist beneath me, or to get his hand on something metal.

Boom!

At close range, the bullet shattered a couple ribs and cost me my grip on dinner. I scrambled to my feet to find a flashlight in my eyes along with the barrel of a still smoking gun.

Blood trickled down his shirt. It stained the tan fabric and called to me.

"Holy fucking shit, Mal? Mallory, is that you?"

No. I wasn't Mallory, not anymore. I was the hunger and he was the dinner.

Watching the blood make its way down his shirt made me

think of the woman on the other end of that line and how she was right.

You don't want to let the meat dry out.

I lunged, or at least I think I did. It was all a blur, and it blended nicely with the gunshots that followed.

I'm coming, Nate. Your sister is coming, she just needs to top off the tank first.

CHAPTER 7
FRIENDLY MURDER

THE BLOOD FLOWED. It wasn't fine wine, or any other stupid poetic euphemism. It was metallic, hot, and salty. It was everything I wanted it to be. I was deep in it, lost to the roaring in my ears and the pain it washed away, when the gun barrel found my chest.

I'd been shot before, but never this close.

The explosion of heat, gunpowder, and burning flesh pushed me back.

"Shit, shit, shit!" He fumbled with the weapon, the modest sized man doing his level best to keep it between the two of us, while his other hand went to stem the tide, but there was no putting back what I'd taken.

My chest spit the bullet up, the dull metal slug falling harmlessly on the pavement at his feet.

"Hello? Jim, can you hear me?" A cracked phone shined up from the pavement, its screen a blur of colors and fragmented faces. "Jim? Did I lose you?"

You did.

"Vicki! I'm here, call nine one one! Tell them to send the police to—"

That was the last of his message, the phone didn't work

anymore, because it wasn't a phone. It was just a lump of glass, plastic, and metal caught between my fingers.

"Please." Jim's eyes moved between the broken phone, my face, and the rapidly mending hole in my chest. "Please. I don't want trouble. Let me go and I'll get in that car and drive out of here. I promise."

"No."

I was surprised my words worked, typically this far in they didn't. This far down it was only the hunger, the need, and the rush of the blood.

This was different. I should have been crawling over him to take the rest of it, but I wasn't.

I was too busy remembering our first date.

We'd been teenagers at the time. The early kind, all elbows and awkwardness. I remembered when he came by the apartment to pick me up, and how I tried to hide my family. It hadn't worked. Dad had been drunk and wanted nothing more than to answer the door and rough up the fat kid taking out his daughter.

I remembered running past him, grabbing Jim, and dragging my first real date into the parking lot, all while the old man screamed bloody murder from the door.

Bloody…

I shook off the memory, batting it away like a hungry mosquito.

I was here for the blood. If I was ever going to find Nate I needed my strength, I needed a clear head. I needed—

"Mallory? Mallory Evers? It's you, isn't it?" Jim wasn't feeling the wound anymore. The blood trickled through his fingers and down his shirt, but he'd stopped paying attention to it.

He stopped thinking about it because that's what happened when I bite people, but somehow this was worse. This wasn't just some random asshole or grabby drunk. This was my first date.

This was Jim.

"I…"

He saw it in my eyes and lowered the gun. He didn't have the strength to pull the trigger anyway. "It is you… I knew it."

"I'm sorry about your neck, Jim."

"My neck?" He started to take his hand off and stare at those red fingers when I scrambled over to press it right back against the flesh. "What's wrong with my neck?"

"Nothing, Jimmy. Nothing."

"Mallory Evers." He turned the words over in his mouth like they were butterscotch candies, warm and pleasant. It had been a long time since someone had said my name and actually cared. "The one that got away."

"Jim, I need you to focus. Do you have a radio? I need to get you an ambulance, and I need to do it yesterday."

Eyes glassy in the coming dark, Jim slipped back against the pavement, my fingers replacing his on the deadly wound. "Why didn't you call me back?"

I kept one hand on his neck and used the other to feel his pockets. I found cigarette gum, a chain wallet, and a set of car keys.

No radio.

"I called you a bunch of times." He said the words again and again, and each time he did so he lost a little more of what kept him alive.

"Lemme guess, you always got Dad."

Jim tried to nod, but that only made the bleeding so much worse.

"Damn it, Jim. You're gonna bleed out on the damn pavement."

He is, because you killed him.

"I am?" My old friend tried to sit up, but it was clear he no longer had the strength. "That's a shame."

"It's more than a shame. It fucking sucks."

"Tell Vicki I love her, okay?" His head lolled to the side and then snapped back up. "The dinner is gonna get dried out!"

"Right. We can't have that."

"No…" The big man's eyes fluttered, so I slapped his cheek a few times.

"Oh no, no sleeping yet. You never kissed me, remember? You got too nervous."

Eyes that should have been focusing drifted off in the twilight. "I didn't…"

"You did." I put his own hand on his neck, for what little good it did, then found the gun on the pavement. I slipped it in my pocket and dragged big Jim toward the car.

What are you doing?

I'm helping a friend.

A friend you murdered.

I shook those thoughts away, then pushed the heavy man across the back seats. Bits of his life covered the floor, no doubt bouncing around as he drove. Stuffed animals, the kind little kids have, and a spare shoe. It wouldn't have fit on my hand.

Damn it, Jim.

I fished the keys out of his pocket and crawled into the front seat. I wasn't ready for the reminders of life that waited for me there.

A beautiful blond, a little on the chubby side, smiled from a picture that dangled from the rearview mirror. I ripped it down and jammed the key in the ignition.

"Stay with me, buddy. We're gonna get you fixed up."

That was a lie. There was no fixing up Jim, just like there was no fixing up me. The big man's heart had stopped somewhere between the pavement and the car, and I'd simply refused to accept it.

Just like I'd refused to accept what I was.

The steering wheel rumbled gently beneath my fingers,

the dead man in the back seat turning the cushions red. His blood was in me, but it was more than that. It had to mean more than that.

He'd had a life, one that was far worse off for having known me.

I idled on the gravelly pavement, wiping away the stupid tears that came, and I was still there when the flashing lights of cop cars lit up the ruined bar.

I fingered the hole in my shirt, and the perfectly smooth skin beneath it.

This is who you are now.

Sirens switched to static, then commands. I was instructed to get out of the car with my hands up. I wasn't interested in their punishment. Vicki's smiling face stared up at me from the seat.

I had my own punishment.

The picture folded up nicely and slid easily in one of my tiny pockets. I'd take it out again, at the last sunrise. I'd like Jim's wife to watch me burn, because I deserved it.

"Get out of the car with your hands up!"

Sigh.

I pulled the handle and kicked the door open. Judging by the heartbeats, there were at least four of them, and one wasn't long for this earth.

Not that any of that mattered.

I stepped out, my hands in the air, and fingers stretched.

Just be patient, Mal.

"Turn around and get on your knees!"

"No."

"Turn around and get on your knees or—"

Those were the last words I heard. I let go. Vicki was in my pocket, and she'd have her justice on the last day. I promised the pictures as much. She could join the peanut gallery of tortured souls that watched me burn, but for now we had something more important to do.

Nate was out there, and I had no idea where. To find him I'd need to be strong.

To find him I'd need blood.

Gunshots and shouting descended into fear and madness with the unfolding of my jaws.

Tonight I was the monster, and nothing else mattered.

I moved from man to man, no longer seeing them as people, but only obstacles. They were in my way, a challenge to be bested, a body to be brought low. I moved with the power of Jim's blood, the life that it gave, and the drops of precious love he'd had for his Vicki.

She would never know me, but I now knew her. I knew how she smelled, the softness of her skin, and the depth of her love for the dead man in his truck. I was a creature of revenge, pain, and death, and I reveled in it, right up until I found the kid's eyes behind the squad car glass.

CHAPTER 8
WRONG THINGS RIGHT

BURNED AND WEAK, his little face pressed up against the fogging window. They must have picked him up somewhere, but they didn't know what they had. I grabbed the door and ripped it open, the thin metal shearing beneath my fingers.

He looked up, tired, weak, and stretched thin.

He came with memories: memories of Nate, of the apartment, and of blood. No sooner had I put a hand on him, than I received a bullet for my trouble. The metal slug cut a line through my chest, in one end and out the other side.

I got a bullet, but I gave back hell.

There was little room for thinking. The hunger had taken over. I hit him like a linebacker, my shoulder cracking ribs and driving that padded body to the ground.

There was panic in his eyes, fear of who or what I was. That terror drained away beneath wing-like jaws built for death.

"Watch out!"

I wanted to hear the kid's words. I wanted to make sense of them. But they couldn't make it past the blood. It was a thundering herd of wild horses. It came with memories, both

43

beautiful and violent. I absorbed them all, the emotions, the pain, and the dying. I was lost to it when the burning started, and it took the smell of curling flesh to pull me back.

More slugs lanced my chest, but they weren't much more than a nuisance, it was the light from the shooter's flashlight that brought the pain. Pale blue and anything but normal, it scorched my pale flesh effortlessly.

It was like the sun, but so much worse.

I stumbled to my feet, but the light followed. Skin flaked away, turning to ash beneath the bulb's withering gaze. I turned to run, to make a break for the tree line and leave the man and his killing lens far behind. I didn't make it far, maybe a dozen feet, before the light became too much.

I hit the gravel hard. The killing light passed over me, cutting across the cab and the young man sitting in it.

He screamed.

For just a second, he wasn't some kid, he was Nate. He was my brother, pinned beneath a darkness too big for him to bite or claw his way out of.

I'm coming, Nate.

The confused officer hesitated, not knowing what to do or who to turn his killing beam on.

A little hesitation was all I needed.

I gathered what strength I could and turned back at him fast, aiming low and trying to stay out of the bulb's burning glare. I knew it worked when my shoulder found his legs and when the first knee popped. It was a satisfying sound. My prey was wounded and wouldn't be running.

There would be ample blood to consume.

Jaws flared wide, I pounced, not thinking of the gun or the devilish light attached to the top of it. My fang filled lips had only grazed his thigh before a bullet and burning light chaser ripped through those majestic and bloody wings.

I scrambled off of him and tried to regroup, but the hesitation he'd shown was long gone. This was a man on a mission, and he didn't appear interested in stopping before he'd finished the job.

Blue light scorched my lips, turning their edges to ash and curling what was left like paper in the fire. What damage the bullet did was nothing compared to the unholy fire spewing out of that bulb.

Get up, Mallory!

I tried to move, to block the beam with my hand, but it was merciless and unrelenting. Porcelain skin turned to char beneath the pale blue glow. He fired shot after shot, bullet casings falling like bottle tops on cheap beer night. It wasn't the slugs that took me to the brink.

It was the light they rode on.

Was this my last sunrise?

No, Mallory. Get the fuck up, now!

I wanted to listen to that voice, to follow it, to do what it said, but while the spirit was willing, the flesh was charred and weak.

I'm sorry, Nate. I failed.

My brother was out there somewhere, had he been burned by the sun, or some policeman's flashlight? Was his body a charred and blackened mess like mine would soon be?

Did it matter?

More bullets came, but I barely registered them. All I could see was the light, the final moments of a life that should have ended months ago on my apartment floor. My tired fingers found the crease of my pocket, and the picture that lay inside. I wondered if this would be enough for Jim's wife. It wasn't a sunrise, but it was just as deadly.

I closed my hand around that soft fabric, nails cracked and peeling away.

I'll see you soon, Nate.

The blue light of my midnight sunrise flickered, and then vanished. Glorious night rolled over me like a warm and loving blanket. I blinked at the sudden change, and at the scene playing out in front of me. My little man had found his legs and had thrown everything he had at our angel of death and his killing beam.

The teen threw weak fists, connecting where he could, but it wasn't enough, not yet. He wasn't me. He wasn't Nate. He was dying.

Blue light flashed and the young man cried again, but unlike me, he could move, he could change his position.

What he couldn't do was eat a bullet.

Boom!

His quick and lively body came to an abrupt stop, the blue light and its bullets unthinking in their destruction.

I didn't like kids, but that didn't mean I wanted to see them murdered.

"No!"

There were no flashy moves, no high-speed collisions. The blue light had seen to that, and the bullets that had followed it had sealed the deal. I didn't need speed, or power. I only needed to pick my target, and to get lucky.

Burned jaws, like the wings of a wounded bird, swelled and latched onto his arm. He tried to turn the devil's light, or the gun it was attached to, but my fangs cut that short. Hot and salty blood poured over ashen lips. It soothed the cracks and filled the gaps. It gave me what I needed, and what I couldn't live without.

There was something else in that blood, something more important. There were flashes of Julio, and his partner in crime, images of the children, and more than that, there was a picture of the thing that had done this to me.

I kicked the gun and its killing light away, then scrambled over to his pale face.

"Who are they? Where are they? Tell me where they are!"

Eyes rolled back in their sockets and a quiet heart slowed its beating.

I slammed his head against the jagged gravel, once, twice,

three times, but there would be no words coming from his dead lips.

I let him slip free of my blackened fingers, and in that moment I realized there was still one heartbeat left, a small and weak one.

I crawled over the gravel on tired hands, finding the kid burned and bleeding. The bullet had torn its way through young, pink lungs.

He was dying.

I scooped him up in my arms, his blackened cheek pressed against my chest. I carried him, half-walking, half-limping to the scrub palmettos and slender pines.

We didn't make it far before his breathing slowed to a wheezing gasp.

I dropped my back against a rogue cypress, its thick trunk dark against the indigo night.

"You wanted to be like me. Well, this is it, kid."

His eyes opened, focused yet tired. They brought with them memories of Nate, and of that first morning, and the blur of it all. I couldn't remember the details, but somehow I'd saved him. Somehow I'd saved my brother, and maybe doomed him in the same breath.

No one deserved this life.

Part of me wanted to lay the boy down and let whatever was coming happen, but there was another part of me, a more calculating part, that felt decidedly different.

I needed a connection to Julio and to the rest of them. I needed a way to find them, to get back in, and I had it in my arms.

Mallory…

I knew that voice. That was the sound of guilt and regret. I pushed her away and let my jaws swell. Somewhere beneath those fleshy wings a stinger danced under the stars.

If I could save Nate, then I can save this one too.

It was fractured logic, the thoughts of an addict that doesn't know what stopping is, let alone how to do it.

I let all that go, the guilt, the pain, and the fear. I let it go along with my jaws and the blood that followed.

I didn't know what I was doing, but it felt right, and so very, very wrong.

CHAPTER 9
MOTHER'S DAY

THE SUN.

It was coming. It would always come, again and again, unceasing in its torment. Today was no different. It tugged at the horizon, pink like the fleshy insides of my swelling jaws.

Had I been back in the concrete cave that would have been fine. A boxy dump on the edge of derelict strawberry fields, it was perfect, or as perfect a place as I could get.

My name is Mallory Evers and I'm a vampire.

The thing is, I won't be one for long if I don't find us some cover, and fast.

The young teen shifted at my side, his body covered in a thick blanket of pine needles and palmetto fronds.

The change was coming, robbing him of his warmth. He'd shivered most of the night, but that just meant the end was close. Soon his jaws would tear themselves apart in a rush of blood and pain.

Not long after that, a second tongue would emerge and signal the beginning of his new life in the dark. Maybe he'd find his own concrete castle, his own fallow field?

That wasn't my concern.

You're a shitty mother.

I was a shitty sister too. Just ask Nate. He'd tell you.

If the sun hadn't burned my brother to jerky.

The young boy stirred again, the debris I'd heaped on him having trouble staying where I put it.

That made sense, most of the men in my life tended to have problems staying where I put them.

A memory of Nate's face in the burning sun came back to me, blisters sprouting on his cheeks like the weeds that poked up around our daylight prison.

How far could he have made it?

Nate was strong, much stronger than me, but neither of us could stand the sun.

He's gone, Mal. Accept it.

I didn't want to accept it. I didn't want to accept any of it. I wanted to close my eyes and go back to that night. I wanted to turn the steering wheel and take another loop, come home late and miss him altogether.

Maybe if I hadn't been there when…

The sound of birds chirping between the trees drew me out of that self-pitying spiral. There would be time enough to beat myself up for the roads not taken.

Right now I needed to get my newly minted bloodsucker somewhere safe and I needed to do it yesterday.

I hesitated in the fading dark, my eyes on the tree-shrouded horizon, and dark thoughts crowding my tired mind.

I would have my last sunrise. Once Nate and this new kid were safe, I'd march right out and watch the dawn one final time.

The ghosts in my head would have their vengeance.

But first I'd have mine.

Cute, Mal. Very cute. Maybe don't try the girl-on-fire trick quite yet?

I slipped my arms under the young man, hoisting him up and holding him tight. Back when I'd been human that would have been impossible, but the blood came with its gifts.

One of those was strength, another was smell.

I caught it on the air, drifting between the narrow pines. It was the scent of peeling paint, mildew, and decay.

It was exactly what we needed, provided I could find it.

The boy stirred and I hushed him. "You're new at this and you're dangerously close to my boobs. That's two strikes and it's not even dawn."

He mumbled something under his breath, the change already taking hold. Soon there would be pain, a lot of it, jaws breaking and tendons coming undone. A new tongue would emerge, and if he had them, his tonsils would not be long for this earth.

Frankly, neither of us would be long for this earth if we didn't find a place to go. The pink above the tree line gave way to a tender gold. It was beautiful and deadly. Even now the first hints of sun nipped at my cheeks like so many hungry mosquitos.

The teen squirmed again and this time I let him, the rest of me too focused on finding shelter.

Trees?

I dismissed that thought the instant I had it. The trees were too narrow, too young.

This scrub was all squat palmetto, thick fronds covering the ground like a blanket of fanned out green. It was tempting to climb under them, to hide beneath that verdant shield, but it wouldn't work.

The sun would find a way.

It always found a way.

Go back?

I shook away that thought as well. The bar was an ashy stain on the side of the road, besides, I'd spent one day in the steel coffin. I was not about to do another, and not with the kid.

If I thought he was close before, climbing in that box with him would represent an all new level of togetherness I wasn't remotely prepared for.

No, those options weren't much in the way of useful, so instead we soldiered on. Or at least I did, the kid just groaned.

"Yeah, the jaws hurt like a bitch, but look at it this way, you'll never have to brush your teeth again."

If he heard me or my stupid jokes, he didn't show it. He was too deep now, too far into the pain.

I trudged on through the sugar sand, my eyes constantly turning back to the coming dawn. We were exposed, marching ever deeper into the unknown with nothing but hope and the smell of chipped paint to drive us forward.

Please be something.

I realized I didn't deserve to say prayers, let alone have them answered, but I asked anyway. I asked for the boy, and for Nate. I asked for me.

"Damn it. If you're not going to give me a house, give me something I can use. Give me a tree, or a hollowed-out log, give me a stump. I don't care. Just give me something!"

I didn't know if things like me were worthy of redemption, or safe havens, but I wasn't above begging.

"Please…"

The gold shifted to yellow and I knew I had precious time left. I contemplated marching right into one of the watering holes we'd wandered past, but dismissed that thought as well.

Too shallow.

The sun would cook us just as fast under the water as above it.

What we needed was a cave, but this was Florida, a glorified sandbar. There were no caves.

Just as the smoke started drifting off the back of my reddening neck, I found it. It rose up like a ruined monolith to frontier living. White and peeling like old scabs in the sun, the tiny church house sat tucked beneath a copse of slender pines. Palmetto gave way to tall grass that rubbed up gently against the chapped wood. Old newspapers covered the windows, yellowed bits of forgotten lore, sales from stores long since closed.

I hesitated, my eyes on the tilted cross above the door.

It's just wood, Mal.

Thankfully bare, the wood still stared back at me. Their savior might be gone, but his empty cross still prickled at the hairs on the back of my neck.

The teen stirred again, this time crying out as the first crack appeared in his lips. It was coming.

"Yeah. That shit's about to get really bad. Trust me."

He couldn't do it outside. Neither of us could survive outside. Not much longer. There was only one option, and its chipped paint entrance glared back at us from across the silent palmetto.

Maybe Nate had made it here? Maybe I'd step inside and find him hidden under a pew or curled up in a ball beneath the altar?

Maybe I'd find none of those things, because I'd never make it over the threshold? The kid's lower lip split apart and he screamed.

It would be the first of many.

Do it, Mal.

"Screw it. We're doing this. Whatever happens, happens. It beats dying like grapes in the sun."

Maybe it did, or maybe it didn't, but I couldn't worry about that now. I was a mother, and a rather shitty one at that. A well-placed shoulder against the door and it swung open, the concerning scent of bleach and rot should have stopped me, but it didn't.

I was too caught up in his screams and in finding a dark corner to lay the boy in to notice the soft rumble of a distant engine, or the new smells coming with the dawn. Sweat, leather, and the pungent scent of gunpowder, they were out there and coming. I was too tired to think about that, or what it meant. All I could focus on was closing the door and pressing my back against it, the glorious dark, and the sound of a new vampire being born.

I should have been doing so much more, but I was too tired. I was too tired to care, to think straight, or to realize a trap when I'd walked right into it.

CHAPTER 10
LABOR PAINS

I DRIFTED in the scratchy dark. The boy lay nearby, his lungs gasping for those final breaths as they slowly filled with blood. He was dying, but he'd just have to get over it.

We all died.

The freaks like Nate and I got to live again.

Be careful what you wish for, you just might get it.

We laid under a dusty pew, just in case the roof should cave in and bathe us in killing light.

Even undead brains still subscribe to irrational fears. They just aren't often good at detecting the rational ones.

I should have been thinking about this stupid church, how convenient it was, and the faint hints of bleach and rot in the stale air. I should have been doing all of that, but instead all I could do was rest and count off the final beats of the little man's heart.

It wouldn't be long now.

I closed my eyes in that hazy half-light and thought back to that night, to my brother, and to the end of our lives.

It wasn't much more than a blur of bloody pain and release. I did remember one thing though.

Poor guy, he'd never had a chance.

Coming home late from some club, our neighbor had the distinct bad luck of showing up outside our door at roughly the same time my face completed its first bird-woman routine.

His heart…

I could still hear it now, if I tried hard enough. You always remember your first. The asshole and his convertible down by the beach, the same one who swore condoms meant he couldn't feel anything.

And now Jeff the neighbor.

Jeff, the guy we'd borrowed eggs from once, and stole his wifi more often than I cared to admit.

I didn't exactly remember how I did it, just that I did. That first kill was a clumsy mess, like raw dogging in the back of a shitty car. It was jaws and tongue and so much saliva.

But it was also blood, spectacular blood.

Jeff had been drinking, and his blood said as much. It had come with images, men in tight shirts and some without shirts at all. My neighbor had enjoyed his evening, maybe a little too much, but none of that would matter anymore.

I remembered tackling him, driving that fit little shit to the ground in a single fluid motion. I remembered the sound of his skull thumping on the concrete, and the confused look in his eyes when he realized who it was. That confusion didn't last.

It gave way to fear before descending into panic.

My jaws were good at inspiring panic.

As if remembering the feast with me, those folds opened softly only to close again like the wings of a butterfly, a deadly butterfly.

The boy wheezed. "Don't laugh, little man. You'll have yours too. They take a bit to reach full size, or at least mine did. Who knows, maybe you'll be like Nate?"

Nate!

Thoughts of my brother and the thing he'd become

stopped my musings cold. Nate was nothing like me. Nate was power, corded, strong, and unthinking power.

Was there another Nate laying next to me?

I shuddered.

"On second thought, let's go with smart, okay? I've got one killing machine to worry about, let's not make it two."

Doing a great job worrying about Nate so far. Really, great job.

Frustration overrode the desire to rest and I pushed myself out from underneath that dirty pew.

The sun boiled overhead, mercifully hidden by a roof that showed no signs of crashing in on us.

Yet.

It was the windows that concerned me more. I counted six of them, big ones, the kind that would have easily reduced me to a pile of runny guts had they not been covered in layers of newspaper.

Not one to push my luck, I'd kept us in the middle of the wide room, as far away from those killing openings as possible.

"We just have to make it to night."

If the dying teenager was listening, he didn't show it.

"Oh, don't be such a baby. You'll be fine."

I think…

I ran a finger over the dusty pew and flicked at the rat droppings that had taken up residence there.

"We need a plan."

The boy rolled to one side, and I could have sworn he vomited, but I wasn't about to check. The rats could have that.

"Yeah. We need a plan. We need to find Nate and we need to get back to the concrete cave. We can regroup there. It's safe. Okay, safe is relative, but it's safer. No one comes to that strawberry field. It's basically all weeds anyway. We need to get a car. Hey, kid, can you steal a car?"

Nothing but gasping and vomit.

"I'll ask you again after you're dead."

I would, but I'd need to find him something to eat, because I had no interest in being on the menu.

Nate had proved as much to me in the early going. It was a simple life lesson. Don't let a newborn go hungry. The end result isn't good for anyone.

Least of all me.

"Okay. So to confirm, we need to—"

Snap!

It wasn't much, and back in the 'before' times I never would have noticed it, but now my hearing was better, so much better. Now I heard shit I didn't want to hear, including the sound of footsteps outside the church.

Damn it!

I counted six windows and only one door. That didn't mean there wasn't a second one somewhere behind the altar. If I'd been smarter I would have looked. If I'd been smarter I would have realized this was just far too convenient to be remotely good.

I wasn't any of those things.

I was tired, frustrated, and getting very hungry.

My jaws rippled in the hazy and I tried to count the steps or pick up the beating hearts.

The boy's vomiting didn't help.

"Shut up! I need to focus."

But he didn't shut up. He did the exact opposite. He got worse.

"Damn it. I don't have time for this. We've got assholes at the gates, kid."

Again, if this meant anything, the kid didn't show it. His body was in control and kicking out the last vestiges of a mortal life.

Shadows moved along the newspapered windows. Long and stretchy, they walked with purpose. I got the impression they knew exactly what they were doing and where they were going.

They were coming in here.

Click.

The sound of a twisting handle sent the unfamiliar shudder of fear twisting in my dead heart.

"Crap! Come on." I didn't think. I just grabbed him. My fingers around the kid's shoulder, I pulled him out from under the pew and looked frantically for a place to hide. The altar wasn't much more than a table, and there weren't enough newspapers to cover ourselves with.

I spotted what looked like a closet door and bolted for it, the dying teen leaving a trail of blood and bile in our wake.

He's going to give you up.

I can't just leave him here.

I think you can.

The tiny argument played out in my head the closer we got to the door.

Don't be that person.

I wish I could have said I wasn't that person, or that I knew what it was like to care. I didn't. This kid wasn't Nate. He wasn't blood. He may have come from me, but he'd done that to himself.

He could have run.

Mal! What are you doing?

The truth was I didn't know what I was doing more than half the time. All I knew was surviving. Maybe I wasn't much better than the rats in the walls, but I was a survivor, and that shit was all that mattered.

"Good luck, kid." Against my better judgment, I tossed his bloody body aside and yanked open the closet door.

Bleach!

Big jugs of the stuff laid in dusty soldier-row formations against the back wall. Above them hung a calendar, a nice one with pictures of the sun, doves, and what looked like really well-adjusted kids—rich kids.

The kind that slept in warm beds, got three squares to eat, and did whatever their parents told them.

Even if it included killing vampires.

Names, numbers, and lines of red marked off sections of those pages. Someone had a schedule and kept to it. I couldn't remember what day it was, or read whose name graced those dates, but it didn't matter.

All that mattered was staying alive, finding Nate, and fixing him. There would be plenty of time for my last sunrise after that.

What about the boy?

What about him? He's on his own.

I closed the closet door no less than seconds before the main one opened.

"Look alive, people. We've got one set of footprints and a lot of blood. The Good Lord has graced us with an injured prey. Let's put it out of its misery."

Great, just great.

CHAPTER 11
TEACHABLE MOMENT

THE SOUND OF HEARTBEATS, once missing, now echoed loudly in the otherwise empty room. I counted five of them. Two appeared to be a little worse for wear, older models with quite a few years on them. But the younger ones, those did enough pumping for twice as many.

Late teens or early twenties.

I turned that thought over in my head debating the merits of slipping the door open just enough to get a peek.

In the end, curiosity killed the cat and certainly put me in a bad spot, but I had to know.

Like characters in one of Nate's old video games, they moved in a perfect cosplay of what I assumed was supposed to be a formation of sorts. The boss man was easy to spot, a straw hat on a balding head, and a shotgun in his hands. A brilliant silver crucifix hung from his neck, the man they'd nailed to it long since missing. As if he wasn't bad enough, his partner-in-crime looked just about as determined, if also capable of baking perfect apple pies. A matronly sidekick hung on his right and on his every word. Much like her man, this thick slab of woman was all about overalls, firearms, and intensity.

As bad as those two looked, it was the kids that raised the short hairs on my arms.

Teens.

They couldn't have been much older than my guy, maybe early twenties at best. Except where the other two were cautious, the remaining three appeared hellbent on the killing. Like dogs you'd tied up in the yard only to let go at the first sight of prey, these three moved with hunger and intent. Two guys and a girl, they all shared a very similar look, right down to the same barber shop. It appeared there'd been a special on buzz cuts at the farmhouse hair salon, and these three were more than happy to take advantage of it.

They might have lacked the older pair's firepower, but the rifles in their hands looked well used.

What are you worried about? You can eat a bullet.

I could, but how many? Bullets still hurt and the well-placed ones were harder to recover from.

Worse, the sun was still blazing outside. I might not be able to see it behind the wood and newspaper-covered windows, but it was there.

I knew it was there.

I could feel it.

That silent killer was waiting for me. We had a date, him and I, but that last sunrise wasn't today.

And it certainly wasn't going to be at the hands of Church Team Five.

Think, Mal!

I had been thinking. I'd been thinking the whole time, but I hadn't come up with much. Even if I shot out of the door at high-speed, I couldn't imagine a single scenario that didn't involve me taking at least one, if not two, shotgun blasts to the face before I cleared the distance between us.

The best I could do was wait and hope for an opening.

It turned out I didn't have to wait long.

"I see something." Blondy was the first to spot the boy.

The little farm girl with the dirty denim and itchy trigger finger had a bead on my whimpering pile of flesh and blood in seconds.

"Don't get too close. Fan out and check under all the pews." That was Farmer Bob, the boss man and one that appeared to actually have excellent military cosplay skill. Big Momma and the boys did exactly what he said, while Blondy kept a bead on my almost newborn.

The kid twitched, a bloody line running down his face. Those lips were going to split apart any minute, and when they did, they'd do so with the help of a long and hungry tongue.

Those two idiots were standing next to a bomb just waiting to go off.

Perhaps I didn't need to do anything? Perhaps I just had to wait for nature to take its course.

And the hungry shall inherit the earth.

"He looks small." Blondy kept one finger on the trigger and both eyes on my boy. Farmer Bob, the big papa, joined her, his shotgun cocked and in position. "They come in all shapes and sizes. Just like us."

The young woman nodded. I got the impression she was used to the lectures.

"But the one from yesterday… he was so big."

Farmer Bob waited for an all clear signal from Momma before pulling all their attention back to the boy. "He was, but the Lord delivered that demon right into our trap."

I tightened my fingers on the knob and left deep grooves in the smooth metal. There was only one monster that fit that description, only one that could just be described as big.

Nate!

A stinger that had been content to lay in rest deep in the folds of my throat took this opportunity to drop out and taste the stale air. It was weak, I might not have noticed it if he hadn't mentioned it, but it was there.

Those five had Nate smell on them, not much, but enough to bring back vivid memories of days spent in the stifling heat of the concrete castle.

Those religious assholes had done something to Nate.

My jaws swelled in anticipation of feasting on their salty blood, but first I needed to figure out exactly how to get past the portable fireworks.

"Is this it?" Big Momma used her gun to poke at the twitching little guy. "The other one could have taken a shit bigger than this one."

"I'm thinking he turned this one. Big guy he is, probably found this one in the woods and gave him the tongue, or whatever it is they do."

The matron didn't appear too keen on the farmerly father figure's words. "Is that why you are keeping one? To figure out how they do it? Who gives a damn how these monsters reproduce? I say we go back to the original plan, kill them all."

Funny, bitch, that's exactly how I feel about the five of you.

"You know your enemy," Farmer Bob said the words with an air of authority, but while the kids may have nodded in agreement, Mrs. Bob did not appear to be toeing the line.

"That's bullshit. I don't know why you think it's so important to put our lives in danger when you know damn well it's smarter to just kill them and be done with it."

I couldn't have said it better myself.

The man in charge ignored his wife and turned to the kids. "Whose turn is it?"

Blondy stepped up. "Mine."

"You know what to do, Sweetheart."

The little buzz-cut bitch nodded. "I do."

"Well get to it. Mom, you and the boys peel back the paper."

That one caught the mother off-guard and she indicated as much. "Why do we need to take the paper off the windows?

Sally's gonna chop this little runt's head off. All we need to do is drag him out and get to work with the bleach."

Farmer Bob didn't give her an answer, not right away, instead he leaned his back against the pew opposite the closet, his eyes never leaving the door, or the narrow crack I'd opened.

No, no, no! Sally handed her rifle to a brother, then produced one of the longest knives I'd ever seen. The squared-off machete had been strapped to her back this whole time, largely hidden from view.

It wasn't the metal that made me nervous, anything but. It was the blood on that blade, the dried remnants of someone I'd laid next to for days on end in the oppressive dark of the concrete castle. It was the smell of weeds and wild strawberries drifting through the cracks in the boarded up windows.

The knife smelled like Nate.

The boy's jaws chose that moment to split apart like the wet and fleshy wings of a baby bird. A tiny worn twisted beneath them, like its earthbound brethren after a storm. There was no denying it now.

I'd just given birth.

Cloudy red eyes tried to find focus in that haze, while the young woman readied her blade and the rest of the Christian Killers fanned out to the windows.

It was just Farmer Bob that stayed put, his eyes never leaving the door. "Hang on a second, Sally. Mom, pull down the paper."

"I don't understand why we have to—"

Farmer Bob pointed his shotgun at my closet. "Because we've got company." *You sure do, asshole.*

Slasher Sally and the rest of the crew turned their attention on the closet door, and on the darkness behind it.

Big Momma cocked her weapon. "Shit. There was another one and you never said anything."

"I think this one is smarter. I think it understands what we're saying. I think it can teach us things."

Big Momma ripped the paper off her window sending beams of scalding sunlight into the closest pew. "Yeah, how fast it can die."

CHAPTER 12
DEAD MEN TELL NO TALES

SOMETIMES YOU THINK, you prepare. Sometimes your actions have to be meticulously planned out and organized to the finest detail.

And sometimes you just explode in a ball of fiery hot rage.

I did the second one a lot.

Maybe too much?

But so far it had worked. So far I was the last woman standing, and I aimed to keep it that way.

I threw the door wide and went straight for Blondy. The knife was a threat, but at that angle I figured she'd never get it up in time.

I was right.

Shotguns and rifles that should have erupted in great vomiting bursts of gunpowder and lead didn't.

Family was a powerful motivator.

The young woman swung once, twice, but those little hands were nothing to a monster like me. My jaws spread like the petals of a flower, while a snake-like stinger found its home around her neck.

Salty sweat and a hint of caramel, the girl was exactly

what the doctor ordered. It took everything I had to not dig into her on the spot.

"Nobody move," I said, that second tongue squeezing the buzz-cut snack cake tight.

"I knew it." Farmer Bob didn't look the slightest bit concerned that what I expected was his daughter was now a contestant on 'how many licks does it take to get to the center of a teenager.'

With me? Only one.

Momma had her gun up, but appeared torn at the prospect of hitting her child. The rest of the boys enjoyed a similar quandary.

"Where's the big one?" I asked, my tongue hungry for blood.

Farmer Bob lowered his weapon. "He's not here."

"Of course he isn't." I twisted the blond to face the scalding light. "The sun's up, you idiot. You better have him inside, or in a hole. If you killed my brother I will destroy you. Each of you. I'll turn you one at a time, then leave you to bleach in the sun. And I won't stop there. I'll make you watch each other burn until there's only one left. That one I'll set free. That one will get to live, to feed, and then become the thing they hate. There are so many fates worse than death. So damn many."

I had to admit, I felt pretty proud of that speech. It hit on all the high notes and appeared to put the fear of God into the assembled masses.

Well, the boys at least. I could smell the fear in their sweat, and hear the sound of those little assholes puckering up.

The real concern was neither Momma or Papa appeared to be nearly as afraid. I tightened my stinger's grip, making Blondy do the twitchy I-can't-breathe game.

"I'm gonna ask you again. Where is my brother?"

"He's back at the house," one of the boys blurted out.

"Excellent. Once the sun goes down, we're all going to go

there together." That was a lie. I didn't need all of them. I just needed one, and it looked like I now knew which one was the most likely candidate to deliver me to Nate.

The rest of them were expendable.

"The sun won't go down for hours." Farmer Bob took a step closer, his gun down, but a steely look of determination in his eyes.

I decided then and there I didn't like that balding man and his overalls. There was something about him, about the way he walked, or the lack of sincere concern in his voice. He knew something I didn't, and I wasn't a fan of that.

I wasn't a fan of that at all.

"So what? I can wait." I let my stinger dig into Blondy's flesh enough to release a tiny trickle of blood. I was right, caramel. "The real question is, can she?"

Big Momma took an angry step forward, but a sharp look from her husband put a stop to that. "Yes. She can. She can wait a long time. We all can, but we don't have to."

I let the tip of my stinger lap at the dripping blood. Caramel with hints of something else, something spicy. It was like getting a habanero chaser with your beer. Something wasn't right.

I knew it, and the old man knew it too.

"That's it. Have a taste. I think you'll find it special."

My stinger shuddered, its thick muscles confused and twitchy. "What the—"

"Wasn't sure it would work on you." The old man took another cautious step forward. "But it worked on the bigger one, and if you two are related... Well, it looks like you proved me right after all."

"What did you... What..." The stinger tightened then loosened, Blondy scrambling to be free. I got a hand on her, but the girl appeared ready to shuck that in an instant.

"I knew it." Farmer Bob clapped his chapped hands. "Horse dewormer. Parasites. That's all you are. Parasites.

Sally took the pill. We all took the pills. It took the big one down, it'll take you down too."

"Yeah… Right…" I got Blondy back close, but my stinger was having nothing to do with her. The thick tongue retreated to its home in my throat like a rabbit running for her hole. "I can still snap her neck."

"You can." Farmer Bob pointed his shotgun at my newly minted son's flapping face. "And I can pull this trigger."

Damn it.

This is what you get for caring, for doing the right thing. Dad always said no good deed goes unpunished, and he was right.

It was certainly debatable whether changing the boy had been a good deed or not, but he hadn't bled out in the parking lot, so it couldn't have been all bad.

Yet if he had, they wouldn't have been able to use the kid against me.

Why was nothing ever easy?

My stinger rolled over uncomfortably in my gut. I'd only tasted a few drops of her blood and I felt like vomiting, I couldn't imagine what it had done to Nate.

My brother was not known for being a dainty eater.

Maybe there'd been a fourth child? At least until Nate had found them.

"Here's what you're going to do," Farmer Bob pressed the business end of his shotgun against the unfolding mess of the young boy's jaws. "You're going to let Sally go, and then you're going to come with us—"

"William!" Big Momma did not appear to be in agreement with this plan. "One is bad enough."

"This one talks. This one isn't some mindless eating machine. We can learn a lot from this one."

Farmer Bob appeared to be too busy arguing with his wife to notice the boy's stinger working its way around the shotgun's barrel.

"I hate to break it to you." I let my jaws ripple in the dusty haze. "But she's right. You can't."

"I can't what?" That got the overall wearing asshole's attention.

"You can't learn anything from me, because I don't know anything."

"You're lying." William pushed the barrel deeper into the boy's budding folds, oblivious to the stinger inching up the bottom of the weapon.

Just a little more…

"Trust me. I'm not. I'm a damn bartender, or at least I was. This wasn't something I signed up for. This was *done* to me." My stinger shuddered, and came with the sudden urge to retch.

Keep it down, Mal.

"It doesn't matter. We can learn things from you whether you're willing or not. Mom, pull the rest of the paper down. Let's get this one burnt on both sides. That ought to soften her up."

My stomach rumbled uncomfortably. "Wait!" I let Blondy go. "Wait! I've got a better idea."

Farmer Bob hesitated. "What?"

The boy's stinger tightened around the gun barrel.

"Nothing. I was just waiting for that."

"Huh?"

The kid yanked, pulling the weapon aside even as the shell erupted. He might have caught a few stray bits of shot, but the floorboards swallowed up the worst of it.

What happened next could only be described as organized chaos.

Farmer Bob fell forward, only to find himself in the waiting jaws of a hungry young bird. I wanted to warn the kid, but I had problems of my own.

Blondy proved to be a lot quicker than I'd initially given her credit for. Still, she went down fast with a punch to the back of the skull. It was her machete that helped dispatch Big Momma. The heavy woman managed to get off a single shot before the long blade lodged itself in her chest.

"No! You can't do—" Farmer Bob made the mistake of telling my son exactly what he could and couldn't do. He got a stinger to the ticker for his trouble.

I let the other two boys run for the door, content in the knowing we'd find them soon enough. My little man had already started vomiting up that nasty blood. I put a hand on his back. "That's it. Get all that shit up. We'll get you the real thing soon." My eyes settled on Blondy. "We'll get you all manner of good things soon."

CHAPTER 13
TIMEOUT

THE KID STOPPED PUKING some time in the late afternoon. It was one of those things where either his stomach just got too tired, or he ran out of whatever it was the second tongue and face folds didn't like in the old man's blood.

Dewormer? Wasn't that what he said?

It didn't matter what he'd said, because he wouldn't be saying anything again. I stacked up the old guy and his august woman wife in the corner like the discarded wrappers they were.

The real challenge had been keeping the kid off Blondy.

"Hey!" I snapped my fingers a few times to get his attention, the boy still having trouble with complete thoughts. "Eyes over here." I pointed to mine in the newspaper faded light. "Do not eat her."

He opened his mouth to say something, but the second tongue gummed up the works.

"Yeah, yeah. You're hungry. I get it. I'm hungry too, but the Swiss Miss here took some bad drugs that will screw you up something fierce if you get them in your system."

He frowned, his infantile lips quivering like a nest of baby birds waiting for their worm.

"Don't give me that. I told you I'd help you, and I will. I'm helping you right now." I pointed to the newly re-newspapered windows. "I risked burning my face off because you can't sit still." I pointed again. "Me, I did that. I did that because you keep bouncing around like a jackrabbit."

Again he frowned, but this time his snake-like tongue tried to sneak a free sample Blondy-negative.

"No!" My stinger was faster, much faster. I had experience, age, and motivation on my side. I was also a right bitch when I wanted to be. And I really wanted to be one now.

My stinger hit his and knocked it aside with next to no effort. The problem was he wouldn't keep his tongue to himself for long. He needed to feed, and I did too, but we also needed Blondy. We needed to know where Nate was, and what they might have done to him. None of that we'd get if she was dead.

As the saying goes, Dead bitches don't tell stories.

That's not how it goes, Mal.

I shook that offending thought away, and instead focused on the task at hand, keeping the boy from eating her face like backstrap.

That turned out to be a full afternoon's affair.

In the end, I had to settle for sticking him in the closet with the bleach and pressing my back against the door.

"No! You're going to stay in there until I let you out."

"I… don't… wanna."

"Tough shit, you little murder imp. People who can't keep their tongues off the tasty blonde girls on the floor don't get to leave the closet. That's just how it is. I didn't make the rules."

His under-sized hands banged on the door. "You… just did."

Shit.

"Fine, so I did. Whatever. Here's the deal, I can't keep her safe and you from setting both of us on fire. I'm just one remarkably awesome woman, but even I can't handle that. I'm going to let you out when the sun goes down. That's going to be soon, I suggest you close your eyes and try to rest. Spend that time thinking about how good that first one is going to taste, because believe me, it's going to blow your socks off."

The pounding stopped, my little man growing tired in the late day's light.

Shit, I was tired too. I was tired of keeping him alive, and of watching the blonde bitch just lay there.

I could hear her heart beating if I focused on it, a strong and hammering thump that rang like the dinner bell for a meal we couldn't have.

Yet.

I slid down against the closet door and toyed with the gun I'd taken off her. I'd never been much for firearms, and even less so now, but I felt better with it near *my* hands and not hers. The squared-off machete, though? That was another story entirely. The knife felt good in my fingers, strong, sharp, and lethal. It had cut that big woman down with all but zero effort.

Thanks to that, the blade and I were pals.

Someone's heart accelerated and I set the wicked weapon at my side. "Nice of you to join us."

I had to give the girl credit. She didn't panic, in fact she didn't even sit up right away.

Playing dead is a lot harder to do than it looks.

"Come on, cut the act. I can hear your chest pounding like a kickdrum. I can smell your breath and practically feel the neurons in your stupid brain firing. You're awake, so let me give you the update."

The girl opened angry eyes.

"Whoa, sister, dial the intensity back a few notches for your own safety. Remember who put your old man and his wife in the ground."

"I do."

I let my lips ripple once for good measure. "I'm sure you do. I'm also sure you're full of righteous fury. You want me and the kid dead."

As if perfectly timing his contribution, the kid chose that moment to bang on the closet door. I banged back. "Shut it."

Blondy started to pull herself up and those icy cold and hate-filled eyes went straight for the gun, and her momma-killing blade.

"And you," I put a hand on both weapons, "you need to think long and hard about what comes next. The sun is going down soon, and when it does, I'm gonna let a little someone special out of timeout. He's pretty damn hungry. Hell, if I'm being honest, I am too. But where I have fine motor control and understand what it means to pace myself, the boy in there is gonna be like a sugar-starved toddler on Halloween. And I promise you, you smell like a big, fat bowl of candy."

I'd expected that to soften her up, and it did, but not as much as I'd hoped. I'd had my heart set on a nice blubbering fool, what I got was a young woman kneeling on the dirty ground, her hands in her lap.

"Cute. Pray all you want, sister. I'm the only god in your world right now."

"What do you want?"

I picked up the machete and placed it across my lap. "I want a goddamn hamburger. I want to taste something other than pennies. I want a face that doesn't unfold like Japanese paper cranes."

She opened her mouth to speak, but I stopped her before she could get a word out. "No. I know it all. I know I'm a monster, and that I shouldn't exist. That I'm a damn abomination. Whatever. I made my peace with that." I pointed the machete at the window. "One of these mornings I'm going to do it. I'm going to get my brother straight, and the kid too, and then I'm going to see the sun rise. I'm gonna watch the pinks, reds, and golds. I'm going to bask in that shit, because I deserve it, but when I go out it's on my terms and not yours," I pointed to the bodies, "or theirs."

She didn't say anything, and if I was being honest, I might have gotten a bit too punch drunk on power, because I hadn't noticed just how quiet my little man had gotten.

Good moms know that sudden quiet is bad news. I did not.

Blondy's knuckles whitened against the ever-darkening blue of her jeans. The sun was setting, even if the newspaper made it hard to see.

"What do you want—"

"I want to know where my brother is. I want you to take me to him, to the big one, and I want you to realize that you can't win."

"I—"

"No." I shook my head. "You're acting like you think there's still a play for you. Like there's some way out. There isn't. There's nothing remotely like that. Your only move is to guide us to wherever you are keeping my brother. Do that and I won't let the kid eat your face. Don't..." I let my jaws snap open like a hawk in flight. "Don't and I'll eat it myself."

I had to admit, even if it was a little melodramatic at points, it wasn't a bad intimidation speech. It had worked well enough for her to make a sudden run for the door. She didn't reach it of course, even running low on good blood, she was no match for me.

The problem wasn't stopping her, the problem was taking my back off the closet door, and letting the kid know the sun had almost set. Looking back on it, that was exactly when things had gone sideways.

The boy erupted from his tiny prison like he'd been shot out of a cannon. He hit her hard, juvenile jaws wide and tongue flailing like a cantor's arms.

Shit.

CHAPTER 14
VANILLA WAFERS

ONE TIME, as a young girl, I was attacked by a dog. Little Mal was out on the trail, just doing her thing and enjoying the outdoors, the fact that she also happened to be smoking a joint was entirely beside the point.

The dog didn't seem to care at the time. It was far more interested in sinking those jaws into my leg. Maybe I looked like a deer, or whatever it was stupid dogs liked to sink their teeth into. It didn't matter, he hit me and I went down.

That was basically the same scene playing out in front of me, except this time I was the idiot guy trying to pull the living weapon off the girl.

It turns out it was a lot harder than it looked.

Infantile jaws latched on fast, but poorly. They didn't get closure before the stinger hit. That was a rookie move, and I suddenly realized just how lucky he'd gotten hitting the old man with it before.

The girl was equally concerned, but in a more simplistic, visceral, I-don't-want-to-die kind of way.

I didn't want her to die either. We needed her alive and functional, capable of walking, talking, and showing me exactly where my brother was.

We did not need her in the kid's stomach.

At least not yet anyway.

I wrapped my arms around that little leech and yanked him back, those tiny fangs leaving bloody scratch marks in her neck and chest.

Vanilla…

The girl smelled like vanilla, like those little cookies I used to steal from the store when I was younger.

It wasn't the smell that got me going, it was the fact I was hungry too. How long had it been? How many hours had gone by? Twelve? Twenty-four? It was impossible to tell. What was very clear was that it had been a while, and the idiot kid just reminded me exactly how much I needed it.

Do not lose your cool, Mal.

My jaws unfolded and a well-placed stinger slipped out from beneath those fleshy wings.

Keep it together…

But I didn't want to keep it together. Sitting there, holding back the feral kid I didn't want anymore, I wanted her. I wanted vanilla wafers. I wanted to bathe in them, to shovel the whole box in my mouth and let the crumbs run down my chest.

Nate! Think of Nate!

I did think of my brother, and his face before he raced off into the sunlight. It stayed my hands, but only for a second, because that visual brought friends. New images came to life in my head, images of torture, pain, and worse at the hands of Farmer Bob and company.

In this scene, Blondy wasn't the victim, she was the aggressor, the villain.

That skinny buzzcut bitch was the monster in my story and this was my opportunity to put her down.

My stinger snaked back and forth, drawing her eyes like ants on spilled soda. I imagined how it would taste, like those little yellow cookies, hard but soft, forbidden, yet so alluring.

It's not like you'll drink all of her…

That's right.

I wouldn't.

I had control, unlike the child writhing in my arms. I had control enough to know when to stop and when to drink deep.

To drink very deep.

Buzzcut Blondy could take it. She was tough, tough enough to put that blade up against the boy's neck, tough enough to kill a broken thing barely alive.

If she was tough enough for all that, she was tough enough for me.

Like a rattlesnake on the prowl my stinger zeroed in on its prey, and in doing so drifted over the blade in my fingers.

The blade with a hint of Nate's blood on it.

Nate.

A memory I thought would send me into a righteous fury didn't. I needed to see Nate again. I needed to know he was okay. There was only one way to do that, and that was with Blondy.

The girl has to live.

"Son of a bitch!" I snapped my tongue back like the retractable cord of some cheap vacuum cleaner, cranking my jaws shut behind it, and forcing down the hunger my newly minted son couldn't seem to get his brain around. "Here!" I shoved my wrist in his flailing mouth, grimacing at the pain, then sighing at the smooth release.

Blondy glanced at the door, her hands on the scraping wounds the kid had left.

"I wouldn't do that if I were you."

"I…" Blondy pushed her head up. "I'm not afraid of you."

"Bullshit. You're terrified. And you should be." The kid started sucking a little too hard and I had to fight the urge to rip him off. I needed him stable, even if it cost me a little in the process. "I hold your life in my hands."

"My life doesn't… It doesn't matter."

"Oh, yeah?" I pulled my wrist free and let the kid go. He crawled a few steps and then sort of curled up in a happy little ball. I remembered my first time, and the bliss that followed.

Enjoy it, kid. It gets shorter and shorter from here on out.

Blondy glanced at the door again.

"So tell me," I licked my second tongue across the wound to seal it, "tell me why your life doesn't matter? Is it because the Pop's and Big Momma are starting to decay? Is it because you don't have your knife? Is it becaus—"

"It's because I'm already fucking dead, that's why. Whatever I do now is all I am." I let my jaws close slowly.

Her heart sounded fine, so did her lungs.

Wait… There it was, the lungs. She wasn't breathing like the others had, like the guys in the bar, or the cop, any of them. There was a whistle in those fleshy sacks of blood and tissue, and it wasn't the cheery kind.

"Cancer."

The girl nodded.

"What the hell? Why go around with the Church Team Five if you've got fucking cancer? Why not just—Oh, shit."

The girl nodded again, this time more slowly.

Farmer Bob wasn't killing vampires all the time. He was studying them. He was learning from them. He was trying to fix someone the only way he knew how.

"I can solve that." I pointed to the kid in his blissful ball of blood stupor. "I can totally solve that. You take me to Nate, to my brother, and I'll do for you what I did for him."

The girl shook her head, but her eyes said otherwise. Her eyes said maybe, and I could work with maybe.

"You don't have to decide right this minute, but you do have to get your ass up. We're burning midnight."

Blondy's eyes went to the machete, then back to me.

"You can try, but trust me, I'm faster. I'll always be faster.

I'm not the killing machine my brother is. I can think, talk, and understand the concept of delayed gratification. I think when the kid wakes up he'll be the same way too. I think he'll be like me. That's two sane, rational, semi-adult monsters that just want to free their rampaging and supremely destructive quasi-sibling before he becomes some backwoods pharmacological test subject."

"If I give you back your brother, do you promise to leave?"

"You got a car?"

She nodded.

"Then yeah. You give me my brother *and* the car, and I promise you'll never see me again, and if you don't want to die of cancer, I'll do that too."

Blondy pulled a bloody hand back from her chest. "I'm—"

"If it's all the same to you, I don't want to know your damn name. In fact, the less I know about you the better. You can call me Red, and this is Junior. I'm gonna call you Blondy. That work?"

"Yes."

"Good. Okay, Blondy. We need to get a move on. I don't know what it is with this place, but all of you appear to want me dead, so the faster I get out of—" I stopped.

I'd gotten soft, stupid, weak. I knew that because I hadn't thought about people coming back, coming back in bigger numbers, with killing flashlights, firearms, and big damn trucks.

Blondy might have, but it was hard to tell by looking at her. She was like a buzzcut angel outlined by the brilliant headlamps of one monster truck that had pulled up outside.

"On second thought." I let my jaws explode open. "Maybe we screw all that and I tank up before the murder posse comes to try to avenge the backwoods pharmacist and his bride."

Blondy shot for the machete. We clutched it together as the

first bullets shattered the newspaper and sent a hailstorm of glass raining down.

I decided right then and there that, should I make it back to the concrete cave, I was never leaving again.

CHAPTER 15
HIGH BEAMS

THAT WAS REALLY STUPID, *Mal.*

I let that thought do the flogging, while the rest of me fought for control of the blade and the buzzcut blonde beneath it. I had to give her credit, she was certainly spirited, but you needed more than a positive outlook to put a stop to me.

My stinger found her neck and squeezed. Those slender fingers immediately left the machete and went straight to the serrated flesh cutting off her air.

Vanilla Wafers…

It was hard to stop, even with the bullets and falling glass. It was hard to say no to something so sweet, so rich.

Then don't? Take it. Take her. There will be new people to follow, a new way to find him. Your brother is out there, revel in that. Maybe a celebratory drink is in order?

I let the stinger's sharp edge dig in nicely, sending a trickle of glorious blood dripping down her tender skin.

Yes.

It was everything I thought it would be and then some. It was water to a woman dying of thirst. It was salvation.

It came with hope, and with clarity.

Memories drifted like some metallic chaser, sliding into my head even as the glass rained down.

There was a house, a farmhouse.

It was impossible to tell how far away it was, but I got the impression it was close.

Blondy moved from room to room in these fractured visuals, unknowingly showing me a life that had little to be proud of.

I'd seen the horrors of religion before, back when Mom had taken a stab at being saved. Saving wasn't about love, it was about control. I didn't know that then, I sure as hell knew it now.

Shifting scenes of manipulation dressed up as caring paraded past. Blondy didn't know it, but I was doing her a favor. I was freeing her from all this shit, from all her weakness.

No, you aren't.

The scene shifted to a single fortified door. It looked metal and industrial, the kind of thing you'd use to keep a rampaging murder beast behind.

I had experience with such thoughts.

Something moved in the door's tiny window and I willed her to show me. I had to see him. I had to see Nate.

That never happened, because the kid woke up before I could finish.

The kid woke up and decided to join me. His stinger found her heart just like it had before, and just like last time, it wasn't remotely delicate.

The bullets may have stopped, but the death was just beginning.

"No! I need her to take us to Nate!" I struggled to release my own tongue and get him free, but the damage had already been done.

The cancer wouldn't kill her now, we already had.

"Damn it!" I ripped the kid's stinger free and all but

stuffed it in his face. "That was my best chance to find Nate! Do you understand? That was my best possible chance to find my brother!"

"I…" The kid's jaws contracted smoothly, and for the first time since the change his eyes no longer resembled someone living in a meth house. "I'm sorry."

"Whatever." I pulled him aside and tried to stay below the high beams. "We have bigger problems right now. I think the rest of the parish is here to finish us off. Must be her brothers called in the cavalry."

For a young man that looked like he had a permanent case of bed-head, the boy caught on pretty quick. "What do we do?"

I have no idea.

It was a different experience, talking to someone who could hear me and understand my words, someone who could reason.

It gave me something I hadn't had in a long time.

It gave me hope.

"We get the hell out of this killing box. Listen, you've had a lot to drink. You're going to be good for a while. Those bullets out there—"

He thumped a fist against his chest. "They'll bounce right off me."

Hope fading…

"Yeah, no. No, they'll hurt like a bitch, but your body will spit them back up. Too many of them will still take you down though, and you don't want to go down, trust me."

The boy nodded.

"Good. I say we make a run for the tree line. I go right and you go left. We run hard and meet back up in the dark under the cypress." I shoved my hand in his face. "You smell me?"

"Yeah. You're like those funny cigarettes my cousin liked to smoke."

A couple of truck doors opened outside. They came with

the sound of robust hearts, the smell of gun oil, and something else.

Something familiar I couldn't place.

"Cloves? Huh. I never thought of that."

The boy nodded. "Do me. What do I smell like?"

"Honestly? You smell like a horny teenager."

"Oh."

Boots crunched on already crumpled grass.

"Listen, Fabio, it doesn't matter. The goal is to reach the tree line, after that we meet back up and find her house." I pointed at the dead blonde on the floor. "My brother's in there. I know it. He's all that matters to me. You understand? All that matters. You help me find him, and I'll give you a place to stay when they turn the daylight back on. You got it?"

Again, it was all coming at him fast, but the kid seemed to be following. I got a few of those vigorous teenager nods and they appeared to indicate as much, or just that he'd grown tired of listening to me talk.

The sound of dogs came next, their panting tongues and machine gun tickers.

Shit.

Dogs were fast enough to chase us into the trees.

We deal with them.

"You're surrounded!" He wasn't Farmer Bob, but he might as well have been for how close he sounded to the backwood pharmacist slowly decomposing in the corner. "You can't escape."

I grabbed the kid's warm hand. "Like hell we can't. You go left. I'll go right. We run for the pines and don't stop running until you can't hear their hearts beating anymore. You understand?"

"Yeah." Excitement played across his young face.

Of course it did. To him this was a game, an adventure. He was still in the early days. His body still felt good, strong, powerful. He hadn't eaten someone he'd loved, or feasted on a poor soul who just happened to be in the wrong place at the wrong time.

Life was new and exciting for him, a verdant field to explore. He was jonesing to sample the whole buffet, plate in hand, and eyes bigger than his stomach.

Things might have been different if Nate had been like this kid. Maybe we'd have been better. We'd certainly have been smarter. I wouldn't have had to do the thinking for two.

I was bad enough at doing that for one.

More boots moved into position around the ruined church. I couldn't see them, but I could hear them, and smell the men that walked in them.

They smelled of sweat and fear.

My favorite.

"Are you ready?"

The kid nodded, his jaws fluttering like a butterfly at rest.

"Good. Do not look back. You hear me? You run like hell no matter what happens. You get to the cypress and then start looking for me. We'll meet back up and find my brother."

"Right."

It was like trying to hold back a greyhound that wanted to run.

"On three."

Click.

"One."

The smell of gun oil hung heavy in the air.

"Two."

The kid snapped his jaws shut and flexed those slender fingers.

"Three!"

We shot up like two blood rich vampires could, taking out what remained of the window on our path to the trees. Guns erupted and I took a few slugs in the chest. They hurt, but not enough to slow me down. Not enough to stop me from getting to Nate, from seeing my brother again, or from reaching the damn pines.

For his part, the kid never slowed. He wasn't distracted by the dogs, the men, or the blood. He wasn't like Nate.

Maybe he wasn't even like me?

Maybe he was better than both of us?

I wasn't far behind him, the dark woods and salvation only a few steps ahead when it hit me.

"Light em up!"

The killing purple light, like a hundred angry suns, took me down harder than any bullet.

The light!

It was a familiar memory, one that was burned into my scalding flesh like a cattle brand.

I lost the kid, and any hope of reaching the trees as I lay pinned beneath the spotlight like a butterfly under glass.

Nate!

Skin blistered and popped like water boiling on the stove. There was no way to escape it, and no strength to run.

Damn it, Mal! Do something, don't just lie there and die!

I wanted to do something, but my arms and legs couldn't do much more than fold-up like some broken insect.

Do not let them win! You're stronger than this.

Maybe I was? Maybe I wasn't? Maybe this artificial sun would be my last dawn?

Fuck it.

I forced my eyes open.

Maybe not…

CHAPTER 16
FANGS OUT

THIS WASN'T how I imagined it would be. Perhaps I'd watched too many cartoons as a kid, too many shows where the hero makes some big sacrifice and is rewarded for it.

That shit only works if you're the hero.

I am not.

I didn't want to admit it, not to myself, or anyone else, but I was about as far from the hero as you could be.

I was a monster, and I wasn't always sure I hated being one.

The blood was life, but it was more than that. It was control. It was taking back something for me. Being alive demanded so much. It ground you down, like gravel under heavy tires. It squeezed. It pushed. Life told you what you were going to do, and that you better like it.

Life had told Blondy what to do. It had told her to listen to her old man and some dusty book. It had told her that cancer was her fate, and to just shut up about it.

The purple light wavered, flickering in and out like a cheap flashlight.

Can't even die with some dignity.

This was supposed to be my moment. The glorious finale where I'd take my seat on the steps outside and wait for the dawn. In my mental screenplay, Nate always sat next to me, a normal Nate, the brother that played video games and emptied our kitchen constantly.

In this version, the monster was dead and gone, and all that remained was the boy who cared.

He held my hand and tried to talk me out of it. He'd tell me it didn't matter, and that we'd find a way to continue. This Nate would get a job and build a new concrete cave. A concrete cave with air conditioning and an honest to goodness floor.

He would make sure we had a life.

In my mind, it always ended the same. I shook my head and let my jaws flutter in the cool morning air.

This wasn't my world anymore.

This was his.

The dawn would bless him, and people like him. It would give no quarter for monsters like me. That was the natural order of things.

In my head, I was poetic. I was strong. I was everything the screaming puddle of melting bitch in the tall grass wasn't.

Goodbye, Nat—

Pop!

It went off like a bad flashbulb on some shitty camera. One minute I was a screaming mess of melted skin and half-blind eyes, and in the next, darkness.

Sweet darkness.

It wasn't the concrete cave, but it was something, and it came with its own soundtrack, a glorious remix of some of my favorite hits: screaming, pleading, and the sound of blood.

The kid!

Half-blind and struggling to stand, I found him moving like an avenging angel. He may have been new to the stinger, but he snapped it like a pro, hooking boots and toppling assholes with a precision that bordered on obscene.

I was too caught up in it to realize just how outnumbered he was, and while he might have taken out that killing second sun, he was in for a world of hurt.

Help him!

I struggled to stand, the subtle realization dawning on me with each passing second. No one was paying attention to the girl they fried.

No one.

Even the dogs didn't appear to care about charred meat.

If the dogs didn't care, then maybe I shouldn't either?

The tree line loomed dark just a few yards away. I could be safe there. I could find Nate. He was out there, in that converted farm house. He was in trouble.

But your son...

I tried to shake away that stupid notion, and almost lost my balance for the trying.

He wasn't my son. He was a thing. Just like me. He was just a monster.

He came back for you.

Yeah, and I didn't tell him to.

Even overmatched, the kid kept fighting, kept trying. Blood and bullets filled the air, and I knew he had to be hurting, but he didn't stop.

He's doing that for you. So what if he was? So what if he did all this for his monster mommy? It didn't change anything. He was just another mouth to feed, another body to find space in the concrete cave, another person to keep Nate from trying to eat.

I don't need this shit.

Those words, my words, and Mom's words, stopped me cold in the bloody grass. The old woman came back to me, just as bitter as she'd always been. Smoke, ash, and eyeliner played out in a memory I'd just as soon left on the cutting room floor.

She was going out again, and somehow I knew when she came back she'd be drunk and missing half her clothes. I knew I'd have to get her to her bed, and listen to all the insults as I did it.

Some people shouldn't get to be mothers.

Some people didn't need fangs to be a monster.

But some monsters are worse than others…

I wasn't her.

I was never going to be her.

Oh yeah? Prove it, Mallory.

I wasn't the kid. I didn't have fresh blood, or the speed it came with, but I did have surprise and the fact that no one paid much attention to the girl that looked like deep-fried chicken.

It didn't take me long to get close enough to take down the first guy, my tired tongue finding his neck in the dark. He dropped hard, but thankfully left me a gun.

And what a gun it was.

I'd never been much of a firearms sort of girl, but holding this thing in my tired hands made me feel like Rambo.

I was suddenly very thankful Nate had made me watch all those late night movies when we were kids.

I squeezed the trigger and ripped through them. It wasn't fair. It wasn't even sporting. It was clouds of red, chunks of flesh, and gun smoke.

The kid spun around and got what looked like a machete blade against his neck for his trouble. He tried to get his stinger out, but the knife man's gloved hand got a grip on it.

"I'll do it. I'll cut his head off!"

I smiled. "No, you won't."

"I've put so many of your kind in the ground. Don't tell me what I can and cannot do."

"See, that's where you're wrong. I'm nothing like my kind."

I squeezed the trigger, rattling off a white-hot stream of

metallic death. It sliced through my son, and the man holding him hostage.

The kid didn't drop.

His captor did.

"Jesus." The boy's body spit up slugs, while his tongue snapped angrily at the air. "Did you have to do that?"

"Yeah." I tossed the gun, almost sad to see the empty thing go. "We need to get to the—"

"The trees. I know. You don't look so good."

I nodded and managed a few faltering steps. "I've felt better. I'll be fine, just give me a little—"

He came out of nowhere, a man with a knife and not much else. I tried to turn, to get my stinger up in time, but it all happened too fast.

The blade bit deep, slicing through flesh already scorched and papery. I tasted blood, my own, and the trees spun. I didn't really understand what came next. It was a mixture of sounds and nonsensical words. There was blood that wasn't mine and small hands.

I remembered the feel of grass against my back and the soft tickle of sand between my fingers.

But most of all, I remembered my mother, her drunken body, and the words she always said. I wasn't sure, but I got the impression I said them too. I said them in the dark and the quiet. I said them and I meant them.

I don't need this shit.

That was the truth. I didn't need this shit, but as the kid pressed his wrist against my broken lips I smiled, and was just damn glad I had it.

Mom would never have understood why I'd done what I had. She was too stupid to fathom sacrifice and what it meant.

I wasn't my mother. I was a different kind of monster.

I was the kind that took care of her own, that made the

bad men suffer, and that would see her last sunrise when she was ready for it, and not a damn moment before.

Right now, there was only one thing on my mind: Nate.

He was out there, and I was going to find him. We were going to find him.

Hang on, Nate. We are coming for you. We are coming, and we're bringing hell with us.

CHAPTER 17
PIT STOP

"WE'RE LOST."

I frowned at the kid in the dark, or at least I would have had my face not still been crinkly as old newspaper.

Frowning hurt.

So did moving.

And thinking wasn't a walk in the park either.

"Not lost."

That was all I managed, two words, and even that was enough to make me regret opening my mouth.

Whatever counted for adrenaline outside the church was now long gone. The only thing left was to deal with the fact I'd been burned like a marshmallow left in the fire way too long.

You need blood.

I did. I needed a lot of it. Whatever a metric-fuckton was, that was what I needed.

You aren't gonna find it out here.

I wanted to growl at that thought, but to do that would have taken effort, and anything beyond limping next to the kid was pretty much off the table.

"Which way from here?"

Take his blood?

Tempting, but more than anything I wanted to punch him in the nose. Still, we had bigger problems.

You're lost.

If I'd been less stupid there'd still be a Blondy, still be someone to strong arm into getting us to Farmer Bob's home base.

To Nate…

But there wasn't. I'd enjoyed that vanilla wafer and left her crumbles on the church floor.

All I had were the memories, or fragments really, the bits and pieces of a life that looked anything but fun.

It was like finding your way in the dark with nothing more than a music video on mute.

Next to impossible at the best of times, and now?

Now, I couldn't do much more than shuffle through the saw palmetto and sugar sand.

"You don't know where we're going, do you?"

I grunted. The irony of it was almost too much to bear. Hours ago I was the one talking his ears off, and now we'd swapped roles.

Sadly, the kid had about as much patience as a new puppy.

You were like that too, in the beginning…

I tried to think back to those first few days, the painful realizations and the blood.

How many people in that first week? How many did I…

Murder?

It was a strong word, but it wasn't exactly incorrect.

Aside from the neighbor, I'd done a number on a bunch of people.

Too many.

I tried to shake my head, but the pain and splitting flesh proved too much. I almost fell over right there, but once again the kid kept me from ending up face down in the sand.

"Aren't you going to… you know… heal?"

I should. I just need blood, time, and someone to stop talking my ear off.

"Y…es."

"Well." The kid looked for a place to put me, then settled on propping my back against a nicely toppled cypress. The rotting wood put out a pleasant, almost cigar box aroma. But it didn't matter how good it smelled, it wasn't blood, and I knew what was coming. "I'm getting tired of carrying you."

I carried your ass through the wet part when the sun was coming up, you ungrateful shit.

"Tough."

He nodded, as if not understanding the not-so-subtle intonation of my words. "Yeah, but I'll manage, you're really light."

That's not remotely what I mean.

"You're really light and you smell so good."

The little hairs on the back of my neck immediately stood at attention, the ones that hadn't been melted off by that damn flood lamp.

In fact, I knew I should be thinking about that lamp, and the fact that all these assholes seemed to know more about killing vampires than I knew about being one.

Still, thoughts like those required blood, introspection, and something other than a hungry wolf admiring you like an expertly smoked rack of ribs.

Don't even think about it, kid.

I tried to snap my jaws open, but only one-side listened, and barely so at that. It would have been comical, had it not been happening to me.

"This is bullshit." The kid shook his head and elected to pace in the soft sand. "What the hell are we doing out here? Why didn't we just take one of their cars? Why didn't we drive away from here?"

Those were good questions, and the answer was the same in both cases.

"Nate."

"Trending alert, your brother doesn't matter as much to me as you think he does."

"Careful."

The kid threw his arms in the air, pristine and without blemish. Oh, to be young and full of blood.

You could take it…

I dismissed that thought as soon as I had it. The kid could put me down. The kid could put me down *hard*.

And how do you know he won't? Get him before he gets you.

"Where is your brother?" The kid pointed at the trees, spinning his teenage arms like a top. "Where is he? Is he out there? Is he in the trees? Where's this farmhouse?"

"I—"

"You don't know. You have no idea where it is. It could be forty miles away from here for all you know."

No, it couldn't be. They walked to the church. Do you think they walked forty miles?

"Close."

"Oh, right." The teenager pretended to hang on my every word and used air quotes like a champ. "It's 'close.' How long have you been saying that for? An hour, two?"

About thirty minutes I think.

"Bottom line is you don't know where he is, or where this farmhouse is, or if there even is one."

"Blondy…"

"Blondy is dead and I'm hungry. I'm very hung—" He stopped mid-sentence, his head up and sniffing at the air.

I noticed it too. What breeze there was had carried it right into our clearing.

Little Mal would have smiled, she would have asked for one with chili and ketchup.

Hot dogs?

The kid followed that smell and the ones that came after it, his feet moving quickly in the soft sand. It wasn't just hotdogs. It was people too, people and gasoline, and the faint scent of old cigarettes.

It was candy, rubber, and spilled beer.

He said the words as I thought them, both of us coming to the same conclusion at roughly the same time.

"Truck stop."

The kid, my kid, didn't waste any time checking on me before following his nose.

"Wait." I tried to push myself off the log but didn't make it more than a few feet before I was right back in the sand again.

"You wait here. I'll be back."

Sure he'd be back. He'd be back just like all those dads that just went out for cigarettes were coming home any minute now.

He's going to forget about you.

"Damn... it... wait."

But the teen was already gone. He'd vanished between the tall trees with blood on his mind and a stinger directing him to it.

Way to go, Mal, your son is just like you.

I stifled a painful chuckle and rolled over to stare at the stars.

How had I ended up here?

What terrible thing did I do to deserve this?

My brain was more than happy to play out its suggestions in excruciating detail. Thankfully, I was too hungry to feel guilty for them, even though I knew the guilt was there. It was still simmering below the surface, riding backseat to the pain, and to the blood.

You need it.

That's great. Tell me something I don't know.

I didn't know where the farmhouse was. I didn't know

where my brother was, and now I didn't know where the kid was.

I was alone in the sand, staring up at the stars and hoping for something to change.

Stupid kid.

Was he really? Had I been much better?

Those were deep thoughts, and I was a 'surface only' girl at present. I needed blood, and I needed it badly.

My thinking had been reduced to functional concepts. I knew how to claw, how to scrape my way over the sand, so that's what I did.

I'd never make it far like this, but maybe I'd get lucky, maybe a squirrel would fall into my lap, or I'd happen across a blind and deaf bunny.

It'd have to be lame too.

I chuckled at the thought, and at the distant sound of cars on the highway. I needed blood. I needed it badly, but a truck stop?

I let that thought roll around in my head like some compact disc that just kept skipping over the jagged parts.

Get up.

I somehow managed to get to my feet, and to grab a slender pine to keep from toppling back over again.

You can do it. One step at a time. One step at a time and you'll get to Nate. You'll find him, but you can't do it like this. You need blood. You need to survive. Someone has to bleed. Someone has to bleed for Nate.

I stumbled toward the smell of gasoline, hotdogs, and blood.

CHAPTER 18
OASIS

IT SPARKLED like how I imagined Vegas might , a brilliant star against the inky night. Cars moved in and out of so many spaces, their engines rumbling and reminding me of a simpler time. A time when it was just Nate and me, us against the world. It hadn't lasted, because my brother was stupid and liked to thumb his nose at the world, but for a time it had been nice.

Maybe we would have ended up with one of those cars, the nice ones, the ones that ran and had cushy seats and actual seatbelts?

I huddled along the shoreline of a massive retention pond. The gator taking up residence in that pond had already made his presence known, but he didn't know what to make of me, so he kept his distance, for now.

We might be getting a lot more time to know each other, because there was no way I could stumble across that lot without looking like some extra from The Walking Dead.

Some parts of the state, that might get you an autograph request. Here in Southwest Whoknowsville? It was more than likely to get you shot.

I did not need to get shot.

I dug tired fingers into the sand and tried to pick up the kid's smell. That little bastard was here, but where I had no idea.

He doesn't look like a campfire marshmallow.

He didn't, which meant he could go wherever he wanted. He could stroll right in those automatic doors.

And wreak havoc.

The kid was new at this and didn't understand hunger. Hunger wasn't a transitory state. It was the new normal. You were always hungry, always looking for that next meal.

There wasn't enough blood in the world.

I knew that, but I was more than willing to bet the kid didn't.

Well, a good mom would have explained that.

I stuffed that admonishment in the mental retention pond that was my life. It would surface later, when things were quiet, to remind me exactly what sort of person I was.

But right now, more than anything, I was hungry.

I counted the cars as they pulled up to park. Lots of bleary-eyed parents and sleeping kids. They smelled like oatmeal and raisins, like some breakfast food, and I had to put a hand on my jaws to keep them folded.

What has gotten into you, Mal?

It was one thing fighting back against self-righteous assholes with guns, but a whole other plucking sleeping kids out of their cars.

I left those dads to pump their gas and their children to sleep, but that didn't stop my hands from shaking.

I needed blood, and I needed it yesterday.

A massive tractor trailer rumbled off the highway, pulling into one of those oversized spaces before killing the high-beams.

The cab swung open moments later to reveal an august gentleman, complete with beard and doo-rag. If I'd looked up trucker in the dictionary I'd have been hard pressed to find something other than his picture.

Bingo.

Without thinking about it, my stinger dropped out and tasted the air. It knew what it wanted, and he was it. That vest and overly stretched tank-top were like the tortilla shell of one human-sized burrito.

Hints of carne asada, complete with lime and cilantro danced across that second tongue.

Mal…

I knew that voice. That was the voice of reason. That was the voice that said: don't eat that man. I wanted to listen to that voice, but instead I mentally fed her to the alligator drifting lazily in the water behind me.

Momma was hungry.

Yeah, well, Momma needs a plan.

I could barely walk, let alone pounce. I needed to get lucky. I needed my human-sized walking burrito to be a good person.

I needed him to care.

Somewhere in the dark water behind me, reasonable Mal screamed out in rage. She didn't like this. She didn't want anything to do with this.

She could die of blood loss for all I cared. This Mal needed to eat, and she needed to do it right the fuck now.

I pushed off, scrambling up the bank and getting as far as the pavement before collapsing on the jagged ground.

This has to work. Please work.

I tilted my head just right, enough to show off some of the scorching, but not enough to think I was well past done, then I waited. I waited for him to look over, to spot the woman laying down in the parking lot and to come to her aid.

All I could do now was hope for the best, hope for what I wanted to happen, hope for blood.

As luck would have it I didn't have to wait long, but also that same luck made damn sure I didn't get what I wanted.

"Oh my god!" The woman's voice caught my ears first, it came with the smell of oatmeal and baby vomit. It also came with soft hands on my back. "Mike! Call 911. I think this girl has been burned. Oh sweet Jesus, honey. Are you okay?"

There more sounds, car doors slamming and the faint beep of buttons being pressed. It all came with motherly smells, and the hint of cotton candy.

I hazarded a peek and found exactly what I didn't want to see. Some middle-aged mom, heavy on the make-up and compassion kneeling next to me, spinning up her husband and a whole fucking hornet's nest. My carne asada burrito lingered for a few seconds before racing inside the rest station as fast as those stubby legs could take him.

This was going off the rails in spectacular fashion and if I wasn't careful in seconds I'd be surrounded.

So much for running silent.

Dad joined Mom, and for a bit, I reveled in their combined attention. It had been so long since someone cared about me like that, and I almost wished I could climb in their car and drive off to a new life.

Dad pressed a phone to his face, the untucked polo shirt and boat shoes giving him a very movie-father look.

He went down first.

I had very little in the way of strength left, but I had my stinger. It moved fast, slipping out and going for the juicy spot behind his khaki-covered knee.

He wasn't carne asada, but he had a nice burger flavor, something left on the grill for just the right amount of time. I tasted sear lines, and a tangy hint of onion. It wasn't much, but it was enough.

He hit the ground hard enough to knock him cold.

It was Mom that really got the party going.

She screamed something and tried to get away, but I was

in gear now and humming. Dad had been just the appetizer, this woman would be my main course. She didn't make it more than a few feet before I tackled her to the ground, that compassionate face splitting open on the pavement.

Mal, stop!

I didn't want to stop. I wanted to enjoy it all. I wanted to soak up every last ounce of Mom and let it swirl around nicely in my belly. Her blood rushed over my tongue, giving me what I needed, but slipping in memories of its own. Fragments of thoughts and emotions hit hard, tightening my chest and squeezing my tongue.

They came too fast to push away: her baby's smile, and the way his eyes lit up when she entered the room, the sound of him crying and the way he suckled at her breast.

I wanted it to stop. I wanted to let go, but the stinger didn't share those desires. It pulled deeper, taking what it wanted and leaving nothing in return.

I drank down first smiles, and that time he crawled across the floor. I swallowed his colic, and so many burpings in the dark.

Stop, Mallory!

I wanted to stop, but at the same time I didn't. I wanted what she had. I wanted everything that made her life what it was. I wanted her warm bed, her husband's hands in the dark.

I wanted it all, but I couldn't have it.

I would never have it.

The stinger detached and I dropped her, almost surprised to find a weak heart still beating. It wasn't much, but I dragged them both to their car, sealing wounds with my tongue and propping each one up in their seat. A concerned little man stared back at me from his car seat.

"Momma's gonna be fine. So's Dad. They just need to rest a little." Maybe that was a lie, I didn't know.

I let my jaws ripple, the infant laughing at the chilling display.

"You're a good kid. A lot better than mine. I see now what it takes to be a mom. If I'm being honest, it looks pretty amazing, in a completely shitty sort of way." I ran my hand through the kid's hair, happy I saved his mom, and stifling the hunger that was already returning to my tired flesh.

There would be no cotton candy, and no stories of dead mothers and fathers, just two worn out parents that fell asleep in their car.

I grabbed what looked like Mom's jacket off the back seat and put it on, adding a ball cap I'd found next to it to my ensemble, then slipped out of the car.

Nate was out there, but first, I had my own son to think about.

CHAPTER 19
HOME SWEET HOME

AUTOMATIC DOORS WHISKED open and I slipped inside, doing my best to hold back the thundering tide of sound. Everything echoed, it bounced off high ceilings and right back into my ears. It was impossible not to hear it: the conversations, the heartbeats, the sound of blood pumping through veins. It was all there, and it called to me. Turnpike rest stops were like enormous buffets with all the trimmings. It wasn't one Thanksgiving dinner. It was a hundred.

Roast beef mixed with curry in the cool air-conditioned space, but it didn't come from restaurants, it came from the people themselves, from all their glorious blood.

Keep it together, Mal.

My jaws wanted to ripple. Hell, they wanted to explode open and send that stinger zeroing in on the first piece of tasty meat passing by, but I didn't let them.

I was in control.

At least for now.

I pulled Mom's jacket up higher, flipping the collar so it would give me a little cover should my lips decide to do the happy dance.

You could never have come here with Nate.

That was true. With my brother I'd have had to avoid places like this, places with people, places with so many good things to eat.

I let my eyes wander over the little shops that lined the mall-like interior. Smiling flamingos and snow globes lined shelves in equal abundance, along with all manner of once-in-a-lifetime merchandise the casual visitor would just have to have.

Where's the kid?

I pushed that thought away, content to wander past a magazine rack and stare at the women on those glossy covers. I bet they didn't have to worry about their jaws unfolding, or just how long it had been since they let their stinger feed.

That second tongue shifted in my throat as if listening to my words.

I tightened my jaws, squeezing it down and forcing that thing to sit quiet like a misbehaving child.

I bet those girls didn't need to worry about their brother, or some son they didn't exactly mean to make.

He saved you.

I frowned at that thought, and my reflection in a mirrored display. I would never be one of the girls on those magazine covers.

And you'll never be a mother.

That one stung, and it got my lips moving. I snapped the collar up tighter to cover them lest someone see.

Who cares? Who cares if they see? Let them. Let them bleed. Let them fear you.

I let my hand down, and the collar with it, the lips underneath settling back into place with little effort.

People rolled past, men and women alike. They moved like schooling fish, like so many tasty tacos herding from the doors to the restrooms before resuming their adventures, their lives.

I want a life.

The chilling finality of that thought hit me like a thief in the night. It stole what joy the blood had brought without a moment's hesitation.

Then leave.

Automatic doors whisked behind me, soft and whispering reminders of the world outside, the world beyond Nate.

Find someone to feed on, maybe someone good to turn?

My eyes followed a handful of men roughly my age, and in seconds my brain was busy building a life around that imaginary world. We were a bloody force of nature. We took what we wanted, when we wanted it. We answered to no one, and had children of our own, violent and strong.

It wasn't till I reached the doors trailing one particular tall, dark, and potential, that I stopped myself.

What are you doing?

I'm having a life.

I stared at those doors, and at the world beyond them.

You can't have a life.

My lips rippled again, but this time I didn't move to cover them. I didn't care.

Why? Why can't I have a life?

I knew the answer even though I didn't want to admit it.

Dead things didn't get to have lives.

I let that sexy potential partner vanish into the lot, fading to nothing beyond the frosted glass.

Dead things didn't get lives, but maybe they don't have to think about their brothers either?

I let that sobering thought linger, not interested in kicking it to the curb quite so quickly.

Was this my chance? Could I just leave and be done with it? Could I just walk away?

I wouldn't have called what I had life, but whatever it was, it would have been easier without Nate.

Go. Leave him. Leave them both.

The doors slid open and a young mother walked in, kids

in tow. She brought with her all those smells, and the guilt they came with. I found Nate's big eyes in her little son's face.

They came with the dark of that empty cooler, the hours spent wondering what happened to him, to the only person who would never stop loving me for who I was.

They also came with the smell of his blood on Blondy's blade.

My brother was out there. I knew it, and I owed it to him to not stop searching. Nate would have done as much for me.

My brother would have ripped the world in two for me, yet here I was losing my mind over glamor magazines and babies.

You know what you need to do.

I did, but I didn't know where to start.

Start by finding the kid and getting somewhere safe—

A high-pitched scream set the whole rest stop on its head. Schools of people hardly paying attention to each other, let alone where they were going, immediately looked up and took notice.

That was the scream of someone seeing a stinger for the first time. It came with a wet crack and the sound of splashing blood.

Women poured out of the rest room like someone had set it on fire. They spilled out over each other as the crowd descended into hysteria.

Shit.

I pulled my hat down and fought the crowd, swimming upstream toward the bathrooms and what had to be the kid. I hadn't cleared half the distance before I spotted highway patrol. I counted two of them, male and female, and both going heavy on the body armor. Their guns didn't last long in holsters and radios immediately crackled to life.

Leave him!

I slowed, letting the police rush in ahead of me.

Let him go. You aren't responsible for him. You aren't his—

The young mother with her toddlers streamed past, headed for the exit and white knuckling her kids' hands in the process.

I wasn't that kind of mother, but I was a mother. I was better than my mother. I was responsible for the kid.

Whatever the hell his name was.

I tossed the ball cap and shucked Mom's jacket. I didn't need them getting in the way.

Trouble doesn't need a disguise.

The smell of blood hit me before I reached the restrooms. It was a funny aroma, an almost spicy tang with a hint of pineapple. It was different, and it was everywhere. I barely rounded the corner before the highway patrol was screaming at him to put his hands up.

Putting up his hands wouldn't have made a difference, they weren't the problem. The problem was his stinger and the jaws that opened like the pedals of a flower behind it. Kneeling in a monstrous pool of blood, he cried tears of joy.

He was lost in the blood and in the memories it dredged up.

"I'm home!" His stinger snaked through what I could only imagine were the remains of a woman. It was hard to tell, because the kid hadn't held back. This was no dainty kill.

This was a goddamn mess.

"Put your fucking hands up!" The closest officer had his gun up and very little in the way of color on his face. His partner didn't look much better.

The only one happy here was the kid, and he was overjoyed. "It tastes like home! All of it! Home."

Home... I didn't have the heart to tell him, but home was something we'd never have again.

Now home was blood and broken bodies.

It was ruin.

It was family.

I let my jaws unfold slowly, each side stretching out like a jungle cat preparing to pounce. The stinger beneath them swelled in the harsh light.

He was home.

He was home with me.

I imagined that little boy squeezing his mother's hand and I hit the man first, my stinger wrapping his neck like a python.

His shock turned to fear and the first shots fired.

I took one in the chest and another in the arm. That's what moms did. They took care of their kids, they kept them safe.

My stinger squeezed, cracking cartilage and splitting tissue. I rode that joy, and the blood that came with it to a new and wildly self-righteous place. I'd barely finished killing him before I turned my attention to his partner and whatever else was on the menu.

CHAPTER 20
SAY MY NAME

THE KID CRIED.

Those were tears of joy and memory. He was lost in it, lost in the blood and something it had brought him, something he needed.

The second cop must have needed something too, because she unloaded, firing round after round at my boy.

Bullets sliced through his flesh without effort, they ripped through the pedal of his jaws and shattered teeth.

They made me angry.

I remembered back when I'd been attacked by that dog, and I remembered what Mom had done about it. The old woman had been lazy, self-absorbed, and an addict, but you didn't fuck with her kids and walk right afterward.

Yeah, I was that kind of mother now. I was the bloody kind, the angel of death with hungry jaws and a tongue that wanted nothing more than to tear her still beating heart from her chest.

The body armor made that difficult, so I settled for tackling her and driving all of that child-hurting mass to the ground. That pretty head bounced nicely off the tile, sending eyeballs rolling backwards and giving me all the time in the world to select the best spot for my stinger.

The second tongue split salt-sweaty flesh and dug deep, swimming in the blood and the broken memories that came with it.

Mommy!

That's who I was.

The world shifted, and I found myself somewhere else, somewhere domestic. There were tiny toddler shoes to press on feet that went limp at their touch.

No!

Little arms threw themselves around my neck. They came with kisses, the sloppy wet ones not held back by modesty or years of conditioning. These were young, carefree, and soul-scorching. I tried to push them back, but there were too many. Tiny feet gave way to even smaller hands and great piles of blocks. They stacked high, so high they blotted out the light and formed a multi-color prison. I was trapped in here, trapped with my guilt, and with my fear.

My kid went home.

I came here.

I returned to my personal hell.

The blocks shifted, becoming the concrete walls of a man-made cave that was my world. I wasn't alone. I was there with Nate, with a bloody and broken brother sputtering on dewormer and the great gouges left by Blondy's blade.

He tried to spit out words, but Nate's speech had long since left him. He was like a whimpering dog, his fingers squeezing mine in the dusty dark.

You did this to him.

I wanted to argue otherwise. I wanted to show off just what kind of mother I'd become, but it was a pale reminder of who I'd failed.

"Just hold on, Nate. Just hold on. I'm coming for you."

Blondy was there, living in these blood memories and using them as a way to dig her blade ever deeper.

"You had a chance. You could have kept me alive. I could have taken you to him. Now what are you going to do?" The buzz cut blonde picked up her blade and wiped it across a red-stained chest.

What are you going to do?

I let Nate go, my stinger retracting with the mother's last heartbeat. It came back with pain, with anger, and with guilt.

It came back with all those things because that was all it knew.

The jaws, the fangs, the stinger, they only knew pain, they only knew ruin.

They only knew how to take.

I collapsed to my knees, taking in the soft sound of crying and the smell of blood, so much blood.

"I… I was home." Tears streaked the kid's red cheeks.

"No, you weren't."

He pounded one of those teenage fists against the mutilated woman's body. "You wouldn't understand. I was there. I know it. I was fucking there and I'm going to go back."

I shook my head, pushing down the guilt and blood memories. There would be time for them later. There would be so many sleepless days spent counting how bad I screwed up, but now I had a kid to collect and somewhere safe to get.

More police would come, and eventually someone who knew what we were, and how to work a killing light.

You have to be the mom. This is your life now.

"You didn't go home. You just found something in the blood, something that—"

The kid lunged, hitting me before I was ready for it. I toppled over, the two of us spinning in a mess of blood and bile.

"You don't get to tell me what I did and didn't do! You don't! You don't even know my name."

His stinger erupted, splitting those jaws in two and zeroing in on my throat. He was fast, but I was faster. I knocked that second tongue away and spun my hips, flipping him and taking the top position.

"I don't care!" I snapped my jaws open wide. "Do you hear me? I don't fucking care if I know you or not. I made you! I can unmake you. I don't need to know your name. Names are for living things, for things with a future." I swung a hand at the mess that was the restroom. "You think this is a future? This is all we are. We are death. We are death and fucking ruin. Everything we touch turns to shit. That's what you signed up for. That's what you are now. That's what you'll always be."

Tears returned to the kid's eyes. "I'm… Billy."

"Whatever." I kicked off, standing up and leaving my son in the mess he'd made. "I told you, names are for things that matter. We don't matter."

"Your brother matters." Billy's words were soft, but sharp as fuck.

I sprung back around but he had a hand up before I could reach him.

"I saw him! I saw him in my head."

"That's not possible."

Billy struggled to his feet. "Why? Why is that not possible?"

"Because Nate is fucking gone. I have to accept that now. He's fucking gone because of me, because of my stupid shit." I stomped on a crackling radio, crushing it like a grape beneath my boot.

More are coming, Mal.

"He's not gone! I saw him. I saw him in—"

"You saw him in your home? Is that what you think, Billy? Is that what passes for thoughts in that broken head of yours?"

"Home isn't always a place." Again he slipped those

words out just quiet enough that I had to pay attention to hear them.

It was an asshole trick, but it worked.

"Sure. Home is a person. Shit, home is a big fat bag of blood. Home is whatever you want it to be. You'll figure this out eventually, but you can't move in with the first girl you lay, and you can't get lost in the first big blood score. You gotta let it go. You were right. We'll get a car and we'll get the hell out of here. I'll get us back to the concrete cave and we'll be safe when the sun comes up, but first we need to move. We need to get the hell out of here before the cavalry shows up." I kicked at the closest corpse. "There might be more of them with killing lights and God only knows what else."

I made for the exit, but Billy hesitated. He couldn't take his eyes off the woman he'd ripped to pieces.

"Come on, there'll be plenty more to weep for. You'll cry yourself a river before you're done, but one day you'll reach a point where the tears don't come anymore. That's when you'll know."

"Know what?"

"That's when you'll know you really are a monster."

I hadn't made it to the exit before Billy spoke again.

"Mallory."

I froze, the already fading Mom blood in my system growing colder by the second. "What did you just say?"

"Mallory. That's your name."

What happened next was a blur. I came back faster than I expected, and hit him with the full force of a woman who'd had enough of this shit. We slammed against the ground together, but Billy didn't crack his skull open. He fought back, jaws expanding and stinger on the offensive.

It didn't matter.

My second tongue pushed the folds of his face aside and dug deep, feeling for the blood I knew was there.

Bingo.

It washed over that serrated thing, soaking into flesh that was always hungry for it. It found a home, and brought with it ghostly fragments of thought.

I don't believe it.

There he was, plain as day and screaming like a banshee. One word rattled off those lips again and again, and each time it did, it cut me just a little deeper.

"Mallory!"

My brother was still out there, and whoever Billy's victim was, she'd seen him. I let the kid go, pushing back and stumbling to my feet. "That's my name, and that's my brother."

Billy nodded slowly, pulling his jaws shut as the first siren's wail hit our ears. "I know."

"Then take me home, Billy. Take me fucking home."

I want to see my brother again.

CHAPTER 21
REALITY CHECK

NATE.

He was out there. He was out there somewhere, and all I had was the kid.

Billy.

I pushed that thought down. Names were for living things, for people that mattered.

The kid didn't deserve a name, not yet.

Covered in blood and staring at the bathroom floor, the subtle hints of realization were just beginning to dawn across his face. Those jaws that had been so hungry for blood only minutes ago now hung limp, barely closing behind the rest of his blood-smeared face. He was in deep now.

The guilt.

It hadn't really hit him before, because before he'd had a reason to kill, now... A monster knelt in that blood, a monster only just realizing what he was, and what it meant. I didn't envy him, but I did need him to move.

I needed him to move now.

"We need to go!" I grabbed the kid's arm and pulled him toward the exit, my feet sliding on the wet tile.

"No."

"Oh, hell no." I dug my nails in harder. "It doesn't work that way. I'm in charge. You go *where* I want you to go *when* I want you to go there."

Billy didn't budge, his knees rooted and his hand in what was left of the woman he'd devoured earlier. The room smelled like soap and pennies. It went great with the subtle aroma of gun oil and tactical vests wafting in from the rest stop proper. Given the sound of those heartbeats and the subtle prickle of adrenaline in the evening air, I got the impression they weren't there for snow-globes or lottery tickets.

The kid squeezed viscera between his fingers like clay. He wasn't really here, not mentally. That first cold one was crushing, and it had taken him down hard. The blood gave, but it took far more.

Somewhere in that broken head of his he was replaying the scene, the moment of sheer bliss when his second tongue hit the motherlode, and the memories that followed. I needed those memories. I needed them to last and to tell me where to go.

Nate was calling my name.

I thought names were only for things that mattered?

That single moment of elation was shattered by the crackle of radios and the sharp sound of clicking firearms.

I turned toward the exit briefly, letting the vision of taking them all down wash over me. They were exactly what stood between me and my brother.

Mallory…

It was my name, but it was Nate's voice in my head speaking it. I hadn't heard my brother speak in so long that it brought a lone tear to my cheek even now.

You've been holding out on me, bro.

I smiled at that thought, but it was short-lived. I needed the kid moving if there was any chance of getting out of here before taking more shotgun blasts to the chest than any sane woman would ever sign up for.

I pulled on his arm again, but this time he pulled back.

"No! I want to go home. It was right here! I could smell it!" The kid squeezed more organs together, their juices running across the floor and down a narrow drain. "I could taste it! Don't you understand? I could *taste* it!"

"And all you're going to be tasting is metal shot and more artificial sunlight if any of these bastards know what's up."

I thought that might move the kid's feet, but they remained planted.

More radios crackled outside the bathroom. They came with boots and the muffled sounds of tactical positioning. I'd watched enough cop movies with Nate growing up. I knew enough to know we weren't going out the way we came in.

"I'm not leaving her." Billy said the words like he meant it. The tough part for him was that I meant business too. My brother was somewhere in those blood memories and the longer we waited to tap into them, the hazier that shit was going to get.

Mallory!

I mentally pushed screaming Nate aside, trying not to focus on the already tattered edges and dropped myself in front of the kid.

"She's dead, Billy. You don't come back from dead."

He squeezed gore between his fingers. "We did."

"Okay, bad example. You don't come back from *this* dead. This dead, they pick up the big pieces and hose off the rest."

The stark reminder of what he had done seemed to hit Billy between the ears. He dropped the pieces of what had been his dinner and lost what little color his cheeks possessed with it. "What did I—"

"You did what you do, what I do, what we all do. This is good. This guilt. It's good. It means there's still a part of you that cares. There's still a part of you that wants to be human."

"And what if I don't like that part?"

The sharp scent of gunpowder made its way into the bathroom.

"Listen, kid. I'll level with you. I don't really know. All this shit is new to me too. You don't get a handbook or a crash course on how to survive any of this with your humanity intact. You fuck up. You fuck up a lot. Sometimes you rip someone to pieces, but sometimes you don't. There's a little kid in the back seat of someone's car right now because I didn't give in. It's not like I deserve a medal or anything, but I didn't kill him, or his parents. You'll get there."

"Car…" Billy said the word as if it held some deeper meaning.

"Right, car. Outside. Listen we need to—"

"Marie had a car!"

"Who the hell is Marie?"

Billy sprung up, pushing me aside and diving into the bits of what remained. For a second I thought he might have been digging in for seconds, but then I realized his stinger wasn't making a grand entrance.

He was looking for pockets.

He was looking for keys.

"Got 'em!" Billy sprung out of the mess with a shiny glint of metal in his red fingers and a wide smile on his face.

He didn't know it, but that was how it would be, the blood would keep him moving forward, but it would eat at his memories, his humanity. It would blend things up, push thoughts in and out like some game of 'stack the tiles' until they toppled down in those agonizing moments before the dawn.

Maybe Marie would visit him? Maybe she would convince him that *he* should see the sunrise?

Hell no.

I pulled him up and grabbed the keys out of his bloody fingers.

If Marie did come, she'd have to get through me.

The kid was my only link to Nate and getting to my brother was all that mattered. The men and women outside the bathrooms didn't matter, not the guns in their hands, or the bullets waiting to be fired.

All that mattered was finding Nate.

I had the kid and his blood memories, and we had a ride.

Things were looking up if we could just figure out a way to get to the car without having our insides sprayed all over the floor like Marie here.

"What now?" The kid asked, those big eyes right back to puppy dog mode, but I knew what was behind them. I knew there was a monster curled beneath that second tongue, a monster hungry for blood and nothing else.

"Right now we need to figure out a plan for getting out of—"

Clink! Clink!

A couple of metal canisters hit the floor, alternating between sliding and rolling through what was left of Marie and the two officers that had stood in my way.

"What the hell are—"

I lost the rest of what the kid said in the flash of light and the boom that followed. I remembered hitting the sink and snapping my head back something fierce. I also remembered watching the kid crash into a stall before vanishing behind its swinging door.

Boots were coming: boots with guns, beating hearts, and so much blood.

The kid…

Somewhere in the smoky haze it came to me. The kid couldn't feed, if he did, he might lose Marie, and losing Marie meant losing Nate.

My jaws unfolded slowly beneath the broken sink. The bones of my skull were already pulling themselves back together. That second tongue surfaced, hungry to feast and ready to strike down the first thing to come into my house.

I was the momma cat now and this was my den.

You come inside? You get my claws.

You try to stay? You get my jaws.

The kid mumbled something from the stall but didn't move.

Good. Stay down. This is Momma's fight now. You stay down and think happy thoughts about Marie, blood, and home. You focus on that and let Momma take care of everything else.

I stuffed those keys in my pocket and turned to face our future, jaws wide and tongue hungry.

Come and fucking get me.

CHAPTER 22
NO SOUP FOR YOU

WHAT ARE YOU DOING, *Mallory?*

The truth was, I didn't know what I was doing. I hadn't known what I was doing for a very long time. I was falling through this bloody and twisted version of life without much of a real plan.

Things happened. I reacted.

Crouched under the sink, jaws wide and stinger out, I was doing what I did best, improvising.

I was running hungry.

I was hungry to find Nate, to put an end to this nightmare of bad decisions, and to see the damn concrete cave again.

I never thought I'd miss that place, yet here, waiting to pounce, and wondering if either the kid or I would survive it, I missed those stupid walls.

I missed the damp ground and the humid air.

I missed my brother's silent presence.

I missed home.

It was a shithole, Mal.

It was a shithole, but it was *my* shithole.

For a girl who'd barely made ends meet for so many years, having anything of my own felt incredible.

It was hard not to imagine it now, to pretend I was back in that hut with the leaky metal roof, but this version was different. This version had bad men, bad men with guns, radios, and faces hidden beneath masks.

Why don't you come in and say 'Hi.' I won't bite…much.

The first man to round the corner, gun up and heart thumping, got more than he bargained for. I hit him low, taking out those knees and enjoying the wet pop they made on impact. I enjoyed all of it more now.

I enjoyed the strength, the power.

I'd been pushed around by so many assholes over the years, now I could push back.

I could push back *hard.*

Ligaments snapped and cartilage sheared, but that was just the beginning. My stinger found the crease between that tactical armor and went to town.

Pizza!

I hadn't had a good pie in what felt like a lifetime, but this guy's blood brought it all back, the sharp bite of crispy pepperoni, the warm cheesy goodness it floated over, and the sauce.

Blood red and hearty, the sauce was enough to give me a head rush.

The whole feast came with new memories, violent and painful ones. There were guns, smoke, and fire, so much fire.

I didn't hang around to get the whole picture. In fact, I barely had time to get my second tongue free before the bullets started putting fresh holes in the stall doors.

Billy!

All that mattered now was the kid. That teenager was my ticket to Nate. He was the only one that knew where my brother was, or at least a way to get to him. He was also my son, and just because I could hate on him, didn't mean anyone else could.

Someone shouted something. It sounded important, but whatever it was, it didn't matter to me.

I leapt, taking a couple of stray shots in the leg before hitting my target. This time I wasn't dainty. I didn't go for the soft spots or the creases between the dark armor. I went for the face and all the tasty bits beneath it.

My jaws latched on, like a calf suckling at her mother's tit. Fangs hooked bone and sliced through tendons, and behind it all, blood roared. Another Italian meal rolled over my stinger, oregano, tomatoes, and something that very much resembled vodka creme hit my stomach like rocket fuel.

I wanted it.

I wanted all of it. I didn't care that it came with memories of kids on swings, of a pregnant wife, or so many hand-drawn pictures they could cover the walls of my mental concrete cave.

I didn't care about any of those things. I only cared about the blood.

I didn't feel the gun barrel wedge itself beneath my chin, nor did I realize his fingers were still moving until they'd found the trigger.

I could heal most everything, but something told me I couldn't put my brain back together.

Thankfully, I didn't have to answer that question, because no sooner had my second dinner wrapped the trigger than the two of us were treated to the kid at high-speed.

Billy hit fast, knocking me and the gun free, then taking position atop the broken man. His jaws wide and eyes full of hatred, Billy was my avenging angel of death, my bloody savior.

Don't let him feed!

It took a second for that thought to register, and almost as long to get my stinger out and around the kid's neck.

Billy fought back, his jaws hungry for the vodka creme feast laid out on the crimson tile.

"Stop! You can't lose home. You can't lose Marie."

You can't lose Nate!

He didn't appear to understand, his eyes unfocused and wild. I couldn't blame him. There was too much blood, and it just kept coming. More bodies rounded the corner, their heavy legs pounding rubber boots on the already slick tile.

There was gun oil, pain, and the hint of ozone.

Someone out there knew what we were, and they had that killing light.

"Billy! We need to go!"

I pulled and the kid pulled back, his jaws flapping wildly and the stinger beneath them fighting for freedom.

"Let go!"

The kid didn't let go, not until a fresh set of bullets tore through his arm and sprayed chunks of his shoulder across the far wall. I grabbed that hungry mess with both hands and ripped it into the closest stall. More bullets shattered the mirror and tore apart sinks. They split the cheap pressboard like matchsticks and found new homes in both of us.

It hurt.

It really hurt, and worse, it made me mad. It made me want to tear them apart, to swim in their blood, to eat that hot metal and spit it back down their throats. I squeezed Billy, holding the kid like I'd comforted Nate when he was little. I held him like I cared, like I cared about something other than death and blood.

Another person might have prayed, pleaded with God or the fates to spare her from all of this.

I wasn't that person. I wasn't stupid either.

Glass blocks shattered above us, the frosted, stone-like cubes tumbling down in chunks. They came with the sound of people, the smell of gasoline, and the tantalizing hint of freedom.

I pushed Billy up first, practically throwing his bloody

body out the newly formed opening before scrambling up after.

Men shouted and boots thundered over the slick tile. We didn't have much time. We had to find the car.

I scooped a hand under Billy, throwing what remained of his shoulder over mine and limping into the massive lot. Lights flashed and police cars blocked most of the exits.

"Billy!" I slapped the stunned teen a couple of times with my hand. "Wake the hell up! Which car is *her* car?"

The kid's eyes fluttered and his jaws with them.

"I'm gonna need more than that." I dragged us into the morass of vehicles, doing what I could to keep the both of us below the door line, but it was slow going. We'd taken too many bullets, lost too much blood. We needed to find the car, and we needed to find it now.

Shouts from the entrance of the rest stop echoed across the lot. They knew we were out here and if we didn't get the hell out soon, then it didn't matter how many bullets we could eat, they'd always have one more.

"B...blue." Billy stuttered out the answer only to get clipped by the side mirror of one very red sports car.

"Blue?!" I stumbled a few more feet, the distant sound of heartbeats, boots, and anger driving me forward. "You're going to have to do a lot better than blue!"

"Four doors."

More sirens wailed in the distance. It appeared we'd spun up a hornet's nest and didn't have much in the way of plans around what came next.

We were reacting.

We were trying to stay alive, or what passed for living.

We were a mess, and I wasn't sure we'd make it out of the lot.

I stumbled a few more feet and thought about the retention pond, but that was back the way we came, on the other side, and past far too many metal teeth.

I pushed Billy up against the side of a silver sedan and tried not to panic.

Think, Mallory! Think!

I needed blood to think.

I needed blood to survive.

I needed blood to find Nate.

I hesitated, turning back toward the rest station and the gun-carrying evil pouring out of it, when Billy tugged on my arm.

"There…"

Barely blue and more or less rust-covered, what I assumed was Marie's ride sat under a streetlamp.

It was ugly as sin, but in that moment, I could have kissed it, and him.

"Good work," I pushed him toward the quiet vehicle, "Now, keep thinking of home and not how we are getting out of here. Let me worry about that. You don't let go of Marie."

Or Nate…

CHAPTER 23
WHEELS UP

I JAMMED the key in the lock and almost lost it when the metal turned. The subtle clunk might as well have been the singing of angels for how good it sounded to my ears.

"Get in!"

I pushed Billy up against the rear door and yanked the driver's side open.

For as old as the car was, it was clean. It came with the smell of chemicals, sponges, and damp rags. A little pine tree hung from the rearview mirror, long since devoid of scent, but its cheerful message reminding me to stay positive written in a swirling script.

I didn't have time for positive. I only had time for getting the hell out of here before the rest of the state's law enforcement personnel descended on us like hungry locusts.

Speaking of hungry, I needed to keep Billy from eating anything until we got what we needed.

Nate.

I shoved the key into the ignition and turned the engine over. Whoever Marie had been, she'd kept her car in decent shape. The throaty monster under the hood roared to life and gave me hope.

I should have known it would never be that easy.

Never.

"Hang on, Billy. We're gonna…" My words trailed off in the rearview mirror's reflection. The kid wasn't in the back seat.

Where the hell—

A muffled scream from the car next to me provided all the details I needed. Billy's jaws were open wide and pressed up against the glass, while on the other side some teenager looked like she was vacuuming up nightmare material for a lifetime of therapist bills.

"Damn it!" I threw my door back open and reached for the kid, but that was roughly the same moment her glass broke, and everything went to shit.

Like the blood addict he was, Billy scrambled to rip the rest away and crawl inside. His fingers already frayed, he clawed at the door locks, throwing them up only to have the young woman pop them closed again.

His stinger shot out faster than I expected, and had the girl not hit the deck she might have already made it to first base with my near feral progeny.

Billy scrambled to get through the window, his mind on one thing, and one thing alone, the blood.

He'd taken too many bullets, too many shots to the sensitive parts, the ones that bled. He was running low and couldn't reason, couldn't think clearly.

Billy couldn't fathom that to eat now might cost him home, and any memory we had of Nate.

That was not an option.

We didn't have time for screwing around, the men racing across the parking lot made that abundantly apparent. Billy wasn't going to respond to words, or anything remotely civil.

I let my jaws unfold, the stinger beneath them dropping out like a snake coaxed from her basket. She licked at the air and tasted the myriad of intoxicating flavors. Screaming as she fought to get the far door open, the girl was like spicy rum, a warm liquor that wanted nothing more than to run down that stinger and make its home in my belly.

No, Mallory! Think of Nate.

I pushed that thought back for a second, preferring to enjoy the complex aroma of exotic rum and how it would dance across my tongue.

It was the sound of boots, shouting, and the smell of gun metal that brought me back.

It wasn't Nate. It was survival.

I peeled my stinger away from that tasty treat fighting to free herself from the steel coffin and looped it around Billy's neck. It was a simple move, one he'd been busted by more than once, and frankly should have seen coming.

I was knee deep in that smug thought that the kid managed to swing around and deck me.

Don't get me wrong, I'd been punched before. I'd made stupid choices and gone in for the wrong assholes, but this was the first time I'd been completely caught off guard by it. The parking lot lights spun as the pavement raced up to greet me.

The kid got yanked down with me, my stinger still hopelessly clinging to his neck.

That was when the girl broke free, our spicy rum treat with cutoffs and a midriff running between the cars like an extra from some horror movie.

Seeing the girl clear must have given them all the assurances they needed, because that was when hell started raining down. White-hot metal shattered glass and tore holes in doors. The nose-wrinkling scent of gasoline filled the air and put my already tired heart in high gear.

"I said come on!" I grabbed Billy's shoulder and scrambled to my knees. Together with a confused and hungry kid, I pushed the driver's door back open. This time I shoved the kid in first, taking a few grazing shots for my trouble.

"Get down!"

Of course the idiot didn't get down, he scrambled up the passenger seat like a golden retriever out for a summer drive, his jaws wide and his stinger tasting the air. He wanted this. He wanted all of it. Billy needed blood and he didn't care where he got it.

I threw myself into the seat and fought for the gear shifter.

Just get it in reverse!

Rat, tat, tat!

More bullets made their home in Marie's trunk, slicing through the soft cushions before embedding themselves in the sensitive electronics, and us.

Thump!

The gear shift dropped into place and I slammed both feet on the gas. The sedan didn't seem too keen on listening, but flooding her engine provided ample motivation. We exploded off the mark and if I hadn't turned the wheel hard we'd have ended up embedded in the trunk of whoever'd been unlucky enough to park behind Marie.

More glass shattered and I took a bullet in the hand. Tiny bones and tendons I really needed ripped apart against the fake leather steering wheel.

I shoved the mess under my other arm and used that hand to throw us into drive.

Billy screamed something, but I lost his words on the rush of adrenaline and smell of blood. My jaws swelled, catching the wind and embracing the madness of it all. Billy tumbled forward, falling beneath the dash as I gunned it for the exit.

I didn't see the other cars as much as I felt them. We moved like a dented pinball, bouncing off vehicles in a mad dash for the on-ramp, and the highway beyond it.

Go, Mal! Go!

I knew it wasn't enough. Even if we reached the toll road, they would follow. We'd done too much, taken too many lives. The noose was already around my neck, except it wasn't a rope, it was a stinger.

It was my stinger.

Someone backed out in front of us and I swerved, hitting the grassy stretch that lined the retention pond. It seemed like forever ago when I'd couched in that muck and given an alligator the stink eye. What I would have given to be back there, and not here, running for my unnatural life.

Marie's tires spun in the slick grass, then caught, launching the car forward like a badly aimed slingshot. We hit the road, throwing sparks and doing what we could to keep from shooting right back off it again.

The kid didn't budge and for once I was thankful. I forced my jaws closed and slammed on the gas, pushing Marie's sedan to the limit. The car grudgingly agreed, racing down the dark road.

"You can get up now."

The kid didn't move.

"If you want to stay down you can, but the bullets are done. I promise I'll get you some blood. I'll get both of us some blood, but first we need to ditch this ride before we're—"

Lights flashed in what remained of the rearview mirror.

"Shit, Billy! Get the hell up. We need to find a place to ditch this car and fast."

Billy didn't move, and that's when I saw it, plain as day on the back of his skull.

A bullet hole.

"Shit. Shit. Shit!"

I pounded on the wheel and screamed at the fading night. I needed him. I needed him to help me find Nate.

You're a shitty mother. I let that thought carry us around the bend and directly toward an elevated stretch of tollway. The water beneath it moved slowly, a languid river that made its leisurely way to the ocean.

It was dark and it was deep. That was all that mattered.

At a high enough rate of speed, even Marie's sedan would ignore the guard rails. I counted on it.

I grabbed Billy's shirt, happy to feel him shudder beneath my touch, then swerved hard. Dark water and an uncertain future raced up to meet us. There was a roar of thunder and the rush of bubbles and then nothing but sweet oblivion.

CHAPTER 24
IN TOO DEEP

RUSHING WATER AND DARKNESS.

This wasn't how I was supposed to go out, but maybe I didn't get to choose?

It took me longer than I cared to admit to remember I didn't need to breathe, but that didn't make fighting my way out of the busted up sedan any easier, nor did it make getting a hand on Billy anything other than a pain-in-the-ass.

The kid was in bad shape, a broken and twisted version of his once proud self. Was there a limit to what could be fixed?

Damn it, Billy!

I wanted to scream at him. I wanted to scream at myself. I wanted to go back in time, grab stupid Mallory by the front of her jacket and throw that bitch right back in the concrete cave.

Stay here! Do not leave. Do not walk out that door.

I shook my head, pushing aside the last bubbles from a dark and dying car before kicking for the surface.

She wouldn't have listened. She knew everything. Hadn't I heard? Mallory was the high priestess of blood and brilliance. She shoved her brother in the car with nothing more than a burner phone for entertainment. She drove him to the bar and acted surprised when he got out and started doing what he did.

Take your rabid dog out for a stroll and see what happens. Play stupid games, win stupid prizes.

I'd done exactly that, and was somehow surprised by the outcome. I was like one of those idiots who plays around with a pistol only to be stunned when it puts a hole in their leg.

Or their head.

That sobering thought brought my attention back to Billy and the gently bleeding hole in his skull.

Would it heal? *Could* it heal?

I dragged my hands through the water pulling for the surface, then hesitated. The cops would be coming. They'd get people in the water. Our best course of action was to ride the current, let it take us away from this place.

But Nate…

My brother would have to wait.

Shows how much you care about him, or the kid.

Had I been able to, I would have loved to snap my jaws open and skewer that thought in the drifting dark, but I could no more impale it than I could pull the coming sun out of the sky. I was right. A good sister would have done more.

And mother…

Nate's face filled my mind, crispy on the edge from an already terrible dawn. I watched him slam the metal lid shut, sealing me in my tomb before racing off into the fiery morning.

What happened to you?

That image melted away only to be replaced with more and ever worsening visuals. Blondy and the rest of the Bible-thumping evil brigade had hurt him. They'd hurt him bad.

Billy knows where he is.

I tried to cherish that thought, to let it paint new and hopeful visuals, but the silent weight in my fingers dragged that joy into the inky depths.

Even if he knew, it was a blood memory, broken at best. To make matters worse, given the injuries he'd sustained, he would need to feed again soon.

You're forgetting something, Mallory.

I wasn't forgetting the hole in his head. I just didn't want to acknowledge it.

I'd done as much with Nate, and with my life before this. If I didn't acknowledge the bad things, then maybe they wouldn't exist? Maybe they would drift on, like the broken bits of river grass beneath the surface? Maybe they would find new people's lives to ruin?

Part of me knew I couldn't wish away my problems, but that didn't stop me from trying.

I wished for my brother to be safe, and for Billy to be okay. I wished for a longer night and a shorter day.

I wished for blood.

You have to do something about the kid.

The nagging voice in my head was right. He should have been awake by now. He should have been pulling with me and not be a drifting dead weight.

I needed him for Nate.

And if i was being honest, I needed him for me too.

I squeezed my fingers tighter around his cold flesh.

You are weak.

No. I was alone.

As much as I hated to admit it, I didn't do alone well. I'd made a big show about Nate living with me, but it had been just that, a show. Truth be told, I'd been tired of being by myself, of having no one there, no one who cared.

You did this to him. Just like you did this to Nate.

I fought those memories like I fought the current, pushing them down while dragging myself up.

They came just the same, breaking the surface with me and steaming with reminders of so many sins.

There was something about the hole in the back of Billy's

head, something about that darkness that spoke to me, that whispered terrible things in those quiet moments before the dawn. I kicked for the bank, the muted green of tall trees and dense cattails.

I was in that moment, and I wasn't. In my head, I was back in the apartment. I was irritated, bouncing around like a blood-starved hummingbird.

Nate was late.

The memory surprised me. I remembered it and I didn't. It was like being lost in a dream you knew shouldn't be real but was.

Damn it, Nate. Where the hell are you?

I stomped around the apartment, hungry for blood, and worried. Ever since we'd changed, I'd grown more and more worried. Worried he would leave.

Worried I'd be alone.

It was weak, and I knew it, but that didn't make it any better. If anything, that made it worse.

That was why when the door opened and my brother walked in with some bitch on his arm I'd lost it.

I pulled Billy onto the shore, slamming him against the cattails like I'd slammed Nate against the wall.

"What the fuck is wrong with you?"

"Mal! This is Destiny. We met at the—"

I didn't care who she was. I only cared that she bled. My jaws exploded and my stinger shot out like the crack of a whip. The stripper screamed, but only for a second. It was hard to do much more with my second tongue down her throat.

"Mal! Stop! She wanted to be like me, like us!"

I tried to shake the memory away, turning Billy over gently to inspect the hole in his head, but the longer I stared at it, the deeper I went.

"You can't just do that, Nate! You can't just—"

He swung and I ducked, and in seconds the brother-sister

melee was on, except this time it was different. This time he'd brought a woman into my apartment.

"I just wanted someone else!"

Five words.

Five words was all it took.

My jaws gently unfolded, the stinger beneath them lashing out and tasting the damp air, and the blood.

It had been the same way then, yet somehow different. I remembered pinning him, scrambling onto his back like a spider monkey and sending my stinger into the base of his skull. I remembered the blood, and then the crack of that melon against the floor.

No! I didn't. I didn't do that! Nate couldn't speak. None of this happened...

I remembered my tongue digging into this head and tasting the sour fruits beneath. I barely remembered stopping, pulling back and trying to will the bone back together.

You did that, just like you're doing it now.

Billy!

The teenager hung limp in my arms. My stinger already in the base of his skull, hunting softly, digging for something.

I tried to pull it back, to deny it that ill-gotten fruit, but it never reached the brain, instead it settled around a mush-roomed lump of metal.

Like some elephant's trunk or an industrial magnet, it popped out the bullet, dropping it on the wet sand.

I pulled the kid close, clutching him to my chest even as the sky took on a pinkish hue. I was both here, and back in the apartment, a bloody and broken Nate in my arms.

This was why I deserved my last sunrise, why I deserved to be burned away like so much ash.

I was the bad sister, the evil one.

Nate moved in my mind, as did Billy on the sand. One would never speak again, would never ask for a new companion. One would be so broken that he would be stuck with me, and I would never be alone again.

The other said my name.

"Mal?" Billy's jaws quivered in the coming dawn.

"Yeah."

"I have a headache."

I let my face fold shut and squeezed him tighter. "I know."

He tried to push away, but I didn't let him. I didn't want him to see the distant pink and the day it would bring.

It would come soon enough, and when it did, we would burn.

That's what this world did to evil things, it burned them.

It turned them to ash.

CHAPTER 25
PUMP HOUSE PONDERING

IT WAS hard to tell who was screaming, me or the kid. Perhaps we both were? It didn't matter. The sun was coming. She peeked above the misty cypress, the first hints of her killing rays sparkling the dew and sending the damp night packing.

Just like my stinger in the dark, the sun found our soft spots. It found the gaps and holes from a night spent running. It found them and it dug in deep. Flesh blackened and peeled, the blood beneath hopeless in the face of the inevitable.

Nothing stopped the last sunrise.

This was my moment. The one I'd always promised myself.

I wouldn't be alone. I'd have Billy. The kid would see me through. He would hold me just like I would hold him. Together we would greet the dawn as one.

The weight of too many sins would hold us down, pinning us to the wet grass like butterflies lanced to the board.

You deserve this.

Blisters swelled only to burst beneath the softest morning

rays, they came with smoke, hints of fire, and the smell of burning flesh.

Does he?

It wasn't Billy's screams or his frantic arms that dragged me from my death wish. It was Nate. My brother's face returned, a face that screamed my name over and over again. Trapped in some nightmare of my own making, Nate didn't deserve this.

My brother deserved better.

Billy broke free, his tired body limping out of my grasp. I stumbled after him, confused and disoriented.

Is this what you want?

I didn't know what I wanted, or which way was up. There was only the sun and the fiery hell it rained down on monsters like me.

Mallory!

Nate's face came back again, this time the burned and blackened version, the one that stuffed me in that ruined cooler.

That Nate wanted me to live.

That Nate was worth living for.

I dropped to my knees and clawed at the wet grass like some fox digging for her burrow. Skin sloughed off my fingers in bloody strips, the dawn cooking them to perfection before my eyes.

No! Not yet! I made a promise.

I had made a promise. I'd made so many damn promises. Everyday was a new promise, a new lie.

You are the queen of lies.

I'd lied to myself, to Billy, and to Nate.

I would kill again. I wouldn't stop killing, because that's what I did.

That's what you have to do.

My hair fell out in great clumps as I crawled across the steaming ground.

The river?

No.

The sun would find me. Those killing rays would slip down beneath the cool surface and do what they did. I would boil beneath the lapping waves just as surely as I'd burn above them.

I turned back toward the trees and their shadows. Long palmetto fronds hugged the ground. They weren't much, but maybe they were something? Maybe they would keep me alive?

I wouldn't find an answer to that question, because I never reached them.

Burnt and bloody hands grabbed mine, dragging me over the wet grass with a strength born of desperation.

"Nate?" I croaked the word out, my jaws peeling back like the edges of burning paper.

My vision swam.

It was a twisted landscape of blood and ash. Trees that had once been green now stood out like blackened sticks against the hellfire of dawn.

"Nate! I'm sorry. I... I did this to you. I made you what you are. Me!" The words kept coming, even as he dragged me over the blades of dew-covered grass. "I ruined you. I ruined us. I did it and I see that now. I see that. You need to let me die."

I said the words, but even now I knew they weren't true. The Queen of Lies was at it again, the stinger in her throat playing her tongue like the keys of some pipe organ. She wanted to live.

There was blood to be had. Even now she could smell it.

The stinger shifted in my throat as if aroused by the hints of life woven between the fires of death.

I thought this was your last sunrise?

I wanted to scream at that Mallory, at the deceitful bitch that made her home in my head. I wanted to throw her against the ground and pin her down with my stinger like some blister popping in the sun.

I never got the chance.

Day turned to night in an instant, the fires of damnation silent in a damp dark.

"Nate?" I swung my hands, eyes too badly burned to make out much beyond the watery slurry of skin, blood, wood, and something metal. "Nate. It's me. It's Mallory."

It's your sister…

The day roared outside, beyond the wooden walls my fingers ran across. I could hear it out there, birds singing their melodies of death, bees buzzing and the faint hint of words carried on the wind.

Words!

Words meant blood and blood meant life. It was simple math, but glorious in its revelations.

I clawed gently at the wood walls, listening to the voices. So many words in a language I didn't understand came to me. I drifted on them, carried away by the aroma of sweat and blood.

My savior shifted next to me, clearly thinking many of the same thoughts. He looked so much like Nate, but smaller, less massive. I knew who he was, but I didn't. His name kept dancing out of my grasp. It flittered like the head of a fiery matchstick in the wind.

My son…

Shadows moved along the fiery seam in the door and I waited to pounce. My jaws already unfolded, weak and flaccid, but hungry to feed.

Feed…

There was something about that word, that thought, that didn't ring true.

Something that gave me pause.

What was it?

The shadow narrowed and a vibrant heartbeat followed.

It was strong and capable. It pumped blood with a fiery passion and called to me like cool water to a woman dying of thirst.

I clawed gently at the door, willing him to come inside my spider's web.

There were more words I didn't understand, then the clink of metal. In an instant the door opened and the thunderous nature of our wooden cave was revealed. We recoiled from the light, hiding in the shadows as a monstrous machine roared to life, sucking water from the river in great gulps. The man-made stinger bled the river of its water and robbed us of our meals.

My son cried out in desperation, his jaws flailing as our breakfast moved away, closing the door behind him.

What sort of mother are you?

Those words weren't mine, they were my mother's. They crawled up from some dark place in my head, coming with smoke and cheap bourbon.

You always thought you were better than me, Mallory. Now look at you. You are weak, broken, sad, and worthless. Your son will die because of you, because of your fear.

I tried to push her away, but the old woman wouldn't go down without a fight. She was there in that wooden cave with us, her vile words like the thundering of great pump's metal stinger.

You let them down. You let them all down.

"No."

You did because that's who you are. That's all you've ever been.

I swung my fist in rage, banging it against the metal beast and causing our retreating shadow to stop.

My son perked his head up, those lifeless jaws finding purpose in this fortunate turn of events.

He joined me, banging on the pipes and steel belly of the beast, his eyes and mine, glued to the shadow, and to blood that would sustain us.

Again the nagging thoughts returned. There was a danger here, a danger in doing this, but I couldn't remember what.

All that mattered was the blood.

Nothing was more important than the blood.

The knob turned slowly, the door behind it opening again and once again bringing with it the fiery light of day. It also came with something else, the smell of vanilla, of popsicles on a hot summer day, and the cold kiss of a sundae against chapped lips.

My son cowered from the light, but I embraced it. Like a trapdoor spider lunging out to grab her prey, I pulled our dinner inside, clutching him to my chest and falling back against the dusty floor.

There were more out there, so many more popsicles to unwrap, so much more ice cream to enjoy.

My tired jaws clamped down on his neck and the stinger beneath them burrowed deep. She sucked up blood like the thundering metal beast behind us, reveling in the new memories that would supplant the old.

Billy latched on too, jaws making short work of the popsicle's jeans and finding the sweet meat on the other side.

My son needed this. He needed to heal, to forget the last few hours, to let go of everything.

I laid there in the darkness, the rumbling engine and the thunderous beating of blood lulling me to sleep.

I was almost out when a single word pushed my eyes open wide.

Marie.

CHAPTER 26
FORGET ME NOT

BILLY!

I wanted to rip him off, to push my son away from the blood feast of creamsicles, but to do that I'd have to let go myself.

I didn't want to let go. I wanted to drift away on the blissful sugar rush. I wanted to succumb to the blood, and to the memories it brought.

They wiped out the fire and pain of the last one, washing away his family like the ocean waves stripping the shore.

They will take away Marie.

I didn't care about Marie. Whoever she was, she was long dead, a piece of the world that no longer deserved a name.

But Nate.

Like a child who wanted nothing more than to pull her blankets tighter, I wanted to take this one close, to enjoy his ebbing warmth and the life it brought me, but that did nothing to stop Nate.

"Mallory!"

My brother screamed my name, like some alarm clock just beyond my outstretched fingers. I needed it to stop, to turn off. But to do that, I'd need to come out of my blanket cave.

The concrete cave…

It came back in waves: the cave, the field, and Nate.

Marie had seen Nate.

The kid can't feed!

I kicked breakfast off like so many blankets, forcing an angry stinger to retract and jaws to close behind it.

It was the kid who had no interest in letting go. Blood flowed beneath his jaws, that hungry stinger sucking it up like the metal pipe that made its way down to the river. He wanted all of it, and with each passionate gulp pushed memories of Marie and Nate deeper into the dark of oblivion.

"No!" I kicked at Billy, but he didn't bother to look up, his eyes drifting backward on a sea of orange creme that filled his stomach and his mind.

Jaws open and stinger back to taste the air, I hit him once, and then again. The serrated second tongue sliced thin lines in his cheeks but did little to draw his attention away from such a glorious meal.

The pump engine rumbled. It was a race between Billy's stinger and the great mechanical beast, who could finish their dinner first? With each passing moment I could feel Nate slipping away, any memories of my brother vanishing beneath the sweet taste of orange and the thundering darkness.

Was that how it always was? How much had I forgotten?

No one had mashed a stinger against my brain, yet still my thoughts felt as much. Too many meals had graced that second tongue. They all jumbled together. All the voices, both spoken and not, wore on me.

Drink, Mallory. Drink to remember. Drink to forget…

Nate's burned face faded in the smell of white blossoms and the dark green of so many fruit trees.

"No!" This time I didn't hesitate. I wedged a foot between the kid and his dying dinner and pried the two of them apart. They didn't stay separated for long before he tried to latch back on like a baby stripped from his mother's breast.

I scrambled to pull him away, his stinger fighting to reach the blood trickling out just beyond it.

"No, damn it! No. You can't drink. You can't drink because you'll forget about Marie. You'll forget about home!"

You'll forget about Nate.

Billy's wide eyes fixated on the meal at our feet, his stinger dancing only inches from the red feast. Like two snakes locked in mortal combat, my second tongue wrapped his.

"No! You promised me. You promised me you'd help me find Nate. You promised me…"

But if Billy was going to be of any help, that ship had already sailed. The man's blood covered his clothes and dribbled down jaws that clamored for more.

"Give it to me!"

"You said you wanted home. You said you wanted to go back there. The only way to do that is in your head. Marie is only in your head now, and barely that. If you do this you'll lose her forever. Do you want to lose her forever?"

Billy grunted, his fingers clawing at my arms. "I want the blood!"

"But Marie—"

The kid's second tongue slipped free, grazing our rapidly dying feast. "Marie is dead. Home is dead. There is no going home. You said it yourself. We are death and ruin. That's who we are now."

Damn it.

Hearing my own words used against me didn't help. Logic wasn't the answer, because logic was on his side. Marie was dead, nothing more than a pile of organs on some examiners table, a set of evidence photos for a trial that would never happen.

Marie was no more, and it was torture to think of her.

It was torture to think of all of them.

"You drink him all and you'll have new tortures, new

things to keep you awake through the long and fiery days. You can't escape the pit by digging a deeper hole!"

Billy hesitated, then pulled his stinger back only to send it my way. "You do!"

"I—"

The kid moved like a starving animal, all arms and aggression. I took an elbow in the cheeks and felt a tooth pop free.

"You do nothing but dig a deeper hole. We could have left. We could have taken a car and gotten out of this place! If we had, then Marie would still be alive. She'd still be here. There would still be a home!"

I threw my arms around his neck and dragged him into the dirt beneath the pounding machine. Hungry for water like we were for blood, it wanted nothing more than to suck the river dry.

Home.

If I hadn't dug my stinger in Nate's head, maybe there'd still be home for me? Maybe I wouldn't be alone?

You're never not alone.

Billy and I twisted back and forth in the dirt, alternating between the victim and the victor.

"Billy, listen to me. You can still help me. You can still help Nate. Just tell me everything you remember. Tell me as much as you can before it's lost. Please just—"

The kid kicked away my foot and scrambled on top, his knees tight to my sides and his jaws wide in the dusty haze. "It's already lost! She knew. Don't you understand? She knew about vampires. She knew about things like you and she did nothing. She still served me up to them! Home is dead, Mallory, because Marie didn't care." Bloody tears trickled down flushed cheeks. "She didn't care! She turned me over to them. She gave me up! You think I want to see that home anymore? You think I want to keep living that? I don't. I want it gone. I want to wash it away in whatever the hell that is." He pointed to the body barely clinging to life in the dirt. "I want to make it stop. I want to make all of it stop."

"But you can't!" It was my turn to scream back at him, my own jaws on full display. "You're only trading one pain for another one. Don't you understand?"

"I don't care." He turned back toward the dying man, giving me an opening I sorely needed.

I pulled him close and knocked those jaws aside before they could find my flesh.

I'm sorry, Billy, but I need to know. I need to find my brother. I need Nate.

I need to not be alone.

I latched onto his neck, my stinger lancing through newly restored flesh with the singular grace of a chef's knife.

I needed to take what I could from him, to steal enough blood to find my brother. I had to go deep and hope it was still there, some hint of Nate, Marie, or this mysterious home. The mix of flavors turned in my gut, so many emotions, so many fragments of life. There was a birthday cake, fiery candles, and dark figures hovering in the corners. There was a corner market, bedecked in Spanish signs and awash in the scent of plantains. There was all of that, but what there wasn't, was Nate.

No!

I dug deeper, even as Billy squirmed in my arms. He had to be there. My brother had to be in those memories. I needed him to be there.

I couldn't be alone.

Not again.

Never again.

Billy managed to get a knee between us and push off hard enough to separate me from my meal.

He scrambled toward the dying man, and I chased after him. No sooner had he gotten his hands on the cooling flesh than the door swung wide.

Fiery light spilled in, turning the wooden cave into a death trap.

I grabbed Billy and pulled him backward, clawing my way under the pump and hoping the monstrous beast would shield us from the worst of it.

Men poured in with the light, men with blood, and new lives to consume.

CHAPTER 27
HIDE AND SEEK

DIRTY SNEAKERS SHUFFLED patterns in the dirt, their owners' thoughts focused on the bleeding man on the floor.

Spanish words flowed over me, bits and pieces of them making sense, but the majority lost to the thundering rumble of the pump and the rushing water.

I got coyote, dog, and something that sounded like doctor.

That worked. The longer they focused on him, the less time they'd spend looking at the powerful machine or under it.

Billy squirmed and I tightened my grip on him. He was hungry, but he didn't appear to be stupid. That had been the sun and neither of us were in that headspace now.

The guilt would return, but for now, self-preservation was the order of the day. Callused hands stuffed what appeared to be a wadded-up shirt against the wound, trying desperately to stem the tide of blood soaking into the sand.

More words in Spanish brought new feet, and soon the tiny pump house was awash in smells. Creamsicles gave way to all new flavors, spicy, exotic, more than enough to get my stinger moving all over again.

It was like some all-you-can-eat buffet and I had to fight to keep that second tongue from breaking out of that closed-jaw prison.

Billy did not appear to be suffering from the same challenge. The kid's stinger was out, way out, and his jaws had blossomed behind it. They unfolded in silence, like some flower expanding to embrace the day, except the day was the one thing he couldn't touch.

Or could he?

The chilling finality of that thought caught me off-guard.

Do you still need him?

I knew the answer to that question, even if I didn't want to admit it. Billy was expendable.

He's my son.

That was a lie and I knew it. I was playing house, an elaborate game of dress-up for a world I'd never know. I wasn't going to be the beautiful women in those magazines, or even one of the moms pushing their child around in a stroller. I could call him son, but would he ever call me Mom?

No.

Billy's stinger moved softly in the sand, twisting back and forth like some desert asp.

Grab it!

Why?

The images weren't hard to play out. I knew what would come if he was found.

The sun.

He wouldn't stay here, beneath the river vampire. Billy would end up out there, out in the daylight, and it wouldn't last.

We were in an orange grove, a killing field.

Like the strawberries…

Nate and I had come so close to dying that day—so, so close.

We'd been on our last legs, burned out from running and

the hunt for blood. My brother had raced off into the tall grass when our last car went out, his broken brain spooked by the backfiring engine.

I remembered chasing after him, even as the first rays of a rising sun stung my cheeks and burned my hands.

"The trunk, you moron! We can stay in the trunk!"

Nate hadn't listened. He'd just run.

My brother didn't leap an old barbed wire fence as much as he tore straight through it. I remembered chasing him across the fallow field, my boots sinking in the broken earth. The deeper we ran, the more it burned, and the more I knew there was no chance we'd get back.

The sun was coming, and it would be our end.

"Nate!" I must have screamed his name a dozen times, but it made no difference, my brother was a rabbit on the run. I might have been stronger now, and faster than I'd ever been before, but I was still no match for Nate. The big man had pulled away effortlessly, his feet kicking up dirt and leaving me in a haze.

I remembered the pain of the sun, that burning daystar and its hellish light. The pink sky taunted me. It was like some dancer teasing with hints of flesh and dangly bits, knowing full well that to take the whole thing in would break me.

It had been beautiful in a strange and horrifying way.

The dawn had whispered of potential, of a day that had yet to be written. Birds had chirped in the distance, and tiny butterflies had emerged from the weeds. It had been a time for living things.

It was no world for the dead.

The dead would burn.

We would burn.

I remembered panicking, turning back to the car and realizing I'd never make it in time. I remembered stumbling a few feet and hitting my knees before the worst of it, before my hands started melting.

The sun was coming and there was nothing I could do about it.

Luckily for me, my brother hadn't felt the same way.

Strong hands had grabbed me from behind. They'd tossed me over a wide set of shoulders like a sack of oranges or some toddler at the park. Nate had carried me across that burning hellscape. His face scorched and hands gnarled, he had carried me.

He'd carried me, like Billy had carried me.

I remembered the darkness, the sweet kiss of it when my back hit the sand. I remembered huddling in the corner, beneath a rusty metal roof while the day roared around us. That had been our first day in the concrete cave, and it had almost never happened.

I remembered holding him in the shadows and not letting go.

I should never have let go.

The concrete cave vanished, whisked away by sneakers and sand, and the snaking tip of a hungry stinger.

No, Billy!

Nate had looked out for me, and in turn, I'd looked out for him. I was going to find him, to fix him, and maybe to cure him.

If what we were could even be cured.

I would do the same for my son.

Billy cared about me. He could have left me to burn in the dawn, but he hadn't.

I wouldn't leave him now.

The kid's stinger had already slipped free from the confines of our hiding place, and even now appeared poised to pounce on the nearest unsuspecting ankle.

There was blood in that ankle, blood and ruin. There was

no way he wouldn't be found, and even though they were weak, they had the sun at their backs.

They would destroy him.

I grabbed his second tongue, my hand slicing along that serrated edge. At first he fought it, but it didn't take long for him to realize there was something else to snack on in the dark beneath the thundering pump. I didn't fight it, and instead pulled him closer. His stinger no longer a liability, I let it lap at the tiny wound like some cub from a twisted nature show.

All that mattered now was watching those sneakers, watching them leave. Creamsicle made it out, carried in the hands of so many men. Our buffet filed out after, one at a time until it was just Billy and me in the shadows of the hungry pump.

We can do this. We can find Nate. We can survive.

The kid drifted in and out, my loaner blood and the excitement of the day proving too much for his exhausted mind. It wasn't long before he slipped out of consciousness and dozed in my arms.

I envied him, because sleep had no interest in coming for me.

All I could do was stare at the burning sand and the sunlight trapping us beneath the steel beast. Nate was out there, somewhere, and I had so little to go on. There was a tiny grocery store, something Spanish, and the name Marie. Was that really Maria?

Did it matter?

It took hours of running the same loops in my mind for that dogged brain to finally calm down. I let my eyes close, only to snap them back open again what felt like a few seconds later.

The sun hung low in the sky, its light sliding under the door orange and faded.

Rest, Mallory. You've earned it.

I had. I'd earned it all and then some.

I let that thought, Billy's body, and the rumbling pump carry me into that soft oblivion.

That's where I was, that almost half-state, somewhere between awake and not, when a pair of sneakers returned. I should have noticed them. I should have realized they were there and done something.

I hadn't.

I was too busy drifting toward sleep to notice when sneakers became knees, and then knees turned into a face.

He stared at me, dark eyes and brown skin.

Somewhere in the back of my head, conscious Mallory was in panic mode. She wanted those jaws open and stinger out, but the rest of me was too tired to listen. The rest of me wanted to sleep and digest the blood already waning in my belly.

That Mallory almost won out, and she would have, had she not heard one word escape his chapped and sun-burnt lips.

"Vampira!"

One word was all it took to open my eyes wide and jaws to match.

A single word changed everything.

CHAPTER 28
SPLIT DECISIONS

I HESITATED.

Why?

Had it been any other person, I would have run them through. I would have split their face in two and devoured the sweet blood beneath. I would have done all these things without hesitation.

But that wasn't what happened.

What happened was the man bolted, leaving the pump house door swinging and our future very much in doubt.

"Billy! Get up!"

The kid rolled off me, his eyes still closed and the rest of him clearly deep in the caressing arms of a blood-aided sleep.

We didn't have that luxury. Whoever that idiot had been, he knew what I was, and he'd tell others. The longer we stayed here the more dangerous doing so became.

The sun…

I clawed my way out from beneath the pump, almost missing the thundering roar of water being sucked up from the not-so-distant river.

What time is it?

I remained well-clear of the late daylight pouring in, but

took comfort in the fact the few shadows I could see had lengthened with the passing of the day.

We'd slept but the sun was still up.

"Billy, we need to move."

The boy groaned and rolled back over, as if by turning he could bore his body deeper into the dusty ground.

We weren't worms.

And there were no caves in this swampy place.

I let my jaws unfold and stretch like some yogi on a mountain top. My stinger dropped free behind them, tasting the orange blossoms, the fertilizer, and the glorious smell of blood.

They're coming back and it won't be for beers.

I got tired of wasting my words and instead dropped to my knees and fished a hand under the pump to grab the kid.

As predicted, he used that opportunity to push himself deeper. Like some animal intent to not be removed from its burrow no matter the cost.

Billy wanted to sleep.

It was too bad he didn't have a choice.

I scrambled underneath after him, wrapping a hand around his shoulder and pulling him toward the exit. "We have to go."

"Five minutes…" he mumbled, the words mixed with dust and sleep.

"We don't have five minutes. We have to go. The shadows are long, that'll help, but we've got to run."

A tired teen opened one eye and stared unfocused at the light streaming in from outside. "It's still day."

"Right, day means people. It means *lots* of people."

Billy's jaws rippled. "Great. Wake me when they get here. I'm hungry."

That's it.

I forced my jaws wide, even underneath the silent pump

they were a sight to behold. Billy's face might still be growing, but mine was the real deal, powerful and terrifying.

The kid only rolled his one open eye and turned his head away. "Like I said. Wake me when they get h—"

Thump!

The sound of something hitting the metal roof caused us both to turn our heads toward the door.

Whatever it was, it wasn't alone. A second and third followed it, and at least one came with a shatter.

Gasoline!

The acrid scent hit my nose and sent my stinger packing. It appeared Billy got the memo too, as those sleepy eyes weren't sleepy anymore.

"Is that—"

I nodded, doing my best to back out from under the pump and pull him with me. "Yes! Come on."

Together we scrambled free only to greet the dancing tips of flame licking at the door frame.

"What do we do?" The kid grabbed my hand. He was so strong, but still so weak. He needed me.

He will always need you.

It was all I'd ever wanted, and I hated myself for it.

Flames emerged like prowling shark fins between the panel walls.

"We run."

Billy pointed at the late day sun and the sea of smoke and green beyond the door. "Run?! Run where? It's still light outside. The damn sun is still up."

"It is, but we don't have a choice."

Billy pulled back toward the metal beast. "We hide. We hide under here and we let this whole place burn down. We'll be safe."

"No, we won't. You think they'll stop as soon as the building is down? They won't. They'll come with guns."

"Screw their guns."

I put a hand on the back of his skull. "You mean the guns that put a hole in your damn head? You got lucky. You got damn lucky. You won't be lucky again. I'm sure of it."

Black smoke leaked from the walls, pooling in noxious clouds against the metal roof.

"We can't run." He stared at the green of the orange trees and the waning sun behind them. "It burns! I… I can't do that again."

He was determined, but also still so young, so afraid.

He always will be.

I found Nate in Billy's face. I found the brother I'd broken staring back at me. There had been fear in his eyes too, fear of me, fear of what I could do to him.

Nate's fear had died at the sharp end of my stinger, his brain sliced and diced like onions at the edge of some cooking show blade.

I'd taken his fear with my own.

Of course you did, because you are a fucking monster.

I needed that monster now. I needed her strength. I needed the Mallory that could rip a beating heart from its chest and devour it whole.

"We run."

Billy shook his head, but didn't try to duck under the pump again. "Run? Run where?"

"I'll think of something."

"The sun is still up!"

Flames engulfed the walls and it wouldn't be long before they brought the ceiling down on top of us.

I grabbed both his hands and turned those fluttering jaws to face me. "Do you trust me?"

"I…"

"Do you trust me!"

"Yes."

"Good. Gasoline means cars. Cars give us a chance."

Billy shook his head. "What about keys? What about—"

The roof dipped and ended our conversation. There was no staying in the pump house, no waking up in the dark. We had one choice.

We had to run.

I yanked him into the sun, questioning my decision the instant the first rays hit my exposed flesh. The fire would have been preferable to this.

Anything would have been preferable to this.

Skin blistered and popped, the bloody tissue beneath burning as sure as the pump house walls behind us.

I couldn't focus on that. All I could do was pull Billy and try to find a new place to hide, try to find a car.

Orange trees spread out like toy soldiers, cut in bushy configurations that left no room to crawl underneath, but it wouldn't have mattered if they had, because there were men everywhere.

And a few of those men had guns.

My jaws snapped open only to close the instant the sunlight hit them.

"Vampiros! Vampiros!"

A shotgun blast took out a chunk of tree, vaporizing orange peel and shredding leaves.

"Are you hit?"

Billy didn't answer, but he kept his legs moving, and that was all that mattered. We raced down the track between the fruit-speckled foliage, our bodies practically melting in the hellish sun.

The river?

It would have been fine had I thought to follow the pipe, but now we were too deep in the grove, too far from those banks and the dark water just beyond them.

You screwed up.

I shook my head, even as the blood in my eyes stained everything red.

I hadn't screwed up, not yet.

Yes. Yes, you have. There is no way out. The sun will consume you. It will eat you both just like you have consumed so many before this. It's revenge, Mallory. Pure and simple.

"No!" I pulled hard, yanking Billy between the trees and toward the distant sound of cars.

There was a highway near. I could hear it. I could smell the asphalt, the stench of spilled oil and melted rubber.

"Where are we go—"

"The road!" Branches whipped at our faces, saving us from the sun's killing rays, but tearing at already tender flesh.

Billy cried something, but I lost it in the sea of red that followed.

No one beats the sun for long, Mallory.

Nate did.

My brother beat the sun, long enough to still be alive today. Nate could do this. I could too.

We shot through the last row of trees only to fall face first into a narrow ditch. The cool water was a welcome reprieve, if only for a second.

The sun showed no signs of being outrun just yet.

"Cars!" Billy cried, the kid pulling me up and pointing at a series of beat up domestics that lined the far edge of the culvert.

We clawed our way through the murky water, then up the other side.

Billy's elbow smashed the passenger window of the first sedan we reached, a rusty number with bench seating and piles of clothing in the back.

It wasn't until we were inside that I realized I hadn't thought this through. No keys meant no movement.

All that work and all I'd done is given up one death trap for another.

CHAPTER 29
IGNITION

KEYS.

Keys!

I pounded tired and bloody fists against the steering wheel. "Damn it, damn it, damn it!"

Long rays from a setting sun sliced through the dirty windshield, burning my already crispy cheeks and sending Billy into the pile of discarded clothing in the back seat.

"Drive!" he cried, his bloody skin worse than mine.

The sun, the fucking sun, had done this to us again. How many times now? How many times had it been?

Too many.

That golden bastard sat low in the sky, only minutes from dipping beneath the tree line. Those minutes might be all it took to cook us in our juices.

If the sun didn't get us, the nice men with the hand tools and fiery bottles would be more than happy to finish the job. They poured out of the grove like ants from the mound. Hate in their eyes and fire at their fingertips, it was only a matter of time before they took care of business.

Angry voices shouted muffled words I didn't understand. All those years of Spanish and they'd never covered vampires or 'kill them, kill them all,' but I guessed that's what I was hearing now.

Billy kicked at my seat back and groaned. "Drive!"

"I can't!"

"Why not?"

I turned around. "Because I don't have keys, damn it."

The kid's burned face emerged from beneath a pile of sweat-stained shirts. "Can't you, like, hot wire it or something?"

"No!"

"Crap."

"I know." I pounded on the wheel again for good measure.

Billy's wide eyes and blackened jaws appeared in the rearview mirror. "We should have stayed in the pump house."

"Oh yeah? Was that a better place to get burned alive?"

"It beats some shitty sedan from the—"

A shotgun blast sent pellets across the dash, gouging metal and shattering at least one headlight.

Billy ducked, but I couldn't take my eyes off the shooter, or the pudgy man next to him trying to keep him from unloading another shell into the car—exactly like the vehicle's owner would do.

"Hang tight. I'm going to get the keys."

"What?!" Billy sprung up in the back seat, panic on his slowly mending face. "What are you going to—"

"Can you drive?"

The kid frowned, the edges of his lips burning all over again in the fading sun. "I… I took a lesson once."

"Good enough for me." I pointed at the wheel. "Steering thing," then the floor, "go and stop."

If it was possible, the kid looked even more terrified than before. "I…"

"Figure it out, Billy." I pushed the door open, facing both the fading sun and the anger of men.

"What the hell are you going to do?"

"I'm going to save my son. That's what moms do."

Good ones anyway.

They circled, men with hedge clippers, small shovels, fire, and hate. I'd seen venom like this before. It boiled the heart and hollowed the soul.

It also brought a *lot* of firepower.

Shotgun guy was up on the far side of the embankment, but he wasn't my target. I only cared about the chubby one next to him and the lump in his jeans I just knew had to be keys.

Billy managed to climb into the front seat and slam the door behind me.

The satisfying sound of car doors locking gave me my starter's gun.

You like to pick on vampires? Let me show you the hornet's nest you just stuck your face in!

My jaws split and face unfolded, the burned skin papery thin at the edges, but still terrifying. They hesitated, the same men who appeared more than happy to burn us behind the safety of the pump house walls now appeared to be having second thoughts.

I dropped my stinger out, letting that glorious snake taste the coming night. She smoked with the fading light, but didn't shy away, there were too many heavenly scents to be enjoyed: chorizo beef, piping hot tamales, and the sweet, sweet smell of flan.

The keys, Mallory.

Shotgun raised his weapon and gave me my cue. I lunged at the closest man, driving that spiced sausage of sweat, dirt, and blood to the ground without a moment's hesitation.

Eat him! Eat them all!

My stinger found the soft spot along his neck line and plunged deep, only to be ripped free by white-hot shot.

It shredded flesh and tore muscle, the pain providing a new form of fiery motivation. I took that desire and I channeled it into the next guy, my shoulder taking him down, while the rest of me stayed focused on the prize.

The keys.

Men screamed and panicked, their legs moving to get away, but you couldn't get away from the inevitable.

I knew. I'd tried.

The sun kept rising, but the darkness always followed.

I was that darkness.

I was an unholy mother of monsters, and I needed those damn car keys.

Shotgun man fumbled with shells, the august gentleman next to him making a break for the grove and the safety of the trees. He could run, but I'd find him. That caramel motherfucker was practically sweating the sweet stuff. I didn't remember crossing the culvert a second time, nor did I remember dropping his fat ass just beyond the deep green.

I barely understood what was happening when my stinger found his neck, or why this all was so important.

I just knew I had to have him. I had to have the blood, every last drop. I wanted to swim in it, to embrace the rich velvet and fall into creamy bliss.

A shotgun barrel to the skull put the skids to all of that.

Do it, asshole! Fuck around and find out!

Honk!

My son blared the horn and bought me a second. A second turned out to be all I needed. My stinger cracked like a whip, taking out his eye and a chunk of his face in the process.

The tangy taste of chilled flan lit up the second tongue, and I might have lingered too long had it not been for Billy.

"Keys!"

Shit, keys!

The kid was right. I dug my fingers around in the fat guy's pockets until I found what I was looking for. Keyring in hand, I popped up only to find more trouble emerging from between the trees: more men, more bottles, more burning.

"Mallory!"

It may have been my son screaming, but it wasn't Billy's voice I heard. It was Nate's. It was the last fragment of a stolen blood memory, choosing this moment to surface in the coming dark.

"Find me, Mallory. Please..."

Nate!

I scrambled off the fat man and down the embankment. Shotgun spun wildly, the hot barrel spewing another round and shredding my calf like ground chuck. I limped into the muck and back out the other side, my eyes on the car and the setting sun.

Billy cranked the window down, his hand extended for the keys. "Throw them!"

Men regrouped, finding their second wind with the fire and the broken woman limping toward her ride.

"Throw me the keys!"

I did what he asked, tossing that wad of jingling metal at the open window.

Billy caught them and fumbled through the options. I didn't make it far enough to see him find the key, a burning bottle to the back saw to that.

Fire returned, hungry like the sun but somehow worse. It raced over the arms of a torn up jacket, eating at the burned flesh underneath. It torched my hair and roared in my ears. I tried to pull it off, stumbling in the tall grass to the sound of a thundering engine.

"Billy!"

I didn't know if the kid heard me. All I knew was the sedan could move when it wanted to. The steel beast shot into the empty road like a dog at the racetrack.

"Billy, wait!"

I managed to toss the jacket free, but the fire had done its damage. Bruised, bloodied, and broken, I knelt in the grass. Bright red taillights faded in the distance.

I laughed. Against all odds, I fucking laughed.

I must have been a pretty damn good mother because he ended up being just like me.

Billy was a monster through and through.

Fire flickered on my discarded jacket, its light playing out across the faces of men hellbent to do me in.

I spit blood and forced weak jaws open, a tired stinger emerging behind them.

"Is that all you got? Is that it?" I pounded a tired hand against my chest. "Show me what you're made of, you little bitches. Show me. Show me how many of you it takes to beat a girl? Which one of you wants to ride my stinger first?"

My answer came in the form of the click of metal on metal and the smell of gun smoke.

CHAPTER 30
NIGHT MOVES

I'D EATEN a lot of bullets in my short un-life, but could I take a shotgun blast at point-blank range?

I was about to find out.

"Do it!" I snapped a tired stinger out in the cooling dusk. "Do it! What are you waiting for, you little bitch? Do it. Be the big man. Be the—"

I had a lot of other words planned, things I wanted to shout, to scream from the rooftops. This wasn't how it was supposed to be. It was supposed to be different. I was supposed to have Nate, to cure him, to fix my mistake. I was supposed to solve problems, not make even bigger ones.

I wasn't supposed to be alone.

Whatever it was I had planned to say, the demons I wanted to exorcise from my soul, they were lost to the roaring of a metal beast, its rusty front end, and the wet thump as it blasted the man and his shotgun.

A wide-eyed Billy pushed the driver's door open, narrow fingers clutching the wheel like they could leech blood from the stained leather. "Get in!"

I didn't have to be told twice, I crawled over his lap and

deposited myself somewhere between the passenger seat and the floor. It was dark there, dark and safe. "Go!"

The kid didn't wait for permission. He rammed his foot against the accelerator and left broken bodies and torn-up grass in his wake. At some point, I felt us reach the road, and eventually Billy managed to keep us from hitting all the rumble strips along the shoulder.

He wasn't a bad driver, but I wasn't terribly sure he could stop without hitting something.

"Are you okay?" he asked, the words coming out like some jumble of syllables from a tweaker high as a kite.

"Yes."

That was a lie, but it was a convenient one. Everything hurt.

I'd taken too much sun, too much sun too fast. Skin that should have been mercifully white stared back at me three shades of red, split, and peeling. I'd lost my jacket and felt naked without it.

"You don't look so good."

I frowned at Billy, immediately angry with myself for doing as much. "Yeah. Try looking in the mirror, buttercup."

As if for the first time tonight, Billy realized cars had mirrors. He didn't reach out to adjust it though, his hands stayed glued to the wheel. "Is it bad?"

"No more than me," I said, righting myself in the seat and leaving streaks of blood across the dash and door. "Turn the headlights on."

"How?"

Sigh.

I leaned over the kid and screwed with the buttons, the whole time Billy only clamped down on the wheel harder. I was impressed it didn't snap off in his bloody fingers.

Click.

"There." I sat back, trying not to imagine the bloody red outline I was sure to be leaving on the seat.

"Uh, can you drive?"

I closed my eyes. "Yes. I am capable of driving."

"No, I mean—"

"I know what you mean, Billy. You're on the turnpike. It's like the easiest driving possible, keep it under eighty and just go straight while I figure out what comes next."

"Eighty?!"

A quick glance at the dash told me why it felt like I should be out pushing.

"At least seventy-five, grandma."

The needle inched up from sixty to a solid sixty-three. "How's that?"

"Just don't put us in a ditch or ram into any cop cars."

"Right." Billy's eyes focused on the dark road.

I almost envied him. He had something to focus on, something to stave off the blood cravings, cravings I knew he was having.

I was having them too.

My stomach churned, as if reminding me that pushing out shotgun pellets needed fuel, and my engine was just about on 'E.'

Don't do it, Mallory.

I pushed that voice back down and let her drown in the not so subtle clamor for fresh blood.

What about Nate? What about Marie?

Nate might still have a place in my head, but Marie wasn't much more than a faded afterimage, the leftover outline after the flash bulb snaps.

Marie was gone.

I considered asking the kid, but then thought better of it. Billy was lost to the road and the hum of the tires. I needed him distracted.

He was strong, stronger than me, but just as volatile.

Like mother, like son.

Bright lights glowed in the distance beyond the trees, another rest stop.

The last thing we needed was a rest stop. There was no way they wouldn't be crawling with cops, and if anyone spotted us from the road…

I didn't complete that thought, but let it linger and push me into action.

"Next exit."

"Huh?" Billy scrunched up his face, trying to both watch the road and look at me.

"Eyes on the road, damn it."

"Right, sorry."

"Whatever." I leaned forward, pointing past him and at the green sign coming up not nearly as fast as it should have been. "There. Get off the road there."

"I…"

"You turn the wheel slowly, ease off the gas and take us down the offramp."

Billy did what I asked, and we made it about halfway down the ramp before he panicked. "What is that?!"

"Toll plaza," I said, pulling out the ashtray and searching for change.

"Toll plaza?"

"Yeah, see those baskets? The plastic ones alongside each lane? You put the change in there."

"I'm gonna hit—"

"No!" I grabbed the wheel. "You are not going to hit anything. You are going to run quietly and slowly between the posts. I'm going to throw whatever I can find in the basket, and we're going to pretend we are normal people."

Normal, blood-soaked and burned, people.

Between the ashtray and the floor, I found enough to hurl at the basket. Thankfully, we made it through without hitting the columns more than once, and what little damage we did didn't account for much more than a nice deep gouge.

"Sorry," Billy said once we'd reached the largely empty surface street.

"Whatever. Not my car. We can't keep it either. We need to figure out where we are, and where the concrete cave is."

"What about Nate?"

Yeah, Mallory, what about him?

"I'll figure something out, but this is insane. We have no plan, no direction. We keep this up, and we're going to get killed, or we're going to hurt a bunch of people we don't intend to.

And you're going to feed. You're going to feed a lot. I can feel it, even now.

I wanted to stuff that mental Mallory in her box, but she wasn't wrong. I could feel the hunger building. It was there, chewing slowly, biding its time and waiting for the first opportunity to come out and make itself known.

"Where do I—"

"Just drive," I said, trying to figure out a street or intersection that might give me some hint as to where we were.

It felt familiar, but not, like I'd been here in a dream.

The car rolled slowly past darkened garages and a gas station long since shuttered. We continued to follow the streetlights, avoiding other cars and doing our best to keep the stolen sedan on the pavement and not in some ditch.

"Billy, red light."

The kid just kept rolling, the coming intersection not registering in his brain.

"Billy, stop!"

"Huh? Oh, shit." The kid slammed on the brakes, and we ground to a halt just over the white line. Cars streamed through in front of us, their drivers appearing to be just as happy we didn't impale them as I was. "Pull in at the next opportunity. I'm driving."

Billy's shoulders visibly relaxed, and it only took a little prodding to get him moving once the light turned green.

We squirted out the intersection, the kid taking the first turn he could. Billy wasn't much for parking, but the little grocer didn't have much in the way of customers. This was great because he took at least three spots.

"That's it. You did great, grandma, but I'm driving from here." I grabbed the first thing that looked like a shirt from the back seat and pulled it on. The men's button down was just shy of useless, but it was better than walking around with bare and bloody arms.

At least until you've fed…

Again I tried to leave that Mal in the car, but she joined me in the lot. She directed my eyes up to the poster-covered windows, the Spanish words splashed across them, and the exotic smells drifting on the night air.

It was that Mal, the hungry one, the one that wanted blood, that didn't bother getting back in the car. She walked right up to the door and grabbed the handle, half of her drawn in by the call of the blood, the rest of her lost in a hazy afterimage the past blood had brought.

This was Marie's store, and the blood inside would bring her to Nate.

She knew it.

CHAPTER 31
TOO CONVENIENT

PLASTIC WRAPPED food hung from metal spikes like meat slow-smoking over the spit. Wide bins sat on home-made tables, their shallow walls holding back produce that had blown past fresh a few hours ago. I got the immediate impression this place, with its varied mix of offerings and a wall of coolers housing plenty of cold beer, did brisk business both day and night.

It was the perfect place to go for a pick-me-up.

Which was great because that was precisely what I needed.

Mallory…

The voice in my head urged calm, but I shoved that bitch down a flight of mental stairs. Calm wasn't what I needed. What I needed was blood—biblical amounts of it.

I wanted to backstroke through the stuff, running it over my face and between my jaws. I wanted my stinger to lap it up like some stray cat with a fifty gallon drum of milk.

I wanted all of that, and I wanted it yesterday.

Mallory, remember Marie…

I dismissed that voice and rode that tide of hunger to its bloody summit.

A ceiling mounted TV barked words at me in another language, rapid-fire words that a more composed Mal might have at least tried to follow. I settled for getting the gist of them, my ears working well enough to catch the highlights.

"…sangre y muerte…"

Blood and death. Don't mind if I do. Thank you very much.

That was right about the moment the first hints of tonight's breakfast drifted on the fragrant air. Spicy and exotic, it had a chipotle base that tickled that second tongue. My jaws rippled softly, happy at the prospect of something new, but still enjoying the creamsicle and his tasty memories.

Hard work.

They tasted exactly like that, like grueling work in the hot sun. They made me tired in a strange way, like effort by proxy. What I needed now was something new and fresh, something different.

Something with a nice smoky chipotle flavor perhaps?

I stretched my hands out, running them over narrow shelves and letting the slender muscles in my shoulders relax. They needed it as much as I did.

I needed to feel strong, powerful. I was tired of running, tired of fighting the sun.

I needed to be the one in charge, the one on top.

Judging by the young man working the counter, I'd get exactly that.

He couldn't have been much older than Billy, maybe just a couple of years, but whereas the kid was still awkward muscles and a childish frame, this one was a young man.

A young man with blood.

Thick hair fell over his ears, rounding out a face devoid of baby fat. Dark eyes and heavy brows stared up at the television, his head shaking slowly with the newscaster's words.

More images played out on that small screen, pictures of cars, police tape, and a very empty turnpike rest stop.

There was a warning for young viewers, but I turned

away before whatever came next. I wasn't here for the past. I was here for the future.

I was here for the blood.

Marie.

My mind dredged up an image of what had been the woman. Whoever she was, she was dead, and dead things didn't deserve attention.

I moved closer to my prey, pretending to compare boxes of powdered detergent, but all the while my eyes truly on the prize leaning behind the counter.

I imagined what it would be like to take him down, to ride that strong body to the floor and steal everything from it.

Mallory! What are you doing? This isn't you!

Like hell it wasn't me.

My jaws rippled in agreement.

I was a monster. I knew that now. There was no more Mallory, not really. The woman who cared, who didn't kill, the one who held her stinger back, was dead.

Mal was all that remained.

Mal took what she wanted.

Mal took *all* she wanted.

I set the box down and moved closer, leaving one tiny aisle before slipping down another. I wanted this one to be smooth, clean, and fast. I wanted to down him without a chance to grab a weapon, should there be one. I was tired of eating bullets. Tonight's feast would provide a welcome break from the frantic past.

Nate…

What about him?

I pushed back on that prissy bitch in my head. I would find Nate. I promised as much, but it wouldn't do to find him hungry, would it?

The logic was messy, but I didn't care.

I only cared about the blood, and the tender muscles soaked in it.

Don't do it, Mallory…

I waved off the warning, instead moving to the edge of the row and finding the open side of the counter.

It was a clear shot to my dinner. A quick run, a jump, and everything would come crashing down.

I imagined it twice, then a third time for good measure. My jaws split apart, and beneath them a hungry stinger emerged. It approved of the spicy pepper and the excitement that fresh flavor brought.

It was here, coiled like a viper ready to strike, that the television image flipped and stopped me cold in my tracks.

Dark hair and dark eyes, full lips, and a warm smile, the photo spoke volumes without saying a word.

Marie!

I didn't know how I knew, but I did. I knew because of the blood, because of some fragment of memory still rolling over itself between my ears like a rock tumbling downhill.

That was Marie, and this store was in her memory.

This store is your only connection to Nate.

A hungry stinger snapped back and forth. She didn't care about Nate, or Marie, or anyone else. She only cared about the blood.

The blood…

My prey shook his head, as if struggling to comprehend the newscast playing out above him. He was a sitting duck, a fish in the barrel. It would take nothing to ride him to the ground, to swim in his blood, to be the powerful one.

It would take everything not to.

You are in control, Mallory.

I wasn't, but maybe if I told myself that a few dozen more times I would be.

I willed an angry stinger back into her hole and from there forced jaws closed that very much wanted to remain open.

You're doing it.

I was. I was doing it and it surprised me. Maybe I could

still be that woman? Maybe there was hope for me after all? Maybe not touching the child hadn't been a fluke?

The TV switched to more gruesome images, officers down and covered in plastic.

You did that.

The guilt swelled and my jaws with it.

What did it matter? What did any of it matter? I was damned. I wasn't worth saving.

I'd split open my brother's skull and feasted on the sour fruit inside it.

I didn't deserve to be forgiven.

I deserved to be burned.

I'd long since earned my last sunrise.

It was here, neck deep in a confusion born of blood, spice, and Spanish television, that the door opened.

It took me longer than I cared to admit to realize this, or to pay attention to just who was walking down the center aisle.

Billy didn't prowl.

My son wasn't the cunning type. He was the hungry kind, the one that takes what he wants, and doesn't seek forgiveness.

Eyes wide and pupils even bigger, Billy moved with purpose.

The teen behind the counter had barely looked up before Billy's jaws snapped open. A stinger followed, slender and ready to feast.

There was no image of Marie to stop him, to make him hesitate.

Billy didn't have a brother in his skull trying to keep him from falling off the rails. Billy only had me, and I was a terrible mother.

The kid behind the counter shouted something, but I lost it in the insanity that followed. Billy launched himself like a blood hungry missile, scrambling over the counter and crashing headlong into the older teen. They slammed into a rack of nudie magazines and cigarettes, those typical teenage vices raining down around them as they wrestled on the slick floor.

I wanted to move, but the sharp smell of gun oil caught in my nose. The weapon emerged next, falling out from some hidden shelf beneath the counter. The bigger teen got a hand on it and that was all I needed to see.

Some mothers are born that way, others are made, but they all have one vital thing in common. My jaws snapped open, and my stinger erupted behind them, resplendent in her triumph.

All mothers will bring hell on earth if they think their children are in danger, and I was no different.

I shot out of the aisle like a bullet fired, crashing down on the two of them, hungry for blood and more than willing to take a bullet for my boy.

That's what good mothers do.

CHAPTER 32
LEADS IN BLOOD

I DIDN'T THINK. I didn't have to. All I had to do was surrender to the blood and let the rest happen.

Nate faded, as did anything else that counted for guilt in my broken mind. It was only me and the blood.

The young clerk's pumping heart became like a lover's whispers in the dark, soft words from the boyfriend I'd never have again. It spoke to me, that pounding muscle. It spoke of our future, and how much it wanted my kisses.

Jaws swelled to embrace the warm flesh and revel in the sweet and tangy fear that followed.

His fingers might have been wrapped around the weapon, but he was too far gone to fire it. My stinger danced in the blood, swimming in like some river otter on a warm day. It twisted in the joy of life, at least until the memories came.

They tumbled out broken at first, flashes of light and sound, but it wasn't long before they took shape, coming together to form a kaleidoscope of crazy.

Kids.

There were so many kids.

Young and old, and every possible age in between, they raced in and out of the house barely holding together at the seams. These weren't his kids. They were his friends, his roommates, the ones he'd bounced through life with.

I tried to follow them, to understand their games and the inside jokes they told, but I couldn't keep track of it all.

It was a cyclone of motion and energy, and I missed it.

I missed my brother.

I hesitated and considered letting go, but my stinger showed no interest in that. She wanted the blood. She wanted *all* the blood.

The scene shifted, and the house narrowed, an already small bungalow becoming just a kitchen, a kitchen full of fresh faces. It was like high school all over again. Eyes watched and judged, but they weren't judging me, they were judging him, they were trying to understand a new kid and his place in the pecking order.

The kitchen shifted and became the yard. I remembered swinging, my fists flying free and untethered by morality or guilt. Somewhere beyond the blood-borne memory, my stinger dug deeper, hunting for a path to the motherlode.

Imaginary fists made contact with someone's face. It hurt, but in a detached and airy way. I wanted this. I wanted to put him in his place. I wanted to let them know who was in charge.

Pick a fight with the biggest kid and win…

Those weren't my words, but they might as well have been, they thundered in my head between each pulsing beat of a fading heart.

My stinger felt that slowing and swam deeper, bringing fresh waves of memory and new scenes to life between my ears.

Christmas played out, not once, but many times, and in each instance the faces changed, but one stayed the same. There was a single face in the crowd of evergreen trees and cheap tinsel that didn't change.

Long dark hair framed the peaceful face, and softened lines brought on by stress and life.

"It's so good you are here, Michael." She said the words with caring and with love. I almost choked on them and on the waves of guilt they brought. I wanted someone to say those words to me, to care if I lived or died.

Nate?

My brother would never say those words to me, I'd made sure of that. The stinger that even now busied itself drilling for a succulent heart to devour had seen to that. I had ended that relationship before it had even begun.

Could we have been like this?

I tried to imagine a different life, one with Nate and his family coming for Christmas to a house of my own, a husband who loved me, and twin girls clinging to my legs in the kitchen. I tried to imagine all those things, but they didn't last, they only washed away in blood and memories—Michael's memories.

The dark-haired woman handed him something, a beer? The sweaty bottle felt cold in my hand.

"I have to do it."

It was like watching some movie play out without understanding all the scenes that came before, but somehow I was enthralled by it, sucked up in the story even as my stinger dug deeper.

"No. We can fight. We can—"

She put a finger to his lips, a gentle finger that spoke of perhaps something deeper and more carnal in the dark of night. "We can't do anything. To even think that risks everyone else."

"The cops—"

She shook her head, those long tresses dancing over resigned shoulders. "No."

"Some of them know. Some of them know about vampires, and they are willing to fight back. They at least try—"

"And they die, or their children die. I'm not risking it. I'm not bringing more death into my house."

I tossed back the beer, forcing down the watery crap even as the bubbles burned my tongue. It was hard to tell where Michael began and I ended, and that was exactly what the stinger wanted.

That was exactly what I wanted.

"So you're going to do it? Just like that? You're going to turn him over to them?"

"I don't have a choice." Her eyes pleaded with me. They wanted me to see what she saw, that the good of the many outweighed the good of the one.

"There's always a choice, Marie."

Marie!

My stinger hit the heart and found a companion there, a young tongue hungry for blood and lapping up memories by the mouthful.

"What about the pastor? What about—"

Marie ripped the beer out of my hand, out of Michael's hand. "I'm done discussing this. You are either with me or you're not. What's it going to be? Are we all going to die? How many of the children are you content to murder? Four? Ten? All of them?"

Michael hesitated, even as I tried to pull my stinger back and Billy's too.

"I guess if you can murder one, then I can too."

Tears swelled in Marie's eyes. "Where's Billy?"

Billy!

The kid knocked me aside, as if watching the same show I was, and was just now getting to the good part. I felt my stinger detach as strong fingers clawed at my jaws. Billy wanted him. My son wanted all of him and wasn't willing to share.

He knows Marie. He knows Marie!

The words played in repeat in my blood-addled brain. They beat like the heart slowing in Michael's chest.

Marie! Marie!

I hated her. I hated her for Billy and for Michael. I hated her for who she was and for the choices she made. I hated her for the Mallory I saw in the mirror of her soul.

Stop him!

I hooked my arms around Billy and pulled, fighting to detach my son from the revenge he wanted, he needed.

I knew what it was to want such things. It hollowed you out and burned away joy like the sun stole life.

I wanted to give him his justice, but we needed this kid.

I needed him.

With a strength born of frustration and anger, I tore Billy free, tossing him aside and putting myself between him and his meal.

Blood-red eyes glared up at me. They swam in anger. My son wanted nothing more than to do to me what he'd done to Marie. "Billy, stop! He knows. This guy knows Marie. He's got to know where Nate is!"

Billy's jaws swelled, blood dripping from an angry stinger. "I don't care."

"Hell yeah, you do." It was my turn to snap my jaws wide, and the stinger beneath them to raise its sharp end. "You very much care. You touch him and I will end you. I will show you what real pain is. I will break every part of you and let it heal, only to break it again."

"I Ie—"

"He is a means to an end. That is all. He's how I find Nate. You want your vengeance? You can take it… *After* I'm done." I pulled my stinger back slowly as he did the same. "I find my brother, and you can do whatever you want with him. I don't care, but now, I need to fix him up. I need to keep him alive, so I can find Nate. My brother is the only thing that matters."

Billy nodded slowly, his bloody jaws closing gently.

"Good." I turned back to the teen, listening for a heartbeat and hoping we hadn't already gone too far. I found one, but it wasn't much. "I think I can close the wound, but he's lost a lot of blood and—"

Click.

Cold metal pressed gently against the base of my skull. The hands behind it trembled as he spoke. "No. I'm not doing it. Michael is mine. Give him to me… now."

"Billy…"

The gun cocked against the bone. "Now, Mallory."

CHAPTER 33
THINK HARD

"I WANT you to think really hard about what you do next."

Billy's hand trembled, the gun in it shaking against the back of my head. "He's mine."

"No. He's not. In fact, if you don't stop screwing around he's no ones. I know you've only been dead for a few days, but normal people don't come back from a lot of blood loss. I figured you might have forgotten that. If I don't do something soon, he's going to die."

"Good." He pressed the gun harder against my skull, trying to offset the shaking by just pushing more. "I want him to die. I want all of them to die. I don't care anymore."

I placed a hand against the young man's neck, relieved to confirm what my ears had already told me.

He was still alive, but for how long?

"Which is it, Billy?"

"Huh?" The gun barrel's pressure relaxed just a little.

"You just said you want him to die and that you don't care. These are two competing decisions. You care that he dies or you don't care if he lives? You really need to think your words through."

I couldn't see them, but I could hear his jaws unfolding behind me. "Shut up! Just shut up. You want revenge. I get to want revenge too."

"Your revenge is fine unless it stops me from getting mine." I let my jaws open just enough to slip that stinger out and taste the air. There was a lot of blood, but if we moved fast we might be able to close up the worst of the holes.

Billy's momentary hesitation faded and he went right back to trying to push the gun through my head. "You don't understand! You don't understand what they did to me! What they—"

"I don't have to. Here's how this is going to play out. You're going to take that gun off my head, and in return I'm going to get to work patching him up. I promise you it will hurt—a lot—and when I'm done you can interrogate him."

"I…" Billy's voice broke. "I don't know how to—"

"You just ask questions, flare your jaws, take a lick here and there. The questions are what's important, get him thinking about it, it'll make the blood memories more vivid. I want to know where Marie found Nate. I want to know exactly where, and I want this human GPS to take us there. After that's done…" I let my words hang like a limp stinger in the stale air. "Well, after that's done then I really don't care what happens to him."

"How can I trust you?" Billy's voice betrayed him again.

I'd known people like Billy my whole life, because I wasn't much different. Trust wasn't easy for me, or for Nate, but sometimes you had to soldier through it if you wanted the good things on the other side.

I took my hand off Michael's rapidly cooling body, blood dribbling out across an already crimson floor. "I tell you what. I'll trust you. I'll trust you to do the right thing. You're going to take that gun off my head, and in return I'll keep Michael here from dying, just so you can do him the honor later."

"You promise?" The gun's pressure came off ever so slightly, but it was enough for me.

I twisted, turning my head and my hips and letting my stinger do all the heavy lifting. She cut a hole through his wrist like a drill press against cheap wood. Blood and snapped tendons joined bits of broken bone and a dropped pistol on the floor.

Billy screamed and I kicked the weapon away, but I didn't stop there.

You gonna let him do that to you?

It was Mom's voice that pushed me forward, and her smoke-shrouded face that coaxed me into slamming his body against the floor. Billy scrambled to get away, but I had a brother and knew how to wrestle. I also knew how to grind his stinger into the cheap tile with my knee. "Who the fuck do you think you are, Billy? Who?"

"Mal, I…"

My jaws swelled like a falcon in flight. "I want to hear this. I want you to tell me who you are. I want you to tell me why you think you get to live after pulling a stunt like that."

"He… Marie…"

I brought my face down close to his, my stinger poking gently at the edges of a frantic eye. "It's a straight shot from here. Did you know that?"

Billy squirmed but couldn't manage to get himself free.

"It is. It's a straight shot to your brain. Your eyeball would heal… eventually, but if I slice and dice just right, then your brain is fucked. It's permanently fucked. You know how I know that?"

"Mal, I didn't mean to… I wasn't going to—"

"I know that because I've done it. My brother made a bad decision, a really bad decision, and it cost him his mind."

Billy's already pale skin took on an even whiter shade. "Mal, I—"

"Now the question is, was your decision bad enough to cost you yours? What's it going to be, Billy? You gonna drool over yourself the rest of your unnatural life, or are you going to start playing for the right team? Are you Team Mallory? Or are you Team Billy? I know which one has a future. The question is, do you?"

"I'm sorry, Mom."

Three fucking words. All it took was three fucking words to rock me to my core and send me right back to the bar, to the cop, and to the cypress tree where I took Billy's life and gave him this one.

I made him.

How could I end him?

You did as much to Nate.

Nate was family.

Billy was blood.

"Whatever." I pushed the kid away, turning my attention instead to the older teen on the floor. "Get me what you can from the bathroom. I need paper towels. If you can find some bleach, get it. We need to clean this up and I'll need some time to seal up the holes in his neck.

Billy pressed a hand against his face, almost surprised to find my stinger not lancing it on its way to his brain. "Paper towels?"

"Yes, paper towels. Bleach, and a fucking mop. Unless you want to clean all this up with your tongue?"

"No, but I don't—"

"Now is not the time for thinking, Billy. Now is the time for doing exactly what Mal says."

The kid got to his knees while I turned my attention to my human GPS. He was in rough shape, but his heart was still beating, at least for now.

"Billy…"

"Right. On it." The kid sprung up and headed for a door

beside the coolers. "I'll see what I can find. I never really came here with…"

We both froze, the rumbling sound of a motorcycle engine pulling up out front stopping us cold like a pair of deer in headlights.

"Shit! Billy, did you lock the door?"

"No! I was supposed to lock the door?"

I scrambled to my feet. "No, you weren't supposed to come inside. You were supposed to wait in the car. You weren't supposed to come back after I freed you in that bar. You were supposed to let me die. You're a stupid fucking kid, Billy."

"Mal," Billy pointed to the distant glass where more motorcycles rolled up, heavy bikes, big ones with equally large riders, "What do we do?"

"Shit, shit, shit!" I grabbed Michael's collar and snapped my stinger into his neck, dragging it back in such a way as to close the wound. It wasn't much, but it was enough to keep him from bleeding out. The big stuff would have to come later. "Take him and hide behind the counter."

Billy hesitated, his eyes on the door and the big men heading toward it. "I can take them."

I ripped off the blood-stained button down and frowned at the black bra showing through a decidedly ripped up top. "I'm sure you can, but the bodies are piling up, and that's going to bring the cops down on us like a fucking hurricane. The cops here have killing light, do you want to spend your last sunrise under some purple spotlight from hell?"

"No, but—"

"Then shut the hell up and do exactly what I say. Stay behind the counter. Don't move. Don't speak, and whatever you do, do not let them know what you are."

Billy's jaws rippled in frustration.

"Exactly. Keep that shit on lock down." I pushed the kid

behind the counter, hoping to hell he'd keep Michael alive while I got these lovely gentlemen in and out of my life. I tugged on my bra straps and wiped what I could off my face, letting my jaws close and my stinger retract just as the door swung open.

Here goes nothing…

CHAPTER 34
BIKES AND BAD BOYS

THINK, *Mal.*

What was there to think about? I counted at least five guys on bikes moving to the door.

They're big.

They were big. In fact, at least two of them would have given Nate a run for his money. They didn't scare me now, but they would have back then, before…

I'd had run-ins with guys like these in my younger years, rough times it would have been generous to call stupid. Rough times that had needed a little brotherly intervention.

Before you put a hole in his head?

I wanted to put a stinger hole through that thought, but it slipped away at the jingling of the bell that hung on the door.

They came in rowdy and loud, bringing with them the smell of stale beer, sweat, and cigarette smoke.

It was a heady combination, but what was worse was the gentle undercurrent of fried chicken. I had to put a hand against my jaws to keep them from rippling at the juicy flavor.

No!

Why?

That question hung between my ears without a good answer, uncomfortable in its honesty.

You can take them.

I pushed that one away. I might be able to take them, but the tangy hint of gun oil told me at least one of them was packing.

Let them get what they want and then leave. Do not engage, Mallory. Do not engage.

"Hey, guys," I said, the words coming out before I could stop them.

Great. Excellent work not engaging.

It was hard to stay angry at myself. It's not everyday one gets to talk to fried chicken.

They were like five buckets of the stuff, the good pieces, nothing shitty, and not the slim pickings after Nate had cleared through it either.

This was premium breasts, thighs, and wings—so many wings.

"What can I get for ya?"

What can you get? Mallory, you can get bent. This is insanity. Just shut the fuck up and let them buy their beer or whatever else they want. Stop talking!

There was a mixture of grunts and blank stares, but at least one guy zeroed in on the skinny girl in the torn-up shirt hovering near the counter. "Where's Mike?"

"Uh…"

Yeah. Where's Mike, Mal?

"He skipped out for something. You got me tonight. What do you guys need?"

The big guy in charge checked all the typical biker boxes: leather, tattoos, and a doo rag to cover hair that appeared to have long since blown off from years on the road. I pegged him for late fifties, and the gray in his beard seemed to be frequent enough to agree with me.

"We need a lot of things."

"Well, we got it." I pointed to the coolers where plenty of cold beer sat quietly waiting to be consumed. "Or perhaps some cigarettes?" I kicked my thumb back toward the stacks behind the counter.

What the absolute fuck are you doing, Mallory?

I didn't know what I was doing, but the stinger did, she shifted softly at the base of my throat. She was hungry and very much liked the idea of the fried chicken on the menu.

"Hmm, that sounds like a good idea." Without much more than a look his guys hit the coolers like beer buying locusts. They scooped up enough for me to wonder exactly how they'd carry all that on those bikes.

The second they opened them, I realized they weren't going anywhere.

Shit.

I took a few gentle steps back, trying to keep me between them and the gap behind the counter, the gap that presently held a barely living Michael, and a Billy that wanted to put him in the ground.

A quick glance back confirmed my suspicion. Billy wasn't really doing much to help him, but he wasn't actively hurting my only chance to find Nate.

That was progress.

What wasn't was the impromptu chicken place the little grocer had turned into.

The big guy slipped right past me and put his bulk against the counter. Elbows leaning hard, he pointed at the rack of cigarettes. "Um, Missy? We're gonna need some assistance."

I stepped back over Billy and his would-be dinner, doing as much without looking at either of them. "Yeah. Which ones?"

"Well, you see, I'm not sure. I'm gonna need to try out a few."

"I've got a better idea." I grabbed four cartons off the narrow shelf and dropped them on the counter. "How about you guys take all this stuff and roll out of here? I won't tell Mike. It can be our little secret."

"Oh, ho, ho! I love it." The big man scooped up the cartons and tossed them back to his crew. "So, Mike chickened out, eh?"

Chicken…

I thought my jaws closed, willing them to stay shut even as the tantalizing scent of perfectly fried chicken danced on the night air like some five bucket masterpiece of oily perfection.

"He's just out running an errand. I'll tell him you stopped by."

"An errand, eh? That's nice. The thing I can't figure is why he'd leave a sexy little thing like you all slutty behind the counter. You'd think he'd want to keep that for himself?"

My stinger practically danced at his words and at that building tension in the store. This was what it wanted, and maybe it was secretly what I wanted too?

Visions of a blood-splattered store played out on repeat in my head. Ripped-up bodies laid in aisles like the discarded buckets they were, devoid of contents and nothing more than a flavorful hint of what had been.

No! You worked in a bar for years. You can do this. Get them the hell out of here, Mallory. Get them the hell out of here now.

I grabbed the register and ripped the drawer free. I didn't make a show of it, but that was more than enough to turn a few heads. "I have no idea why Mike missed this, but I know why he left me here." I turned the contents over on the counter, popping open the bill holders one by one and making a more than modest deposit on the smooth surface. "I think he left me here to give you this and direct you to the door. How's that sound?"

The big guy's eyes moved between me, my chest, and the modest pile of cash I'd deposited on the counter. They also lingered a few seconds on the bent metal edge of the register drawer. There was a complex calculation running through his head and I just hoped it tallied up in my favor.

No you don't. You want chicken, don't you, Mal? You want to lick your fingers clean...

I shoved that thought back to live with the stinger that wanted it, then pointed toward the door. "So, what's it gonna be?"

You could tell this turn of events had not been what they were expecting. It wasn't often you came in to shake some place down and had the new girl hand over everything without a second's hesitation.

He stared at me, then at the register. You could tell the rest of the crew wasn't keen on walking, not when there was a tasty piece of trim in groping distance, but I got the impression this guy knew enough to know a good thing when he saw it.

He tossed cartons to one of his buddies and then stuffed fists of cash in his pockets.

"There you go. I knew you'd see the light. You guys go have fun, paint the town red for me."

They moved toward the door slowly, not quite sure what to make of this string of good luck, but not quite willing to shake their fists at it either.

They'd barely reached the exit when the ceiling mounted TV switched back to the news.

"We caution viewers. The following scenes may be too graphic for..."

It was me, decked out in red and racing through the rest stop parking lot. The details were grainy, but there enough there to make out the key pieces. What's worse? There was Billy and the stolen car. The picture went to static just as his jaws unfolded.

Fuck.

If anything, that should have done it. That should have cleared the shop and sent those guys packing, but it didn't. In fact, it appeared to put gears in motion, gears I didn't want in motion.

"Time to go, guys," I said, hoping to get them in motion again. "I'm closing up."

A shared look between them sent a shudder down my stinger.

"No. I don't think so." The big guy put his hand on the door and turned the deadbolt shut.

Thunk.

"I wouldn't do that if I were you." I let my jaws swell. "I'd walk out that door while you still have feet that work."

Someone fished a narrow flashlight out of his pocket. The hint of ozone I'd missed before hit my nose immediately.

"Nope," he said, turning that metal cylinder over in his hand. "I think we're staying right here."

CHAPTER 35
ONE BAD APPLE

"THAT SHIT DOESN'T WORK on me." I pointed at the flashlight, lying through my teeth and doing my best to put on a terrifying display. My jaws stretched to their limits, the stinger beneath them rising like an angry cobra from its basket.

"I think it does." The big man slipped his own killing light out of his pocket. "I think it works damn well. I think that's why your people ran. I'm not sure why you didn't get the message, but we're happy to tell you again."

"The message?"

The fifty-something asshole nodded his head, that stupid doo rag dangling behind it. "Yeah. This is *our* town. We don't want you here, and we're going to show you what happens to those of you that try to break those rules."

He's seen more of me... Nate?

I dismissed that thought the second I had it. These guys weren't interested in telling me anything useful, and I certainly didn't want to be at the receiving end of that much concentrated artificial sunlight.

The door?

It was locked, but since when did that stop me? If I'd wanted to I could have busted right through that glass.

Billy...

The kid was behind the counter with my one path to Nate. There was no way in hell I was leaving those two behind.

Fight it is, then.

My eyes latched onto the flashlight and my stinger shuddered at the memory of those damn things. "I'm not here to make trouble."

"That's funny." The boss man slapped that flashlight against his palm. "Sure looked like you were game for trouble on TV. I'm betting you were the same one that slipped outta that preacher's trap."

He knows.

"Listen." I raised my hands slowly. "I'm not here for your town or the stupid people in it. I'm here to get my brother back. One of your fellow assholes took him and he's important to me. I get him back and I'm gone. We'll be in the wind. You'll never see us again."

"Why don't I believe you?"

I took a cautious step forward, closing the distance between us.

Watch it, Mal...

"I have no idea why you don't believe me, and frankly I really don't care. If I wanted you dead, I'd have done it by now, and if you really wanted to try and cook me to a crisp, you'd have all those flashlights humming. The point is, we haven't done either. We're talking like human beings."

"You aren't human."

I stopped at the end of the aisle, trying to do my best to keep everyone in front of me. It wasn't working great. At least two of them had made their way into bordering aisles, putting me right in the middle of a perfect pincer move.

Shit.

I shook my head. "I was."

The big man hesitated, as if processing my words slowly. "That's bullshit."

"No, I assure you it isn't. I hate these fuckers just about as much as you do, maybe more. You think I like the fact you all smell like fried chicken? You think it's fun to hide from the fucking sun every damn day?" I let my stinger crack like the end of a whip. "You want a snake in your throat, a little second tongue that listens worse than the first? I can tell you from experience, you don't."

"You are nothing but monsters and thieves."

I lowered my hands slowly. "That's a funny thing to say coming from a guy that likes to shake down shitty little grocers."

"That's different." His calloused thumb grazed the on-button.

"Whatever. Listen, I don't care. Like I said before, I don't care about your stupid town or the people in it. I'm not here for your blood. I'm here for my brother. The second I get him, I'm gone, and believe me, you want me gone."

The big man laid his thumb down on the button but didn't press it. "Is that a threat?"

"Yes, but not for you. Like I've said at least twice now. I do not care about you or your people. I want my fucking brother and I want safe passage out of this place. I want to get back to what I was doing, namely surviving, and figuring out how to fuck the everliving shit out of the guys that did this to me, to us."

It felt oddly good to say it all out loud, to put words to the thoughts that had been rolling around in my head for what felt like months.

I truly didn't care about the asshole standing in front of me, or his fellow chicken-flavored sacks of skin. The fact that I had a premium family meal laid out in front of me was only mildly alluring.

That's bullshit, girlfriend. You are hungry as hell and they smell so good.

I stuffed that thought down, right back in the hole it had climbed out of without a moment's hesitation.

Clear head, Mallory. Clear head survives this. Clear head finds her brother.

"So, let me get this straight." The big man kept his dark light pointed directly at my chest. "You want me to let you go, and in return, you promise you're going to just find your brother and leave town, no problems. Is that right?"

"Yup."

He placed a hand on the stubble on his chin, running his fingers over the gritty flesh. "Hmm. So I take it whoever has your brother—provided he hasn't been burned to a crisp—is just going to turn him over to you out of the kindness of their heart? And that you, the bloodthirsty thing you are, won't wrap those jaws around their neck as payback?"

Oh, fuck no. I'll kill them all. I will swim in their blood. It will soak the ground.

"That's right."

"I don't believe you."

"I think you need to. I think it's your best option. You are outnumbered."

He chuckled, eyes on checking the back door and his men before turning back to me. "How do you figure? I count five of us and one of you."

"I'd say I'm worth more than one of you, wouldn't you?"

"Maybe." He pointed his flashlight down and popped it on, the killing purple light bright against the dirty floor. "But we've got these."

"You do, but I have Billy."

"Huh?"

"Come on out and say 'Hi,' Billy."

I kept my eyes on the rest of the crew, but hazarded a

quick glance behind me to make sure the kid was coming out from behind the counter.

He wasn't.

"Billy, now would be a really good time to come out."

Still nothing.

"Having some people problems?" The boss man toyed with his flashlight, bringing it ever closer to my feet in playful little circles.

"Bill, you need to come out now. You're embarrassing me in front of the idiots."

No Billy emerged from behind the counter, and I suddenly got the sinking sensation he wasn't coming. That fear went great with the slowly rising scent of fresh blood.

Son of a bitch!

More flashlights popped on, those purple lights bringing back memories of the pain sufficient to make my stinger hesitate. Now was not the time to tuck tail. Now was the time to puff up, to look dangerous, to have your fucking son pop up like the goddamn cavalry.

"Looks like it's just us, cutie." The boss man's flashlight skimmed over my feet, catching a few hints of ankle flesh and scorching them like the dawn.

"I guess so." I snapped my stinger, forcing it to stay put. Billy might not be listening to me, but I wasn't going to fold that easy. "The way I see it, this is your last chance. Let me go and I promise none of you will die tonight. You'll walk back out that door with arms and legs still attached. You all can keep your dicks, even if they really don't get much use. I'm offering you all of that, and all I'm asking in return is for you to let me find my brother and get the hell out of town."

The boss man nodded. "Yeah. I heard you the first time. See, I've got a better idea. I think we're going to strip you down and cook you like a pig on the spit. How's that sound?"

"It sounds to me like I'm finally understanding why you smell like chicken."

That did it.

The killing light came hard and fast, hitting me from three sides at once. What these assholes didn't understand was that I'd been burned before.

I'd been burned by my brother, by Billy, and by the sun.

Sure that shit hurt like hell, but you know what hurt more?

Me.

I crashed into the closest guy, riding him to the ground and taking a full wash of purple light for my trouble. Skin peeled like the edges of burnt paper, but his blood went a long way in salving that pain.

CHAPTER 36
FINGER LICKING GOOD

I WASN'T MALLORY ANYMORE. I was feral, hungry, and willing to do whatever it took. I had teeth and a razor-sharp second tongue. That tongue cut through this biker's jacket like cheap tissue paper, plunging deep into the blood beneath.

Fried chicken!

The taste brought back with it a flood of memories, both mine and his. I was little again, my fingers greasy and a smile on my face. The tall bucket sat on the table, bright red and white with heavenly steam rising off the breaded goodness that resided inside it. I wanted more of it, just like I wanted more of him.

My stinger lapped at that secret recipe, all but oblivious to the fiery pain of the fucking killing light. His memories came with the pain, good memories of the wind in his hair and the open road, the thunder of the bike rumbling between his legs. But those weren't the only memories I received. Dark ones, bloody ones, they hid, waiting to pounce, and only too happy to introduce me to the evil in his soul.

There was a flash of stinger and the flaring of jaws I knew

weren't mine, then the whole store spun, because that's what happened when you took a fist to the skull.

I tumbled across the slick floor greeting the nearby shelf with my face.

You're outnumbered, Mallory.

Not if the kid helps.

Like I said, you're outnumbered.

I shook that thought off and the killing light that accompanied it. My stinger snapped wildly, hoping to hit something but getting only plastic bags and dusty boxes for its trouble.

They're here! You can smell them!

All I could smell was the fried chicken and the burning scent of my skin curling.

"Billy, damn it!"

If the kid was back there, he didn't show, what did show was a gun. I don't know how I'd let it slip earlier, but somewhere beneath all that imaginary breaded goodness there was gun oil.

"Shows what you bitches know. I can eat more bullets than you can shoot."

"Not these bullets," the big man said, giving up his position in the confusing purple light.

"Oh yeah? We'll see about that." I grabbed a box of something off the shelf and held it up to block the worst of the glow, then snapped my stinger in the general direction of the Chatty Cathy asshole. I got the satisfaction of my stinger hitting leather and salty flesh before the first shot was fired.

Boom!

The bullet ripped through my side, snapping a rib, and taking with it a chunk of flesh.

"See? I can eat a—"

The pain hit me hard and fast, like what a real bullet should have. My stinger retracted immediately, as if it had been pulled back on a short leash. Whatever it was he'd hit me with, it sent the feral part of me running.

"Hurts, don't it? I bet it does. I bet it hurts a lot. I told you. This is our town, we don't want your kind here."

I clapped a hand against my side, startled to feel my own ribs between my fingers. "And I told you, I don't want your fucking town, I only want my brother."

"Light her up!"

Bullets exploded and a killing light burned. I scrambled for the next aisle, my frantic brain trying to make sense of what just happened. How were they doing this? How was I not healing? What the fuck was going on and where was Billy?

I was alone.

I was alone and it hurt almost as much as the hole in my side.

Think, Mallory. Think and live. Run and die.

My jaws flapped in and out like the bellows of some crappy furnace, the pain driving them like unbridled horses.

I can't…

Like hell you can't. You can. You are more than you think you are. Where's the killer I know? Where's the bloody monster?

She's bleeding herself.

I pressed my hand tighter against my side, grimacing from the pain and trying to think. They appeared to be regrouping, picking aisles, and lining up for their last push. Those fuckers had done this before. Hell, half this damn town seemed to know about vampires, and what to do with them.

Shit.

I scrambled to my feet and caught sight of the light switch out of the corner of my eye. It wouldn't be total darkness, but it would level the playing field just a little.

Let's play in the dark, assholes.

I snapped my stinger out and hit the switch at roughly the same instant that killing purple light came around the corner. This guy's momentary hesitation was all I needed. My stinger on a return trip moved like the cracking of a fleshy whip.

There was no neck in existence that could take that impact. His split, vertebrae shifting like wooden blocks under the fingers of some unruly bully.

That's what I was.

I was the bully.

Two down.

I'd barely pulled my stinger free before the third one came in hard. His shitty purple light stung, but the darkness made it hard for him to see enough to hit the sensitive spots.

Close the distance now!

Wrestling with Nate had been an instructional series in how to lose. The jerk never let me win, but in doing so he taught me so many things: get tight, get close, eat space and gain leverage. I did exactly that, wrapping my arms around this tasty bucket of fried chicken and dragging it to the dark ground. The burning light scorched my jaws, but they found his neck just the same.

Blood, glorious blood, rolled over my lip, a retracting stinger overjoyed to lap it up. Memories exploded like fire-crackers, popping in my head and showing flashes of stingers, jaws, and faces I'd never seen before.

Fear.

He was afraid.

He would die afraid and I loved it. My stinger practically danced in the majesty of his blood and the richness it brought. The luxurious second tongue was just as excited when the dead bolt flopped open and someone made a run for their bike.

Do it! Run, little pig, run because the big bad wolf is coming for you.

I dropped his still twitching body, my hand back to pressing against my side and wondering why it was taking so long to heal. I didn't get much time to focus on that though before I realized I wasn't alone. That last heartbeat cut through that haze with the clarity of a gun barrel shining in the filtered street light. "I told you it would hurt."

"Whatever." I pretended to shake it off, immediately regretting that move when I did. "I can go a dozen more rounds, old man."

"I don't think you can. I think all I have to do is put a single round between your eyes and this is all over. You won't get up from that."

"Try it." I let my jaws swell just enough to give the stinger an easy exit lane. "Try it. Play stupid games and win stupid prizes."

"This is for my—"

I never let him get the words out, sending my stinger at his feet and yanking the closest one out from underneath him. The gun went off, its powerful bullet ending up somewhere in the ceiling tiles.

It couldn't hurt me, not now.

He tried to get up, to turn that killing light on me, but I scrambled on top before the big man could get his hands free.

My jaws snapped like a falcon in flight. "I want this to be the last thing you see. Me. I want you to remember that this could have all ended differently if you'd just been smarter. You didn't have to die."

An empty hand came for my head, but I dropped before it made contact, my jaws and stinger driving him into the slick floor like a mounted insect.

His memories hit hard. Bright and smoky, they came in fragments, There was screaming, fire, and the smell of blood. None of it made sense, but fresh faces, wide jaws, and so many stingers set my head on tilt.

I wasn't paying attention as his life ebbed out in my throat, or how he'd slipped a hand free. I was lost in a movie of broken clips, trying to make sense of all of it, but also drifting on the best bucket of fried chicken ever created.

I didn't notice when the gun barrel pressed against my

skull. In fact, I didn't realize his hand had put it there until he spoke. "This one's for you, Sarah."

"Mallory!"

The gun erupted and took off a chunk of my ear, but thanks to Billy's fast hands the rest of it still had a skull to attach to.

I pulled my stinger free, falling back to clutch my head and try to make sense of what just happened, a bloody Billy standing over me.

CHAPTER 31
ANGEL'S WINGS

BLOOD SOAKED BILLY'S SHIRT. Blood that wasn't his.

"You did it, didn't you?" I asked, my head still pounding from the shot that should have ended me.

Billy didn't answer. He didn't have to. I knew guilt when I saw it.

"Motherfucker!" I slammed a fist against the slick floor, angry at the boy who'd just saved me, and ruined my best chance to find Nate. "I told you we needed him. I told you to—"

"I can take you to her house."

Billy spoke the words softly, as if each syllable took something from him, something deep and soulful.

"How far is it?"

The kid shrugged his shoulders. "Not far, I think. It's hazy."

I struggled to my feet, legs wobbly like some baby deer in traffic. "Fine. We go now."

I pushed for the door, but the kid grabbed my arm. He produced one of those killing flashlights, mercifully turned off, and placed it gently in the palm of my hand. "I... want you to make it stop when we get there. Can you do that?" His dark eyes, ringed in regret, pleaded with me. "Can you?"

I closed my fingers around the metal tube. "I can."

"Thank you, Mal, I—"

"But I won't." I flung the light into the far corner of the room, relishing the sound of glass shattering.

The kid's jaws snapped open and mine did too, twin stingers emerged like something out of an old western.

"You don't get to go out," I said, ripping my hand free. "You don't get to go out like that. They screwed you over. They deserve what's coming for them. They deserve you."

Billy's jaws fluttered in the half-light. They were bigger now, stronger. He was growing, coming into his own.

I needed him. I needed him strong, fast, and focused. I didn't need some blood-swollen bag of guilt.

I needed my son.

He's not your son, Mallory.

I tried to push that thought away, but the harder I pushed the more it pushed back. I was his mother now. I was the closest thing he'd ever have to a mother.

He needed me, but I needed him more.

I just couldn't let him know that.

"I… I just want it to end." Billy's jaws drooped, their ferocity diminishing like the claws of some paper tiger in the rain.

I let my jaws close too, waiting for them to seal up and an angry stinger to retract before I spoke.

"I know. I know you do. If there's a way to make it end, I want to help you do that. But first, I want you to give the rest of these assholes their due." I kicked the closest body, enjoying the sound of my boot on broken flesh. "Can you do that? Can you become my angel of death?"

Billy tilted his head. "Huh?"

"It was just something I heard once. Like, this angel comes down to kill a bunch of people, you know, how angels do."

Billy frowned, suddenly more caught up in my words than the fact I had the door open and was pointing him toward the car. "I don't think angels kill people."

"Are you sure of that?"

The kid hesitated. "I… I'm pretty sure… Maybe?"

"Have you ever stopped to think about what we are?" I pulled open the passenger door. "We are vampi—"

I grabbed his face, squeezing his folds just enough to expose the edges of those fleshy wings. "We have wings. Have you ever stopped to think we might be angels?"

The kid pushed my hand away. "I'm no angel."

"No, Billy." I waited until he was in the passenger seat before grabbing something relatively clean out of the laundry pile in the back and shoving it in his lap. "You're no saint, neither am I, but based on what I know about angels, I'd say we check most of the boxes."

I left him thinking while I grabbed something for me. It was slim pickings in the second seat, but I managed to locate something mostly white that might have been originally at home in the children's section.

I tossed the bloody work shirt and fought to get that undersized garment over my head.

Angels? Really, Mal?

I chuckled at the thought, even as I tugged at the bottom of a shirt that barely reached my waist.

You're going to lose him.

I found Billy still in the passenger's seat when I reached the driver's side. His head tilted and his fingers counting out something, he surprised me with a smile when I sat down. "You know, maybe you're right? Maybe we are angels?"

I smiled back and shoved the key in the ignition. "Oh yeah? How do you figure?"

Billy rolled into a summary of his angelic knowledge. I had no idea if even half of it was right. In fact, at one point I was reasonably sure he mixed up both the tooth fairy and

Santa's elves with something he'd picked up at Sunday school.

Frankly, they all had about the same chance of being real, so I didn't care.

What I did care about was keeping him talking, keeping him giving me directions, and keeping him from thinking about killing light and some silly notion he had involving death.

Denying him his last sunrise, eh? How very Mallory of you.

I tossed that thought out the window on our next turn, preferring instead to listen to Billy explain his fractured version of why maybe we really were angels.

The commercial district with its darkened store fronts and derelict gas stations gave way to narrow streets and houses shrouded in shadows, all while Billy kept talking.

I'd touched on something and now I couldn't get him to think of anything else. He kept peppering off directions, a right here, a left there. That was how the blood memories worked. It was good not to think of them. They did their best work when you weren't paying attention.

You planned this, didn't you?

I chuckled at the thought, and at Billy's gesticulations in the seat next to me. This was a lucky break, a good turn, and if I wasn't careful, the kid might start calling it a sign from God.

I didn't need any of that. I needed Nate, and I needed to not be alone.

Sitting there next to Billy and weaving deeper into the empty back streets, I realized what I'd missed.

I'd missed this.

Nate had been a talker before, a big time talker.

Right up until you put a hole in his skull. Tell me, Mallory, was that God's plan too? Is that what angels do? Or demons…

The kid pointed anxiously to a modest home at the end of the windy street. Tall oaks ate the sky around it, swallowing stars and sinking the already dark home in a sea of indigo hues. A couple of bikes lay in the wild grass, rusty, but not unloved. Beyond them, a wide front porch sat smothered in kid's toys, like some store had been gutted tip to tail and poured out across it. Again, these weren't unloved, but they also weren't new.

Nothing about this place was new.

Paint chipped from the sills and mildew made its home in the eves.

The house was old, but very much lived in. I pulled past it, then swung around, killing the lights at the last minute.

I didn't see any other cars and it was only the sound of the gentle breeze through the leaves that reached my ears.

Billy got quiet. I could almost feel the thoughts running through his broken head. This place was heavy with memory. Blood or not, this place had purpose and meaning.

"This is it?" I asked, turning off the engine and letting the car settle.

"Yes."

"This is Marie's house?"

The kid nodded, the rest of his head appearing to be caught up in a wash of feelings.

"Okay. I think it might be best if you—"

Billy ignored me, pushing the door open and wandering out into the damp evening air.

"Actually, Billy, I think it would be best if you stay in the car."

The kid shook his head slowly. "No. I am the angel of death, remember?"

Shit.

"I was just using that as a metaphor, you know, to get your mind off that stupid desire to kill yourself."

The kid nodded, not looking back. "I know. You said they deserve me. You said they deserve what is coming for them. I remembered something. The blood on the door that told the angel of death to pass by the house. Do you smell any blood on the door?"

"What the fuck are you talking abou—"

"No blood meant he'd kill the firstborn inside. It was a mercy killing, Mal. I see that now. I see what I have to do."

"Billy…"

The kid's jaws swelled beneath what little moonlight broke through the trees. "I have to do it. I have to show them mercy."

"Billy!"

"I have to kill them all."

CHAPTER 38
STAIRWAY TO HELL

BILLY BOUNDED up the loose steps, taking them two at a time until he reached the top.

"Wait, don't—"

He didn't wait and he didn't stop. He moved like a kid possessed, like a person trapped in memories and living them out in realtime.

The screen door swung free on its hinges, and Billy didn't let some silly thing like locks stop him from getting through the front door.

He tore wood from metal and pushed into the darkness, his jaws wide and his stinger out.

He *was* the angel of death.

Way to go, Mal.

I didn't bother pushing back against the guilt. I deserved it, and I would do it again if it meant I'd get here. I'd get one step closer to Nate.

There was only one endgame—save my damn brother.

Anything after that was gravy.

Really? Thought you were going to find the guys that did this to you? I thought you were going to fix Nate? What happened to all that?

I didn't have an answer, what thoughts I did have washed away in the heady aroma of children, so many children.

It was like Halloween all over again, except this time I wasn't stealing other kids' candy at school. I was swimming in a bucket of my own.

I tried to pull my jaws in, but it was just too much. This was more than the cotton candy baby in the back seat. This was so much more. This was ice cream with sprinkles. It was candy bars, the king size monsters only rich kids seemed to find. It was hot caramel without the idiocy of an apple.

I practically floated up the steps on that smell, soaking in it, and surrendering to its whims.

I didn't remember stepping inside, or letting my stinger emerge to gorge herself on the sugary air, but I did both.

I did both without thinking.

Billy was somewhere else in the house, his feet pounding on the hardwood.

I didn't pound.

A true angel of death is soundless.

I prowled, slipping between discarded toys and around a couch that held so many intoxicating aromas. It wasn't hard to imagine that couch full of kids, their faces plastered to the nearby television and the bright glow reflecting off of it.

I ran a hand over the crumb-covered fabric, not feeling the grit as much as embracing the life it had held.

Life mattered, because I wouldn't last long without it.

Children, Mallory…

I let my jaw swell all the wider, embracing this dark moment and new menu.

So what?

Guilt crept up, finding her way into my thoughts like an unwelcome house guest.

This isn't who you are.

I sent my stinger out to poke at the couch cushions, to

tease the sugary hints of long dried sweat and skin from their creases.

Maybe this is exactly who I am? I put a hole in Nate's head. Me. I ruined his second chance at life, and now I was on my way toward ruining Billy's.

I let that thought roll over on repeat a few times, giving the guilt something to cling to as I made my way past the couch and toward what I assumed was the kitchen. Somewhere along the way I found a handful of pictures on the wall, glossy ones, like something taken by a cheap camera and a shaky hand.

So many little faces stared back in the gloom, their plump cheeks exciting an already hungry stinger.

I paused somewhere along the second row.

Marie…

It had to be. Even though I'd only seen her in pieces spread out on the bathroom floor, there was enough to go on in that still frame. Billy was right. This was Marie's house.

Marie's house of tasty treats…

The stinger had moved on, like some diamond back rattler hunting for her next meal. She pulled me into the kitchen, losing us once again to so many smells. Food had been eaten here, but that held no allure for me. Not the honey still sticky on the cheap counters, or the bowls of slowly souring milk water in the sink.

Food was ash and filth.

Blood was everything.

It didn't take long to clear the kitchen. It was empty, just like the rest of the downstairs.

Billy's sudden silence drew me like a moth to the flame. Was the good eating up there? Was there a chocolate fountain just waiting to be gorged upon?

Those thoughts dragged me back past the TV and onto the stairs. I climbed them swiftly, not pausing to admire more photos of Marie and her candy-wrapped brood. I was restless. I was an angel of death without her purpose.

The steps gave way to a creaky landing, and from there yet another narrow hallway loaded with toys.

If I'd been paying more attention, I might have noticed the mess, I might have put more of it together.

I didn't.

I was a creature of blood.

The stinger dragged me from one room to the next, each time reveling in the scent of so much candied goodness, only to hiss in disappointment at yet another empty bed.

There were no heartbeats.

There were no children.

There was no Nate.

I found Billy in the last room, the furthest one from the stairs. He sat on the edge of an unmade bed, the sheets twisted in his hands.

Just like before, there was so much candy, but something else caught my nose and unset the stinger. My second tongue didn't like it, just like it hadn't liked the smell of Nate's old clothes after we changed.

That was Billy, before he became my son, before I gave him this new life.

Red tears welled in his eyes, his jaws closed and his stinger hidden behind them. "Why? What did I do?"

"I don't...I don't know," I said, letting my own jaws close, those wings retracting like the feathers of a bird realizing she was not going to feed tonight.

Billy tightened his pale fingers around the scratchy fabric. "What could I have done? I did everything she said. I was the good one. I was always the good one. You believe me, right?"

"Yes."

"I was. I swear I was. I... Why would she give me to them? Why the fuck would she give me to them?" Sheet tore effortlessly between his fingers, loose threads dangling only to be cast aside by Billy as he stood. "I'm glad I did it. You know that? I'm glad I tore her apart. I'm glad I ripped her to pieces."

"Billy—"

More tears, and now stomping. He paced the empty room, kicking toys out of his way with each step. "No. I'm glad I did it. I want it gone. I want to bury it all. I want to burn it down. Yes! Burn it down. Will you help me? Will you help me burn this place to the ground?"

"Yes, but first, where is Nate?"

"Nate?" Billy tilted his angry head. "Nate? Who the hell is Nate?"

"My brother. You saw him in your blood memories. You saw him because Marie saw him. Where is he?"

The kid shrugged his shoulders, then pushed the bed out of his way in a fit of rage. "I don't know and I don't care. Don't you understand? It all started here."

"For you. It all started here for *you*. It didn't start here for me. It started when I broke my brother. It started when I drove my stinger through his skull." I barely realized it had happened, but no sooner had I said those words than my second tongue had made an appearance.

"Yeah? Maybe you should have left that bullet in mine." Billy's jaws swelled, wide and powerful in what little moonlight made it through the window shades. "Maybe it wouldn't hurt anymore?"

"It's supposed to hurt. Living is supposed to hurt. That's the penalty for being us. That's the price we pay for this." I spread my jaws wide. "You want to be an angel? You pay for these wings in blood."

"Maybe I don't want to be an angel, not anymore..." He let his words hang in the air, but his body language was still speaking. His weight shifted and his hands no longer seemed so relaxed. Billy was looking to pounce.

I planted a foot to match him, my stinger on full display.

"I made you. I brought you back from oblivion. If I recall, this is what you wanted. This is the world you begged for. Now you have it, and all you do is weep about it. Grow up. Grow up and help me find my brother. If you want to die after that, then fine. We can watch our last sunrise together, but not until we find Nate. Not until my damn brother is safe."

Billy moved to jump, but stopped suddenly. It wasn't hard to see why.

Headlights filled the gossamer curtained windows.

We weren't alone.

CHAPTER 39
LIGHT 'EM UP

BILLY REACHED THE WINDOW FIRST, pulling the curtains aside before I could slap his hands free.

It was too late. The wash of dingy yellow light flooded the upstairs bedroom and lit us up in the process.

Whoever was in that car knew we were here.

I suddenly got the impression that this might not have been the best plan after all.

"What do we do?" Billy's jaws almost quivered in time with his frantic eyes.

"Do you know them?"

"I have no idea who they are."

Shit.

I grabbed his arm and pulled him away from the window. "Whoever they are, there's a good chance they knew Marie. If they knew her, then they might know where Nate is.

Nate…

I pushed thoughts of my brother down, hiding them under mental rocks so I could focus on the task at hand.

No one dies tonight.

I don't need blood memories. I need the real thing. I need to press the flesh and make it bleed.

I need to know where the hell Nate is and I need to know now.

Billy turned his attention to the window as the sound of car doors closing echoed through the thin glass. "We should—"

"No. This isn't your plan. This is mine. You are going to stay here. You are going to stay in this room until I come get you."

"Like hell I am."

The sound of car doors closing turned to boots on tall grass. I counted at least three heartbeats. Loud but muffled, they rumbled against my ears.

"You can't keep your shit under control. You are staying here."

"I can too keep my shit under control." Billy's jaws closed in the soft light. I had to give him credit, at this angle he almost looked human.

He almost looked like a living boy.

Hmm, it might work…

I rolled one very questionable thought over in my head a few times before deciding I had nothing better to work with.

"Okay," I pulled him to the bedroom door, then stopped to put a finger against his sealed jaws, "You can come, but you have to promise me to keep those closed. No matter what, you keep your jaws closed—tight."

Billy's eyes went wide. "What are you going to—"

"I'm not sure, but you are my insurance policy. For that to work, I need you to listen to me. I need you to look human, innocent. Can you do that?"

Billy's face softened. "I think—"

"Perfect. Like that. Now, where the hell is the breaker?"

A newly repurposed Billy dragged me into the hallway and down the stairs. Flashlights, mercifully normal ones, flickered from outside the front windows. They were close.

"Billy!"

The kid pulled hard, dragging me into the kitchen and back out again, ripping a door open to deposit us in a laundry room. A gun metal box lay recessed in the wall. I ripped it open and threw the main.

Thump.

We had our dark, now to see what we could do with it.

The front door opened and it didn't take long for the hushed voices to make it to us. I couldn't understand the words, but I didn't need to. It was the smells that set my jaws in motion.

Farmer Bob!

It wasn't the man himself. I'd left that asshole dead in the corner of an old church what felt like a million years ago. No, this wasn't Farmer Bob, or even Blondy, but this smelled like them. That same rustic terrible they'd filled the church with was here too. Back then it made me afraid, now it made me angry.

My jaws swelled, the stinger beneath them dropping out like a hungry viper on the prowl.

Billy hesitated. "I thought we were supposed to keep our jaws closed?"

"You are." I pushed him up against the breaker panel. "You stay here until I call you."

"But I—"

"No buts. None. When I say your name you come out of that door and you run like someone has lit a fire under your balls."

"I don't understand—"

I put a hand over his rippling jaws. "You don't have to understand. You have to keep your face closed. That's all you have to do. Keep those damn wings tight and your stinger hidden, and I've got a chance of getting what I want. Can you do that?"

The kid nodded.

"Good. I know this shit is hard. I know it is. Once it's

all over, once I have Nate and we're back in the concrete cave, I promise I'll give you a choice. I promise you can decide if you want to keep going or not. I'll honor whatever decision you make. Hell, I'll help you do it. You understand? I'll hold your damn hand while you burn if that's what you want, but I won't do shit if you screw this up for me."

I let him go the instant I heard the sound of light switches clicking on and off.

What? Afraid of the dark, assholes?

I gave Billy one last look and hoped to hell he got the gravity of it before prying the laundry room door open and slipping into the kitchen.

The smell was stronger here, as were the heartbeats. There were three of them, definitely three, and they came with the distinct scent of gun oil and ozone.

My jaws rippled at the thought of those damn killing lights.

Chill, Mallory. You have the advantage. You have the dark. You have a plan. You've got everything you need.

I crept along the dingy tile, my feet soundless and my eyes trained on a wooden block of chef's knives.

My stinger shifted uncomfortably, like a dog that had been pulled back on her leash.

I'm not falling for that trick again.

The largest knife I could find in hand, I curled into the dark corner and waited. They moved haphazardly, trying switches and arguing with each other as they moved up and down the stairs. Light, both white and purple, danced along the walls and reflected off the many picture frames that lined the walls.

Be patient, Mal…

The laundry room door creaked open and a confused Billy stuck his head out.

Motherfucker! What did I tell you?!

I didn't dare speak the words, but my eyes bore them into his skull from across the darkened room.

The kid panicked and pulled back inside, but the damage had already been done.

"Did you hear that?"

"Sounded like the kitchen."

Sure did, asshole. Come and get me.

I tightened my fingers around the heavy blade and watched the front room. They didn't disappoint. A couple of heavy bodies thundered back down the stairs, guns up and purple light flashing.

I barely waited for the first one to hit the tile before I pounced. My stinger arrived first. I turned that second tongue on his feet, wrapping the closest leg and pulling. The worm may have wanted to feast, but the gray matter between my ears knew better.

"Fuck!" He crashed down, killing light and gun landing somewhere in the dark. They weren't my concern, not now.

I was the momma bear now. I was the killing fury of a woman very much pissed off. I was a bitch with a knife and a massive chip on her shoulder. I didn't need three of them to take me to Nate. I needed them to know exactly what they were up against and what I was capable of.

I needed them afraid.

Fear makes for bad decisions and that was what I was counting on.

I couldn't hold one of these guys hostage, there was a good chance they'd taken that shit and had it in their blood.

No, my hostage would be young, innocent, and hard to make out in the dim light.

I caught the man's face in the dark, and the panic painted on it. It was a singular moment of clarity before he realized his life would end tonight.

I hesitated, the blade in hand while every ounce of the momma bear in my skull screamed otherwise.

Is this who I am now?

"Vampi—"

I slammed the cold steel home, pushing it through ribs and past organs. It was different, visceral. This wasn't killing to feed. This was just murder.

Murder…

I didn't have time to linger on that thought, or the avalanche of guilt that followed. I ripped the blade free and made for the relative safety of the darkened corners. More light was coming, white and killing. It covered the walls and the gasping man, then frantically hunted for me.

"Now, Billy." I whispered, hoping to hell he heard me.

The laundry room door crept open and that was when the shooting started. Bullets cut through the cheap wood like crepe paper. They shattered plates and ripped the doors off cabinets.

Shit. Billy!

There was no kid emerging from the laundry room, just the hint of smoke and the smell of blood.

Fuck.

CHAPTER 40
THE BEST LAID PLANS

I SQUEEZED the stupid knife in my fingers, whatever idiotic plan I had unraveling before my eyes.

"Stop!" One of the men shouted, grabbing the shooter by the arm. "What if one of the kids are still here?"

"We got them all out," his partner said, tugging his arm free.

"You sure?"

No response.

That was hesitation, and it was exactly what I needed.

Sure, it was a stupid plan, but it was the best I had. I needed those idiots talking, talking to me. I needed them to care.

Well, I needed *one* of them to care.

"Billy!" I whispered, hoping to hell the kid could hear me. "Pretend to be one of the kids. Fuck, you used to be one. Go with it. Come out and—"

I didn't get out much more than that before the kid emerged, blood streaking his pants.

Shit!

He'd been hit.

What was worse, they had the killing light up and on its way to roasting him.

Here goes nothing.

I bolted, tackling Billy and driving him to the ground.

"Don't shoot! That's one of the kids."

The trigger happy one hesitated, instead pulling his killing light up to cook both of us in our juices.

"Keep your jaws closed and look innocent." I slammed a hand over Billy's mouth, then sent my stinger around his neck, my other hand pressed the knife against his throat. "Drop the killing light or I gut him like a fish!"

Hesitation turned to panic as both men trained their weapons on me. "I told you there was still a kid here."

"Fuck."

Billy squirmed in my arms, I couldn't tell if it was an acting job or not, but it worked, the killing purple glow remained at our feet.

"One step, one damn step, and I'll tickle his brain with the pointy end."

The compassionate one lowered his gun, and pressed his partner to do the same. "What do you want?"

"Who fucking cares what it wants?" The angry shooter's thick shoulders reminded me of Blondy. "I don't. She's not supposed to be here. That was the deal. They broke the deal, and they should be punished for it."

Deal?

I let my stinger tighten around Billy's neck, hoping to hell it didn't split his jaws apart on its own. "You have my brother. Give me back my fucking brother and you can have your child. It's as simple as that."

"Brother?" they said in unison.

It was the compassionate one that spoke next. "Are you talking about the big one? The blond guy?"

Nate!

I'd all but given up on seeing him again, on whether he

was even alive. Yet based on the look in those eyes, I knew he was there. I knew my brother was still with us.

Nate was alive.

"Yes. That's my brother."

"Well, he won't be for long. No need to keep him around now that we have you." Aggressive gunman raised his weapon and pointed it at my head. I flashed the blade in the light and let him see just where it would end up. "Think you are faster? Think you can get a shot off before I skewer this kid? How much does he mean to you? How much do any of them mean to you?"

"Whoa, whoa, whoa." Again, the one with the soft eyes and short stubble pushed his partner's gun barrel down. "The kids mean a lot to us. Just like they mean a lot to you. We stopped that trade a long time ago."

Billy fought to free himself, and this time I got the impression he wasn't acting.

"Chill, damn it," I whispered against the base of his skull. "Your jaws need to stay closed!"

The proto-bearded guy took a step forward, his hands out and gun at his side. "You want your brother. We want the kid. Sounds like a simple deal. Nothing too hard."

The aggressive one, the one with Blondy's shoulders and one hell of a chip on them, bristled. "Fuck that. That's not how it works. That's not how it works at all. We kicked their shit out of town. We did it. They knew not to come back, but they did. They did anyway. They're monsters, and sometimes you have to put down monsters."

"Hold up." Again the bearded guy raised a hand. "We can do this. We can make this work. You give me the kid and I'll make a call. I'll get your brother."

"Fat chance." I pressed the knife against Billy's face. "I'm not budging until I see him, until I see my fucking brother."

The gunman sighed and kicked at something on the

ground. "This shit is pointless. Why are we even talking to this thing? We shoot it, then light it up. It's fucking simple."

The other guy waved him off, then retrieved what looked like a phone from his back pocket. "Hold on. Let me get you something. We'll see if this helps."

He mashed a few buttons on the glowing display with his fingers and the sound of digital ringing flooded the quiet room.

"Hey, Joe, What's—"

"We have a situation. Do you still have the one we fished out of the Sullivan's farmhouse?"

The voice on the other end of the line hesitated. "Uh, yeah, but not for long. I think they made the decision to cook it at sunrise."

Nate!

"We're not going to do that," Joe said, holding the phone up so I could hear it.

"Uh, we can't reall—"

"I need you to put it on."

Again there was hesitation on the far end of the line. "What?"

"I need you to put it…him. I need you to put him on. Just put the phone on speaker."

"Uh. Are you sure? I mean—"

"Do it."

It was a few tense seconds before the voice returned. "It's… it's quiet. That's odd. Thing's been wailing like a banshee for hours, and now silent. No idea what Doc did to it, but I'm not sure what to—"

"Nate!" I shouted, not caring who would hear, not caring about anything but my brother. He was there. He had to be. He'd been screaming my name. I'd seen it in Billy's stolen blood memories. "Nate! Nate, it's me. It's Mallory!"

The voice on the other end of the phone crackled. "Who the fuck is—"

"Mallory!" Nate's voice boomed through the speaker, followed shortly thereafter by the sound of chains and cracking concrete. "Mallory!"

I tried to stop it. I tried to stop the tears, but they came anyway. Bright red and stinging, they ran down jaws swollen with hunger and joy.

I thought I'd lost him. I thought I'd lost the one person that would never leave me.

"Holy shit, whoever that is, they spun it up like a hornet's nest. I gotta—"

"Thanks. That's all we needed. Stay by the phone." The bearded guy mashed the button and killed the connection, plunging us back into that hazy darkness. "Okay. I did what you asked, now you do what I ask. You give me the kid."

Billy pulled harder on my stinger. Enough such that I was starting to question just how much of this was acting.

"No. I said I want my brother here."

The gunman trained his weapon on our heads. "Fuck it. I say we shoot her."

"No!" Joe put a hand up. "No! You risk hitting the boy."

"So? Sometimes things happen."

"That's not who we are." Joe stuffed his phone back in his pocket. "That's not what we do. We take care of our own. We aren't like those things."

I felt Billy's jaws ripple. Thankfully neither of them were looking at that moment.

"Damn it, Billy, you're going to blow the—"

"He's lying," the kid whispered. "He's lying They don't care about—"

"I know." I tightened my stinger around his throat. "I know and I don't care. I only care about my brother."

"Okay." Joe pointed at Billy. "You want your brother and I want the boy. I think we can work this out. He's not that far away. Shouldn't take more than twenty minutes to get him here."

"Are you fucking crazy?" The gunman's finger found the trigger but didn't squeeze. "Are you negotiating with one of these things?"

"I am." Joe pulled the phone back out of his pocket. "I'm going to get your brother in motion, but I need you to do something for me. I need a show of good faith. I need you to take your tongue off his throat."

It was my turn to hesitate. I pressed the knife against Billy's head and whispered, "Fuck this up and you are dead to me. You understand? I will tear you to pieces and feast on the insides."

Billy nodded and I released my grip on his throat, my stinger unraveling slowly.

"Son? Are you okay?" Joe turned all his attention on the kid.

"Yeah. I'm fi—"

"Then duck now!" Joe popped on the killing light and turned it on the both of us.

That was the moment this all went to shit, spectacular shit.

CHAPTER 41
NO MAN

AT LEAST ONE GUN EXPLODED, fire and anger erupting from its barrel. I took the worst of that, the bullet slicing through flesh and bone, but as bad as that was, what came next was worse.

Billy.

Billy did what Billy did, and my best chance for finding Nate collapsed beneath his fury.

The second his jaws opened and the first hints of blood caught the night, I knew it.

Those guys were dosing on something.

Billy's stinger emerged and he rode that tongue and its victim to the ground. I didn't have time to focus on that because I had a gun barrel in my face, and a host of other problems.

"No, Billy!"

I didn't know if the kid listened. All I could do was hope, hope and hide behind the kitchen table. I flipped that heavy pressboard mess and wedged myself behind it. The sawdust took bullets so I didn't have to.

Think, Mallory!

My jaws rippled, wide and ready to attack, but they didn't

have a target, they didn't have something they could wrap themselves around.

"Get it off of m—" Whatever words my link to Nate said, they vanished in the wet thump that followed.

The room filled with the sour smell of brains.

"Fuck!"

I popped up to find the gunman had turned his attention to Billy. That was all it took to engage those stupid motherly instincts. I scrambled over the table, throwing myself at that asshole before he could get another shot off.

We hit the slick vinyl together, a twisting mix of arms, legs, and anger. The gun erupted again and I was reasonably sure it took a chunk of my elbow with it.

It didn't matter.

Only one thing mattered now.

Nate.

Billy kept pounding, his bloody fists wrapped around the nice guy's shirt and driving the whole of his smashed face into the ground. My son was in another place, a dark place. Billy didn't think about the blood, or the hunger. Billy had a stronger motivation.

Billy was living on revenge.

The asshole's gun slipped under my chin for a second, and would have spilled my own sour fruits across the wall had I not pushed it away just in time. The stinger came next, driving that gun-wielding hand to the floor and the stupid weapon with it.

Sadly, we'd forgotten about the light.

Purple rays from that stupid ultraviolet cannon lit up my face and took my eyes with them. The kitchen went black beneath the fiery sting of that killing bulb.

"Fuck!"

I didn't think. I just swung. I swung my head like a wrecking ball, smashing a nose and knocking a few teeth loose in the process.

Blood!

The blood was everywhere. I couldn't see it, but I could smell it. He was a chicken man, a slow-roasted chicken man. It was like those times I'd gone to the grocery store with Mom as a kid, the fat birds hanging from their spits and turning slowly behind an oven glass we never got to open.

You open it now...

I could. I could feast on this fat bird. I could let his juices run wild and free down my face, but I would regret it.

I would regret it because there was something rotten in that meat, something nasty.

He'd been dosed. I knew that smell now.

The stinger didn't care. She went for it. She swam like a snake in the river, twisting in the devil's runoff.

It took all I had to keep her from drinking, to force that second tongue to listen to me and not the blood. I sent her in loops around his neck, enjoying the pulse and the frantic pounding of a heart that knew its beats were numbered.

I couldn't see, but I could feel.

I could feel his terror.

Burning light splashed across my side, the flashlight no doubt spinning on the floor. I let it go, no longer caring what happened beyond the man in my arms.

He panicked, his bloody lips screaming like a baby, but that didn't stop me. If anything, it gave me strength.

How many men had come before this one? How many held me down? How many? Fuck them. Fuck them all.

His shoulder moved and an arm with it. He was reaching for something.

The gun!

My stinger wanted to release herself, but I held her fast. I still had hands.

He got his fingers on whatever it was, but they didn't last. Even with a shredded elbow, it was easy to overpower him.

Little bones broke in a hand that wouldn't heal. He wasn't like me.

He was weak.

I was strong.

I was everything he could never be, that none of them could ever be.

Again he screamed and this time I scrambled over his back, hooking my legs around his waist and pressing my wide jaws against the base of his skull.

"It's over," I whispered, my vision returning to a blur of muted colors and my lips tasting his sweat. "I own you."

He tried to sputter out something, but my stinger held the words in his throat.

"Your only words from here on out are going to be the answers to what I want to know. You're going to tell me how to find my brother. You're going to tell me how to do that or I'll make sure you suffer a fate worse than death. I can do that, you know. You see the kid? He used to be like you. He used to breathe. Now he swims in blood and licks at brains. I can make that your life. I can make that your life then leave you out to face the dawn. How does that sound?"

It must not have sounded good because the gunman started twitching like a man possessed. He wanted out in the worst of ways, so I tightened down harder, hooking my legs in deep and letting my stinger do the rest.

"Let go of him, Mallory."

Billy?

I blinked once and then again, trying to make the world come into focus, but it continued to swim like a shitty hotel watercolor. "Billy, you didn't drink any of the—"

"No. I didn't. I need you to let him go and stand back so I can put a bullet in his head."

"No! I'm going to find him. I'm going to find Nate. I'm going to find him and this one is going to take me to him."

I couldn't see it, but I could hear Billy's hesitation, the way his finger rattled against the trigger. "Mal—"

"Please! Please just do this for me. Just this thing. Just this once. I can't do it anymore, Billy. I can't pretend anymore. I miss him. I miss him and I hate myself for it."

"Mal, you're—"

"No, Billy." I tightened my stinger, hoarding my prize like a jealous child. "I'm not arguing with you anymore. I'm telling you. You don't know what it's like to have a brother, to have someone you care about like that, to have a piece of you that's missing, that has been ripped out and dragged away. I'm tired of missing him. I'm tired of being alone. If this asshole knows where he is, then I'll squeeze the information out of him. I'll squeeze him until—"

"His heart just stopped beating."

"No, it…"

It had. His heart had just stopped beating. My stinger practically danced at the news, unwinding rapidly to plunge itself deep in his dead dying flesh.

"He's dead."

Billy's cold recognition of the obvious struck a chord and I lashed out. "No! No, he's not dead. He's not dead at all. He's not dead because I get to fucking laugh at death."

"What are you doing, Mallory?"

My stinger quivered in the hazy half-light. "You think you're special? You think you get to be my only child? Is that what you think?"

Billy's finger trembled on the trigger. "You're not… He's been dosed with that…that stuff. It's running through his veins. I can smell it. You don't know what's going to happen if you—"

"That's right. I don't know what's going to happen, but I know one thing. I know he's seen Nate. I know that much, and I know something else. I know he's going to tell me what I want to know."

"How do you know that?"

I pointed at the purple light flickering from the end of an angry bulb. "I know that because I know how to make him hurt. I know how to make him burn."

My jaws swelled and the fangs beneath them caught the gentle moonlight. They wanted this. They wanted it like they wanted to live.

"You're going to tell me what I want to know," I whispered, my stinger piercing his rapidly cooling chest. "You're going to tell me everything."

CHAPTER 42
TOXIC PERSONALITIES

THE POISON WAS THERE. Like a snake in the tall grass it waited: patient, hungry, and evil. It curled my stinger and burned at its sharp edges. The tongue wanted out. It tried to push back, but I was having none of that.

"You don't get to pick and choose. I decide. I decide for the both of us."

An enthralled Billy knelt opposite me, his wide eyes taking in the spectacle he hadn't been conscious of before, the miracle of rebirth.

Those same wide eyes pivoted to the door and to the car beyond it. We had a new ride, a better one, but I knew that wasn't what he was thinking.

He was thinking he had a way to get away from me.

I pushed my stinger deeper, ignoring the pain and forcing her tip to stay closed. There would be no tainted blood for us, not today.

A mother has to conserve her strength.

"I know what you're thinking, Billy."

The boy turned his head back fast, too fast. He moved like a kid with his hand stuck in the cookie jar. "What?"

"You are thinking about leaving me."

"No! No, I was just…"

"Nate wanted to leave me. Did you know that?"

Billy shifted uncomfortably on his knees, once again those eyes drifting to the door then back again. "I…"

"He did." I placed a gentle hand on the dying man's chest, coaxing the stinger with my fingers. "He found someone new. Someone to share his life with. Some skank to lick his wounds… among other things."

"I'm not going to leave you."

There was sincerity in his words. Real or fake, it resonated, but that did little to quiet the voice in my head.

He's going to run. He's going to run because that's what they all do. They leave you. They run from you.

My stinger swam upstream, fighting against the stagnating blood and whatever it was he'd poisoned it with. I wanted to vomit, but what I wanted didn't matter.

All that mattered was Nate.

It's not going to work. It takes too long to turn them. Too long. Nate will be scorched at sunrise. You heard them. Sunrise.

I pushed the stinger faster, urging it on with images of fresh blood, tasty blood, the good stuff I would reward it with after this was over.

"Will it ever be over?"

Those weren't my words, not in my head. They were Nate's. My brother's words came back to me the deeper my stinger traveled, they came back to me and brought their own visions with them.

"Will it ever be over?" Nate asked, perched on the edge of my couch, his big hands clenching and unclenching in frustration.

"No. I'm sorry, but it won't. This is life, bro. This is just how it is." With my back against the kitchen counter, I watched my brother spring up from the couch and pace yet again, the big man leaving footprints in the recently vacuumed carpet.

"It's bullshit then."

"It is." I nodded, not so much out of agreement, as out of habit. Nate was just learning the world and how it worked, and these sorts of revelations always came with pain. The good lessons were never easy.

"I don't get it, Mal. How come you put up with shit like that? I mean, why don't you do something? Why don't you say something?"

"Ha!" I barked a laugh before shaking my head. "Because I like eating." I pointed at the cheap popcorn ceiling. "And I like having a roof over my head. This shit matters. All of it matters."

My brother sighed, then slammed a balled-up fist against the arm of the couch. I winced, not so much for his hand, as for the furniture itself, and my deposit. "It's bullshit. That's what it is."

"No. It's called sacrifice."

Nate hesitated, those big, round eyes finding mine. Like any good brother, Nate didn't like to see me hurt, but like any youngest kid, he didn't really understand sacrifice. He didn't grasp what life demanded in return for living.

Life demands blood.

The vision stirred, like a spoon through coffee laced with cream.

The blood was pushing back. The poison still in it didn't like me there, and my stinger agreed. She wanted out just as much as Billy did, her sharp tip constantly pulling for the exit.

No. We're doing this. We're doing this now.

It had to be faster, all of it had to move faster. I couldn't wait for him to change. I couldn't drag his slowly blossoming body from one place to the next. I needed answers.

I needed them now.

I pushed my stinger deeper, the broken body beneath me jerking and twitching. Billy started to move and I snapped a hand out to grab his arm. "No. You need to see this. You need to understand."

"I don't—"

"You need to understand sacrifice, Nate," I said, no longer seeing Billy, just my brother. The big man knelt across from me, the way he had been before, before I put my stinger through his skull in a fit of panic.

Big hands lay folded in his lap while wide shoulders slumped in the dark. "I understand sacrifice, Mallory."

"No. No, you don't. Do you know what I gave up for you? Do you know what life was like before you?"

"I—"

"No. You couldn't. She didn't hate me back then. Mom didn't hate me. She didn't love me, but we had an understanding. Then you came along, her big boy, her little man. You sucked the air out of the room and the love out of Mom."

"Mal, I'm not—"

My stinger stirred, finding the spot it wanted and urging me into action. Things were different this time. The poison in his blood was fighting everything, and in doing so churning up the water like unruly kids in a public pool. The change would come fast, too fast.

"You're going to have a front row seat for sacrifice now."

The gunman's mouth opened and eyes that didn't yet see blinked.

Nate vanished and it was only Billy at my side, a frightened child, his eyes on the thing sputtering beneath me. "What… What's happening to him?"

"This is sacrifice. You'll get a chance to experience it yourself in a second. He's changing too fast. It won't last. He'll burn himself out, the poison and my blood will fight and only one of them will win. The loser will be him, but he's lucky. I only want to know one thing." I leaned in, my face just inches from lips that had already begun to ripple and peel. "Momma just needs to know one simple thing."

"Mal…" Billy tried to pull away but I held him fast.

"Momma just needs to know where her brother is." I ran a finger down his nose, helping the jaws stretch and peel. An infantile stinger emerged, pathetic and weak, much like the man beneath me. I tickled its sharp edges, my finger slicing open the serrations like I knew it would. A drop of my blood sent him into convulsions. The poison and the blood, they were fighting to the death in that broken sack of skin.

If I was going to get the winner I wanted, I needed a sacrifice.

Billy pulled again, managing to get to his feet before I pushed them out from under him. The kid was strong, but he was afraid. He was confused.

"It's okay, Billy." I hugged him close, bringing my son's face up to mine. "It's all going to be okay. I need you to do something for me. I need you to show me how much you love me."

Billy became Nate, and Nate turned back to Billy. I was lost in the blood and my memories. I was angry at the boy who wouldn't listen and at the one who had tried to leave. I was angry at both of them for not understanding one very simple truth.

Sacrifice.

I snapped my jaws wide and sliced a perfect line in Billy's neck. The kid fought back, but he wasn't ready for what came next. He wasn't ready to have his virgin neck pressed against the budding jaws of my newest progeny.

Billy wasn't ready for life's greatest lesson.

Sacrifice is everywhere. If you want anything, you have to be willing to give up something for it.

"You still want to leave me, Billy?"

The kid fought back, and would have broken free had the two of us not held him down. The gunman's simple jaws latched on, the poison and the blood waging war on his lips.

"This is sacrifice, Billy. This is what it takes to get what you want in life. It takes blood, passion, and everything you can give it."

My son's wild eyes slowed and his hands stopped fighting.

"Good. Now you understand."

Now you understand what it takes.

CHAPTER 43
ENOUGH

I LET it go longer than I should have, but Billy only fought for so long, eventually he gave in to the inevitable.

"That's enough." I pushed the kid free, tossing him aside to get a look at my fresh-faced newborn.

It wasn't pretty.

The newly made vampire's jaws flapped wildly, unable to close. This wasn't Billy, this wasn't a new thing learning the ropes of life. This was the fucking poison.

This was a nightmare.

I grabbed his throat, pulling the infantile stinger out with my bare fingers. "Hey! Momma needs you to talk. Momma needs you to tell her things."

Wild eyes darted in haphazard patterns, clearly struggling to come to grips with what was happening to the body they lived in.

I snapped my fingers. "Up here. Keep those eyes up here and on me."

He did as he was told, blood and bile running down his malformed face.

"That's it. That's what I want. Now, it's simple. I know what you want. You want blood."

He tried to shake his head, but his jaws fought him.

"N…"

"Ssh." I pushed a hand against those revolting lips. "Save your strength. The poison you ingested. The shit you thought would save you from things like me? It's killing you now. Maybe fast? Maybe slow? But it's killing you just the same."

Weak hands clawed at me, but I pushed them away.

"You want the blood, don't you?"

Jaws that appeared to have forgotten speech mouthed the word.

No.

"Oh, that's cute, but you do. You *need* it. That need, it's deep down in your gut now, festering. It's eating a hole in your soul. You can smell it, can't you? You can smell Billy, hell, you can smell me and the man who came here with you." I tilted my head at his partner's dead body. "You can't have him though, cause he took the poison, too."

It was like negotiating with a feral animal, his every movement jerky and uncoordinated.

"Was I like this?" Billy asked, the kid's wounds already healing.

"No. You weren't. You started slowly. You took forever to get your jaws underneath you. This one took the express train and it's eating him alive."

There were voices in my head, soft ones, quiet voices that questioned who I was anymore.

I squeezed the life out of them.

I am the queen of lies and pain.

"What do you hope to get out of this?" Billy asked, his eyes drifting back to the door and the darkened street beyond it.

"Isn't it simple to see? I'm going to find my brother." My jaws swelled and my stinger dropped out behind it. "I'm going to find Nate. I'm going to save him."

"And then what?"

What does he want to hear?

I grabbed Billy's hand in the dark. He pulled back, but only a little.

He wants you to be with him. He wants you to be with him till the end.

"And then we go home."

"Home?" The kid said the word with hope in his voice. That hope was all I needed to hear.

"Yes, home. I'm going to take you home. We'll be safe at home. There won't be anymore assholes, no more Maries, or Farmer Bobs, or dickheads with guns. The concrete cave can be our home, our haven. Do you want that?"

He didn't answer, but the way he squeezed my fingers back told me he did. "Good. Now find their cell phones and get his gun."

"What are you going to do?"

My stinger snapped like a viper. "I'm going to get directions. Don't you know?" I turned all my attention back to the shuddering thing on the floor. "Women aren't afraid to ask for directions."

Will he know enough? His blood is poisoned, what will that do? Can you get what you need?

All these questions and more raced through my head looking for a place to land. I didn't let them.

It didn't matter.

My last sunrise was inevitable, Nate's wasn't. Nate and Billy could be fine, they could find a way to live with this, to live together.

The kid would be good for him, better than I was, better than I ever could have been.

My stinger snaked along his chest, the dead heart beneath it fighting out the battle between the poisons competing for control of his destiny.

Which of them would win? Which would seize control and grind the other into dust? It didn't matter.

All that mattered was Nate and answers.

Billy moved about behind me, gathering phones and weapons, and doing his best to make sure the killing lights were off and turned away. It was good to keep him active, to give him something to do.

The last thing he needed was an idle mind.

Which was funny, because the one thing the ruined man beneath me needed was a mind at all.

My stinger touched his throat, gently peeling aside the layers of flesh like some lover in the dark. He wanted me to stop, but at the same time he didn't. His stinger coaxed me forward, drawing mine into its den.

It was the poison that struck first, burning that second tongue and bringing its own brand of hellish justice. The poison brought with it memories of the church, and of Blondy.

Blondy…

How many more had I killed since her? How many more would I kill? Did any of it matter?

All that mattered was Nate.

I pushed past his stinger, repeating that mantra as I did. My brother was all that mattered, not the poison, and not Blondy or the rest of them.

I closed my eyes, using my knees to pin his arms down. He wasn't going anywhere, not anymore.

He was mine now.

The blood churned beneath his flesh, even more unhappy than before. My stinger hungered for it, but was it safe enough to drink? Had enough of my infection made it so?

His head swung from side to side. It was the last gasps of a man refusing to accept what he was, what he'd always been.

There was no escape from the inevitable.

That's what I was.

That's what we all were.

We were the night that follows the day. We'd long since shucked our humanity like the husks of so much summer corn.

Why had I clung to it? Why had I insisted on pretending to be something I wasn't?

My stinger's tip opened gently, not so much to ingest blood as to give it. Just like before, I had to seed the ground, make it fertile.

He took it from me without a moment's hesitation. This man who acted like he would rather have died than be turned, accepted my blood just like he'd accepted Billy's. I gave of myself and in turn pushed back the poisonous tide just enough for something more.

These weren't someone else's blood memories, borrowed bits of the past. These were the deepest thoughts and desires. These were the fears, the worries, and the failures. All manner of things turned in his head, too many to count. I felt love, pain, regret, and ecstasy.

I pushed past those to something more concrete, to something of substance.

I got what I wanted, the hazy visions settling into movement and faces. At first they didn't make sense, but it didn't take long for them to form into something more concrete.

Vampires!

So many at once it hurt my eyes to try and follow them. They came in waves, like the crashing of a red and angry tide. In this fever dream, our gunman huddled in the corner, his bravado cowed by the blood hungry beasts at the door.

"Trev! Get the fuck up and fight!"

It was impossible to find the source of the voice, but I knew fear when I felt it. This rabbit was cornered and couldn't do much more than soil himself in the dark.

Show me Nate. Show me my brother.

The waves of hungry red death at the door faded, his mental camera taking me deeper, down winding stairs and into the dark underground. It was wet here, wet and cold. Stained concrete shined beneath the killing light of so many purple bulbs, but I didn't focus on that. I focused instead on the one thing that mattered, a cell.

The narrow vision didn't afford much of a view, but there he was just the same. My brother hung from the wall, chained up and surrounded by so much killing light.

Nate…

He couldn't hear me, but he looked up just the same, his lips mouthing the word I would have heard had I been there. It was a single word, one I never thought I'd hear him utter again.

"Mallory."

I pulled the memory back, driving it out and into the sunlight. I had to know. I had to know where he was.

A monstrous water tower hovered above like some pregnant flying saucer over the squat building.

It was my sign.

It was all that mattered.

And it shattered the instant that newborn stinger decided to fight back.

CHAPTER 44
FAMILY TIES

I TRIED to pull my stinger free, but that asshole held it tight. He didn't want me to let go. There was something he wanted me to see.

Memories shifted, blending and twisting like stirred coffee until it wasn't the water tower anymore. It was some backyard. Quiet in the evening darkness. So quiet, even the crickets had moved on to nicer pastures. It was just me and a beer, the good life while the kids slept. Suzanne would be out in a minute, most likely with a fresh one herself and a plate for the burgers.

Burgers…

The intoxicating aroma of sizzling beef on the grill was almost too much to take. I wanted it. I wanted it like I'd never wanted anything in my life, but the memory didn't take me there.

My lips never tasted that little slice of home-cooked paradise.

All it would taste was death and pain.

I leaned back in the porch rocker, watching the grill work its magic and taking in the tall grass and toys in the yard.

There were so many toys. I really should get on the kids to clean them up, but I didn't. They were just having fun.

Fun?

I struggled with the concept, trying to use another gulp of beer to lubricate its descent.

Fun didn't matter. Life didn't matter. All that mattered was finding Nate.

Finding…

Suzanne poked her head out the back screen door, those short auburn curls bouncing in the humid summer night. "Almost ready?"

"Just about."

"You want another one?"

I crushed the can with my fingers. "Yup."

"You got it."

Another beer. That was the last thing I said to her. The last words I'd told my wife was that I wanted another fucking beer. Not that I loved her, or that she and the kids were the greatest things to ever happen to me, just that I wanted another fucking beer.

The screen door swung shut, inside Suzanne busied herself clunking around in the kitchen and humming, humming some song that had found its way into her head.

I didn't listen. I only watched the gentle waves of heat rise off the grill.

The first one appeared not long after that, a pale white face against the indigo night. He was tall enough to tower over the fence.

He didn't say a word, only stared.

Vampire!

I knew what he was, even if this guy didn't. I knew what he was and I wanted to run, but the memory didn't know any better.

I settled on watching him, daring him to do something. This was my yard, my house, my wife, and my kids.

Do it. Come on my property, asshole.

He would. He would do a lot more than come on my property, and he wouldn't be alone.

Burger meat sizzled, fires leaping up from beneath those roasting patties.

"Suzie, go check on the kids," I said, never taking my eyes off the stranger beyond my fence.

My wife didn't answer.

It was only a silent house that responded, deathly silent.

The next few seconds were a blur of memory and emotion. They moved in gap-filled still frames. There was a kitchen, and an unopened beer on the counter. There was also something else, something slick on the vinyl floor.

Blood!

"Suzie!"

Ever more still frames rattled past.

My palms soaked red and from there my knees. I moved through the house frantically, each scene more disconcerting than the last. It didn't take seconds to reach the kids room. One instant I was at the bottom of the stairs, and the next at the top and standing in front of their door.

I pushed it open and would never forget what I found on the other side, never as long as I lived.

Wide faces, impossibly so, with jaws that flapped like the wings of some sea creature catching the ocean current, stared back at me. Long and snake-like tongues danced in the air, tasting and enjoying the many flavors the room and its occupants presented.

What came next happened fast, too fast. The room spun and the floor raced up to meet me. Swollen jaws red with blood greeted me in the dark, the serpent beneath them red and hungry.

I swung. I swung with everything I had. One fist, then the other, they made contact again and again, but it didn't matter.

I couldn't punch the memory from my head no matter how hard I tried.

My children!

The monster plunged its stinger deep, cracking ribs and puncturing a lung. I was drowning in my own blood, running out of air in dry land.

I should have died.

I wished I'd died.

I hadn't been that lucky. I was blessed with watching the tragedy unfold, searing it on my brain like the grill lines on those burgers long forgotten in the yard.

They devoured Suzie in front of me. Those things ripped her to pieces and gorged themselves on what fell out. She never looked away, never stopped reaching for the beds and the little faces that were too scared to move.

I never forgot her love, or the way she refused to turn away.

Her screams bubbled like those sizzling drips of fat on the charcoal.

I failed the children, mine and so many others.

I failed them because I wasn't strong enough, fast enough, or smart enough.

I failed them because I was an 'I' when I should have been a 'we.'

Strong fingers pulled on my shoulder, yanking me away from the memory and from the dark thoughts that followed. I didn't let them. I yanked back. I had to know what he knew, to see what he saw.

There were more vampires, so many more. They came in waves night after night. They took the children and ate the rest. Families banded together, they sought strength in each other, and in numbers.

Someone discovered killing light and another person gathered weapons. So many more died, their blood added to the ledger, their lives painting the ends of so many stingers like wicks wet with hot wax.

But this place was different.

This place fought back.

This town and the people in it chose a different path. They didn't roll over, they didn't mourn their dead or lament their fate. They didn't bend beneath the hammer's blows. They swung back.

"Mallory!"

Billy pulled and the connection broke, my stinger tearing free from the infantile one slowly curling in his throat. In a battle of poisons, his had won. Dead eyes stared up at me in the dark. Dead eyes that would never see their Suzie, or the children, again.

"Mallory, we've got to go." Billy dragged me to the door and out into the evening air. I could almost hear the burgers sizzling on the grill, or feel the empty can rush beneath my fingers.

It's not real. But it was real. It was very real and very much exactly what I was up against. This town had been through hell and now knew how to bring it.

"We've got to go!" Billy pointed to the car and shoved the keys into my tired fingers. "Come on. They got a text. I saw it on the phone. There are more of them coming."

The subtle hum of an engine in the distance echoed between the trees. It reminded me of Suzie and her song, of the way she danced when she thought no one was watching.

It reminded me of death.

Billy pulled the door open and stuffed me inside before finding his own way to the passenger side. His wounds were still there, but better now, mending slowly in the absence of blood.

We would heal. We would heal, but they never would. The people of this town were a walking scar, a burn mark that would never smooth over.

I jammed the key in the ignition and bit my lip waiting for the engine to turn over. Blood memories faded beneath its rumble and the thump of its tires hitting the pavement. I took us down the street, past the dark houses and beneath the blackened trees. My eyes should have been on the road, but they weren't. My eyes were on the horizon, and on the water tower that dominated the night sky.

My brother was there. Somewhere beneath that monstrosity on the hill. Nate was there and that was all that mattered.

I'm coming, Nate. I promise.

Suzie may be gone, and her children too, but there was one person still worth saving. My brother deserved to live, even if I deserved to die.

One of us would burn in the dawn and for the first time in forever I knew exactly who that would be.

The sky had not even begun to pink, but it would, and when it did, I would be there to greet it.

CHAPTER 45
DISTRACTED DRIVING

NATE.

My brother was close. I could feel him.

Nate was here and I was going to save him, no matter the consequences.

I jammed a foot down on the gas, enjoying the thundering engine of this newly acquired vehicle perhaps a little more than I should have. It suited my mood and my desire for vengeance. It suited them both just fine.

Billy stared out the window, his face a placid mask of stoic fortitude, while anything but churned beneath his pale skin.

How much had he seen? How much could he remember?

"What did I do? Why did she give me up? Why?"

I didn't have answers for him, beyond that Marie was a bitch and a broken person. I would never give him up. I would never turn him over to those men.

I was his mother and that meant something to me.

"It's gonna end tonight. You know that, right?"

Billy didn't turn away from the glass. "Yeah."

Sigh.

I took the next turn gently, my eyes on the bulbous water

tower in the distance. Each turn brought us closer, each turn put us just that much nearer to the end.

Nate.

"I'm going to get him, Billy. We're going to get him. You and me. We're a family, you know?"

He didn't answer. The young man leaned his head against the glass and watched the dark pavement stream by.

"I mean that. When this is over, we're going back to the concrete cave, back to the strawberry field."

Billy ran an absentminded finger over the glass.

"We won't stay there forever, but for a while. We'll stay there while all this crazy blows over. Nate's a good brother. You'll like him. I know he seems big and intimidating, but he isn't always. You guys will get along. I know you will. I just know it. We can fix up the concrete cave, get it all functional and stuff. That'll be good. Then—"

"Then what?" Billy snapped off the glass like it had been electrified. "Then what? Are we just going to keep killing? Keep feeding? When does it stop?"

"It doesn't stop." I pounded a hand on the wheel. "It never stops. That's the beauty of it. It never stops and neither do we. We are fucking limitless. We are without equal. We are ange—"

"Stop. We are murdering things, Mallory. You know that. I can hear it in your voice. You know that and you know we don't deserve to live. Monsters like us? We are—"

I took the next turn harder than I needed to and enjoyed seeing Billy bang his head against the glass. "So what? Marie was a monster, too. Farmer Bob, Blondy, that asshole back there whose name escapes me, they were all monsters. Who gives up a child? Who does that?"

Billy opened his mouth but I didn't let him answer.

"I'll help you. Normal people don't do that. Normal people don't fall for their foster kids like some creepy made-for-tv movie. Normal people don't turn a kid over to… to…"

"To monsters like us?" Billy said, finally getting a word in edgewise. "Mal, you've said it yourself. You've said it a hundred times. You're a monster. We both are. We live to consume, to feed, to rip good people apart."

I flipped the high beams on as we pulled off the pavement and onto a narrow dirt road. Tall pines and scrub palmetto pressed in on the car, threatening to squeeze it like some over-ripe fruit.

The kid had a point, but he also didn't. I needed the angry Billy. I needed the Billy who wanted revenge. I didn't need the broken child, the boy without direction.

I needed the fucking monster if I was going to have any chance at saving Nate.

"I'm gonna level with you." I slowed the car in the sand, hoping it was packed down well enough to not get stuck. "I've been around a lot longer than you and I've met a lot more people. This world isn't easy, not by a long shot, but that doesn't mean there aren't good people out there. They're not easy to spot, or always the same. Some of them do great-looking things for terrible reasons. Maybe Marie thought she was saving the bulk of her kids when she turned you over."

Billy's knuckles whitened against the door handle.

Do not let up, Mal.

I didn't let him respond, and instead pushed us deeper into the narrow pines. "Maybe she thought it was the right thing, you know? Maybe she did? Maybe it was a mistake… or maybe it wasn't. Maybe she fucked up? Monsters do that, you know? Monsters aren't perfect. They make mistakes."

"I'm not a mistake."

Bingo.

"I never said you were. I made you, Billy. I made you, but I couldn't have done that if you hadn't saved me. You know that, right?"

He nodded, half his face illuminated by filtered moon-light. "I—"

"You did. I know it seems like forever ago, but you did. You came in there fists swinging and gave me what I needed, and in turn, I gave you what you needed. What you wanted…"

Billy closed his eyes, then turned away, no doubt reliving those confusing moments. That was what I needed. I needed him focused on why he mattered and they didn't. There was more blood coming tonight, more pain, and I needed Billy ready to bring it, and not tucked up in his shell.

"You're a good person."

"I'm not a—"

"You're a good vampire, is that what you want to hear?" I took the next turn a little sharper than I needed to, hoping the tires wouldn't spin out in the sugary white sand, my eyes on the water tower that now seemed to almost loom over us. The Sunshine State didn't have shit for elevation, but somehow we'd stumbled on just about the only thing that counted for hills in the whole damn swamp. Whoever had built that water tower must have known that, and used every bit of height to their advantage. The monstrous tower hung there, its wide body pregnant with potential above the treeline. I imagined it like a tall cup just asking to fall over. How much water was inside? Enough to level the town? I doubted it, but it didn't hurt to imagine exactly that. It brought a smile to my face, and set those winged lips all aflutter. Maybe we were like that tower, ruinous potential? Maybe we were here to finish what the monsters in that guy's memory had started?

The dirt road ran out, depositing us unceremoniously beneath the behemoth. A small building sat at its base, square and unassuming, and no bigger than the concrete cave. Simple blocks, stacked one atop the next, formed the structure, a steel door the only discernible entrance. We weren't alone. A much larger, almost industrial truck, lay parked up against the fence. Its wheels alone were taller than both of us.

We pulled up alongside that truck and the eight-foot

fence. Beyond them lay salvation, Nate, and an end to all of this.

Night was here, but the day was coming. The day was always coming.

"Well, Billy…"

The kid shook his head. "We can't just walk inside there."

"Why not?"

"Because I'm betting there are more of them inside, more killing light, and more guns. I'm tired, Mal. I'm tired of all of it."

I threw the car in park. "No you aren't."

"How do you know what I—"

"You aren't tired because you know this is the end. You know that whatever happens next is the fucking end. You also aren't tired because this is what you always wanted, this moment, right now. You knew what you wanted when you begged me to change you, to give you the power to fight back. Well, your fucking demons are inside that building and just waiting for you to introduce yourself to them. How's that sound?"

Billy's fingers pulled on the handle, but I got the lock engaged before he could pull it open. "What gives?"

"You think we can just walk in there?"

"I just said exactly—"

I waved him off. "You did, and I agree with you. We can't just go strolling in through the front door."

Billy squinted at the tiny structure. "I don't think there are any other doors."

"We need to get their attention, Billy. We need to make a lot of noise and a big fucking mess."

"I don't—"

I grabbed his hand and put it on the steering wheel. "It's time for you to do some driving, grandma. It's time for you to do some abjectly terrible driving. Can you do that?"

"I—"

I smiled. "Who am I kidding? Of course you can." I put the car in reverse and packed slowly down the sandy road, lining us up.

Billy's face lost what little color it possessed. "What do you want me to—"

"I want you to put *this* car into *that* building. What do you say?"

The young teen hesitated, taking in my face, the tower, and the tiny concrete building. "I... I'm not... Uh..."

"Billy..."

"Fuck it," he said, finally coming around to being the Billy I wanted him to be.

"That's the spirit. Fuck it good. But this time, try to push *down* on the accelerator, okay?"

CHAPTER 46
DRIVING LESSON DE NOUVEAU

"IT'S SIMPLE." I pointed to the steering wheel and the pedals again. "I want you to point the car using this, and make it go *fast* by putting your foot here."

"I know how cars work." Billy rolled his eyes.

"Really? Even the whole gas-means-go part? Having driven with you before I'm not quite sure you have that part down."

The kid tried to push me away and close the driver side door. "Mal, I got it."

"Look at you, all grown up."

He smiled and rammed a foot on the gas only to have the engine roar and the car do exactly nothing. "What the—"

"It's in neutral. Still think you know everything about —"

Billy grabbed the gear shifter and threw it into drive. That was a new one for me, I hadn't taught him that, but he'd picked it up just the same. Billy had picked up a lot of things from me, and not all of them I was proud of.

He seemed to have somehow ended up with my sense of general confusion and inability to make consistent decisions. I chalked that up to a tough life as much as time spent around me, that, and the blood memories.

Blood.

Our newly stolen car shot forward like it had been launched from a cannon, the vehicle headed straight for the chain-link fence and the building on the other side.

We needed blood, and soon. I could already tell that just like the car, we were pushing the red line. We were running too hot without enough of the good stuff to keep us grounded.

The sedan bounced over a rough patch in the sandy road and Billy had to fight the wheel to get it back on track, the fence was only a few seconds away.

I wondered for a few seconds if he'd remembered to buckle his seat belt, and was pleasantly surprised when he ripped through the fence like wet newspaper.

Newspaper.

It seemed like forever ago we were in that old church, surrounded by crazies, and just trying to survive, when in truth, it couldn't have been more than a few days.

Days.

I glanced at the sky, taking my eyes off Billy in the final moments before impact. It was still dark, but the dawn was coming. The dawn always came. Maybe this time I'd be ready for it?

Maybe this time I'd finally do what I'd promised so many times before?

Nate.

I turned my attention to the car and suddenly realized why I should have been the one driving. Billy wasn't exactly great at working the steering wheel. He was still a little crazy on the overcompensating, and as such, wasn't exactly on target with the building as much as he was with the water tower above it.

"The building! Hit the building!"

The car accelerated in those closing seconds, then turned, smashing headlong into the building. Steel met concrete and the two shared a messy embrace. Blocks fell and crushed the hood. That was the moment it dawned on me that we would need a car to get out of here, and I suddenly hoped he hadn't hit the damn thing hard enough to break it permanently.

What he had done, though, was give us a new way inside, and kicked up a hornet's nest in the process.

I didn't wait around to find out who was going to come streaming out of that little box, and instead raced across the damp grass up and onto the hood. A smiling Billy's face met mine through the cracked glass.

"That was awesome!" The kid pounded his hand on the steering wheel in excitement.

"I bet it was." I slipped into the flickering light beyond the newly created opening.

I didn't make it two feet before the first bullets hit. White-hot explosions of pain, they left deep holes in my leg and gut. The blood went to work closing them up, but it was like scraping the bottom of the paint can. There wasn't enough good stuff to work with to do a decent job.

My attacker coughed in the concrete dust and I had him. He wasn't large, in fact, I'd say he wasn't much bigger than Billy, but he knew how to carry a gun, and what to do with it. More bullets exploded out the business end and I was lucky none of them hit anything vital.

I was the one doing the hitting now.

My jaws swelled and the stinger dropped out beneath them. It was hungry and smelled blood. There was a meal in the oven, something like bread with a hint of rosemary. There was something else too, the poison.

I pulled that angry stinger back, forcing it into its hole and using my shoulder to do what my jaws should have done. I knocked him to the floor and smiled at the satisfying wet crack that elicited.

This is easy.

In hindsight, that should have been my first clue. This *was* easy. This was *too easy*.

I put a knee into his chest and listened for the heartbeat, waiting for that frenetic beast to fade away with the spilled blood and brain matter. It did, just like it always did, and for a few moments I stared at his skinny young face. He couldn't have been much older than me.

That wasn't what got me, though. What got me was my reflection in his glasses, the monster with her terrifying wings of blood and ruin. She is what stared back at me from those shiny circles.

This is who you are now.

I hadn't always wanted to be this thing. There'd been a time I just wanted to make enough to have a decent place, maybe find a guy that wasn't an asshole, or at least get Nate to pay his share of the rent.

There'd been a time I wondered about being a mother, about being a better mother than mine ever was, of what it would be like to have a daughter.

Or a son…

Billy emerged from the car, pushing the door open and sliding out of the crack he'd made. "Holy shit, would you look at this place."

I pulled away from the dead man, only now realizing exactly where it was we'd ended up. Computer screens lined one wall, computer screens with views, so many of them familiar. Billy pointed out the rest stop, and something that looked like the church. I found the street outside the grocer, and a few houses that might have been close to Marie's.

"What the hell is this?" He asked, leaning in to poke his fingers at the keys of a nearby keyboard.

"This is a town prepared. This is a place that knows what the hell it wants and that doesn't have anything to do with us."

"Hey, look." Billy mashed some buttons and the displays

changed. Empty concrete hallways, gray and devoid of life replaced more interesting nocturnal vistas.

"Quit it. We need to find—"

My words caught in my throat, and this time it wasn't the stinger that took them from me.

It was Nate.

I'd spent so much time thinking about him, I'd almost forgotten what he looked like. In my mind, I'd reduced him to my brother, to the man he was before I'd changed him, before I'd turned him into that thing.

He was still my brother, but he was so much more now. He sat on what looked like a bench, his hands and feet wrapped in chains that looked like a lot, even for him. His face sagged, the wings of his jaws no longer perfectly closed, but now dangling in some sort of half-open display of futility. He was saying something, repeating it, but the screens offered no audio.

I leaned in closer, reading his lips as his voice echoed in my memory.

Mallory.

I'm coming, Nate.

I grabbed Billy's shoulder and pulled him back. "Where is this? Where is—"

"I don't know. It could be anywhere."

"It's not anywhere. It's close. I know it's close."

The young teen hesitated, taking a moment to turn around in the room and admire the rest of the camera visuals, and a rack of what looked like assault rifles.

"Uh, where?"

"It has to be here." I slammed a hand down on the desk, knocking the keys and taking with them my view of Nate. "Bring him back!"

Billy jumped on the keyboard and started cycling through images while I tried to make sense of this tiny building. This wasn't much bigger than the concrete cave. It made no sense.

How could Nate be here? Was there more to this than I could see?

Billy's frantic keystrokes stopped. "Shit."

I didn't need to turn around and look, I got just as good a view from the hole we'd put in the wall. Headlights, so many headlights, streamed up that dirt road right toward us.

We were about to have a whole lot of company.

CHAPTER 47

COME HELL

"UH, MAL..."

"I see them, Billy." I stood at the hole in the wall our borrowed car had made. I stood there and stared out on the coming end. It wasn't my last sunrise, but it might as well have been. There were too many of them. If those cars were like the ones that had pulled up in front of the church...

I tried to push the thought down, but it popped back up like one of those buoys in the deep water. There was no pushing down the end.

There was only facing it.

"Where's Nate?" I asked, looking past the snaking line of cars and focusing on the distant horizon. It wasn't here yet, but it was coming.

The dawn was coming.

Billy mashed buttons. "I don't know. Are you sure he's—"

"He's here. He's here, I know it."

The kid looked around, leaving the console briefly to push open the only door and finding nothing more than a toilet on the other side. "Well, then he's invisible because—"

Clank!

We both heard it at the same time, that hollow metal

sound when Billy's feet made contact with a stupid steel plate I hadn't noticed before.

We didn't talk about it, we just pounced on it and pulled. The kid found the finger loops first, but I was the one who ripped it up. I was the one who found the steps on the other side. A dull hum rumbled from somewhere in the hazy dark beneath us. It reminded me of the pump house, a mechanized rumble that came with the rushing sound of water.

Nate!

I hadn't taken more than a couple of steps before the screens lit up white with headlamps. The artificial dawn was still coming. Going into a hole wasn't going to stop them. They'd pour down here like army ants, army ants with guns and killing light.

We couldn't stop that.

I got the impression the kid could sense my fear, my frustration. Billy hesitated, his eyes on the screens then back on the hole.

"Go find your brother," he said, turning back to the desk and the images of mobile death rapidly coming to greet us.

"What are you doing?"

"Don't worry about me." Billy grabbed what looked like industrial keys off a hook behind the desk. "I can drive, remember?"

"Not well."

The kid winked, his jaws rippling with excitement. "I know, right, but you don't have to drive well to crash into stuff."

Shit.

"Billy, wait, you—"

The kid hit the opening and raced into the dark. He wasn't halfway to the monster truck before the first bullets arrived.

My jaws swelled and stinger dropped out, licking at the air in hungry anticipation. That second tongue didn't understand, didn't know what I knew. They'd be dosed. They'd be poisonous. I couldn't feast, and neither could Billy. They'd fill him up with lead when all he needed was blood.

My son would starve.

Fuck that.

I grabbed a gun off the rack, and really wasn't exactly sure what I was doing when I pointed it into the mass of oncoming vehicles, but it didn't take a lot of thinking to pull the trigger.

I was just really pissed when nothing happened.

"What the he—"

Boom! Boom!

Someone else had no trouble getting their gun working, or in using it to shoot at my son. Billy took a strafing shot across the side, spinning the kid before dropping him in the wet grass.

"Damn it!" I didn't think. I just ran. I raced out into the night, a useless hunk of metal in my hands. More cars pulled up, trucks too. Their rumbling engines came with the smell of gun oil and ozone, as well as so much tainted sweat. Big purple lights kicked on, their killing beams slicing through what remained of the chainlink and coming straight for us.

This wasn't how it was supposed to be. It was supposed to be different. I was supposed to find my brother, to save him, to fix all the stupid mistakes I'd made. I was supposed to be better than this.

You aren't.

I grabbed Billy's arm and pulled him up, the kid's blood soaking my hand. His wounds weren't healing, not fast enough.

He needed blood.

I pushed my wrist in his face and let those hungry jaws clamp down on it. His stinger dug deep, pulling like the pump siphon from what felt like forever ago. He took more than I could spare, but for the first time in forever, I didn't care.

This was what it meant to be a mother.

It meant to give everything, to give until you had nothing left.

Billy let go, pushing off me of his own accord before mashing down a button on the side of the gun.

The safety!

The kid was back in motion and headed toward the truck, without so much as a word of thanks, but I didn't need it. I had everything I needed in my cold fingers.

"Eat death, bitches!" I squeezed the trigger and pointed, firing off round after round into the bright lights. Head lamps shattered and at least a few people screamed. It was music to my ears, just like the sound of Billy climbing into the cab and jamming the keys home.

"What the hell is this?" He cried, no doubt finding that the differences between a sedan and an industrial vehicle were a little different than he expected.

"You gotta press the clutch and—"

"There's three pedals?!"

"That's the clutch. You gotta push down on the clutch to—"

Gunfire sprayed the side of the truck, pinging off metal and forcing Billy to slam the door. I fired back, my jaws wide and my stinger snapping in the air. It wanted the blood, but was forced to live on nothing but the screams. There would be blood soon enough. I just had to find Nate. I just had to find Nate and get the fuck out of here.

The truck's engine turned over, a lion roaring in the night. More bullets fired in the killing light hit the cab. Wisps of smoke immediately pressed up against the glass and I could hear Billy screaming.

Something broke loose in my head.

No one fucks with my Billy, no one but me.

I fired again, and kept firing, even as the truck started limping forward. I shattered lights and must have hit a few of them. A misty blood drifted in the air and I embraced it. I embraced being the killing machine I was.

"Suck on this, you bast—"

Bullets ripped through the tall grass and straight across my waist, knocking me back and costing me my grip on the rifle in the process.

I'd barely managed to get rolled over before the killing light came. It came like an angry dawn. Blisters boiled across my skin, followed closely by the black and charred flesh. I wanted to scream, to dig a hole into the dirt and hide, but I was pinned down. I was like a butterfly under glass. More bullets came, they cut through so much. Useless lungs collapsed, and jaws snapped like cheese cloth in the wind.

I put a hand up, only to watch fingers get torched in the purple death.

No, Mallory! No, no, no! You've come too far. You've come too far to lose now.

I wanted to listen to that voice and to find some new reservoir of hate to draw from, but my well was empty. Life had sucked it clean and now there was nothing left to give. The truck rumbled forward, only to stall. The cab was nothing but smoke and ash, if Billy was still in it then he was worse off than me.

I tried to roll over and crawl toward the building, toward my brother. I didn't make it more than a few feet before the killing light sapped my will to go on. I stared out at that concrete box and didn't see the screens or the desk.

I saw the concrete cave.

I saw home.

In that burning purple vision, I was there with Nate and with Billy. We laughed in the pink moments before the dawn. We laughed and we looked out for each other. We were a family. We were *my* family. My brother scooped me up in his arms and held me close.

"I'm sorry, Nate."

"I know, Mallory. I know."

More bullets and more pain.

I closed my eyes to the sound of a roaring engine and the shouts of men. I closed my eyes and waited for the end. I didn't know if there was a heaven for monsters like me, but if there was a hell, then I hoped they knew what they'd signed up for.

CHAPTER 48
DOWN THE HATCH

ONE SECOND I was a mess of bullets and burning, and the next, sweet darkness. Billy got the truck moving. It rumbled like a giant metal battering ram. This time he didn't point it at the building, he pointed it at something bigger.

He pointed it at the base of the water tower.

I'd heard plenty of booms in my life, but nothing measured up to the sound of an industrial truck hitting the main support of a monster water tower. The entire thing swayed once, just a little, then the first cracks started to appear. They raced up one side only to vanish in the darkness above. The cracks brought more wavering, and then the sound of water.

The rest was history.

The main tower support bent forward over the truck itself, white water spraying everywhere. I stumbled to my feet in the suddenly flooded grass and tried to find Billy.

That was the moment the world descended into chaos.

Gravity brought the tower's bulbous top down, and while it felt like slow-motion, I was reasonably sure it was anything but. The ball top ripped through trees and smashed palmettos flat. It also exploded open on impact. Water roared, rushing out to flood the dirt street, wash away cars, and throw the men into a panic.

The water also rushed back into the broken concrete of the control building, and while I couldn't see it, I was certain it rushed down that trapdoor.

Nate!

"Come on, Billy," I cried, limping through the hip deep water toward my brother and the dark hole in the distant building's floor.

Billy didn't move, and he didn't push the door open.

"Shit, Billy. Come on!"

Still nothing moved from inside the crumpled cab. That was when I smelled it, the familiar smell of blood, of Billy's blood.

Shit.

I turned away from the partially crumpled concrete cave and limped toward the ruined truck. Men shouted and flashes of killing light lit up the trees, but they weren't after me, not yet. They had bigger problems.

"Billy, are you okay?" I made it to the side of the vehicle and banged on the rusty metal. The bullets that should have been pushed out by my flesh refused to let go. I looked about as banged up as the aging truck in front of me. Whatever it was they were shooting, it hurt. It hurt a lot. My jaws opened and closed like the gills of a fish out of water. I needed blood. I needed blood like I needed air.

But there was no blood to be had.

Unless Billy…

I grabbed the door handle and pushed that thought aside. "Come on, kid, we've got to—"

I lost my words as the door swung open and Billy's crumpled body greeted me on the other side. Windshield glass had shattered and forced its way through his chest. That alone was bad enough, but there was more. There was so much more.

The crumpled canopy sheared in two beneath the weight of the falling tower, the resulting knife edge had removed one of Billy's jaws like the closest of shaves. The other hung limp, like a lover without its mate. Beneath it a stinger dangled listlessly in the misty dark.

Billy!

I grabbed the kid, his blood streaking my hands and sending my stinger into overdrive.

This is your chance. Take what you need. Take the blood and live.

Billy's good eye fluttered open and he tried to speak, but the words just came out as a wet mess of blood and sputtering.

"I got you. This is why we make people get licenses, you know?"

The kid tried to smile, but it didn't work. So much of Billy didn't work. His shoulders slumped and his unbalanced face just kept flapping. He was like a butterfly that had lost one of its wings. His one jaw kept fighting for balance, when all it was really doing was making a mess of everything.

Take what he has. Take what little blood he has left and use it to save Nate.

My stinger slipped out, almost before I could stop it. That second tongue poked at the juicy bits, trying to find the path of least resistance.

No. I shouldn't…

I might have said those words in my head, but my stinger had no interest in listening to them. The second tongue wanted blood, whatever it could get, and it wanted it no matter whose it was.

But he's my son…

I scoffed at those words and at his clawing hands. I was no mother. I never had been, and never would be. I was Mallory.

I was a monster.

I was the girl that ruined my brother, that split his skull and feasted on the brains inside. I was the broken woman who had killed so many so she could live to see another night.

I didn't create Billy out of thanks, or maternal desire. I created Billy so I wouldn't be alone.

There was nothing worse than being alone.

Water roared around the truck, spilling back into the control and no doubt down the trapdoor. Somewhere an angry pump roared.

My stinger was like that pump, angry and frustrated. It wanted blood to siphon and enjoy. It needed it.

I needed it.

So does Billy.

My stinger dug for the deep veins, the tasty lines of life-giving sustenance. Without them I would eventually dry up and fade away.

Without them, I would die.

And what about Billy? What about your son?

"You're not my son." No sooner had I said the words out loud, than I wanted to take them back. His frantic eyes and flapping jaw told me he'd heard them.

"It's not your fault. It's mine. I created you and I never should have. I never should have stuck you in this life. You should have died back at the bar. I should have let you go. I didn't do that. I didn't do that because I can't stand the thought of being alone."

I said it, even as my stinger found what was left of the blood in Billy's broken body.

"I am a monster, Billy." I let my second tongue quiver in that rich vein of life. "I'm a monster and I've always been one. I destroyed my brother and now I'm going to destroy you. I have Nate now, or will soon. You've served your purpose. You got me here. That's what matters. That's all you ever were, a means to an end."

Billy's clawing hands stopped moving. All that was left was his eyes. They stared deep into mine. It was the look of a disappointed child when they'd discovered who their mother really was. My eyes had done the same a long time ago, and they'd done the same thing again when I'd broken Nate.

"Don't look at me like that." I put a hand on his cheek. "This is for the best. Trust me. You don't want to be around me. I'm bad news. Just ask Nate. I am not a good person, and I'm an even shittier vampire. I will get you killed. Hell, I practically have now."

More water raced past, followed by the sound of men, men with killing light.

My stinger tugged at me, hungry to dive into what little blood Billy had left.

"I'm... Sorry, Mallory." Billy pushed the words out through broken jaws. "Not... enough."

I wanted to run him through. I wanted to take every last ounce of blood in his body. I wanted to hate him.

I wanted to do all those things, but they weren't what I did.

I didn't take his blood.

I gave him some of mine.

It was an angry stinger that pushed what it had into Billy's veins, and a pair of tired hands that pried him free from the torn metal. We hit the water like a poorly coordinated cannonball. I tried to stand, but it was Billy that pulled me upright. The kid dragged and I kicked, together we pushed for the concrete cave and the black hole inside it.

I didn't know why I saved him and took myself to the brink in the process. Something told me it was the right thing to do, and for the first time in next to forever, I wanted to do the right thing. I was pretty sure it wouldn't last, that I'd be back to making the terrible choices soon enough, but using Billy's hand to lean on, I had a chance.

Maybe we really were angels?

Billy's lone wing flapped in the whitewater spray.

If we were angels, then we were the fallen kind. The kind you don't dare fuck with.

We reached the black hole in the floor and the rushing water filling it, while outside men shouted and purple light flashed.

He didn't hesitate. He grabbed my hand and together we plunged into the darkness.

We're coming, Nate.

CHAPTER 49
BOIL AND BUBBLE

THE WATER ROARED. Overjoyed to be freed from its lofty prison, it raced down stairs and over metal railings. Waves slapped against our legs and splashed around tired knees, but that didn't stop Billy and it certainly didn't stop me.

"Nate!" I screamed my brother's name, no longer caring who else heard me. "Nate! It's me. It's Mallory."

Flashing emergency lights painted the water orange, giving it an angry and unpleasant glow. The rising tide of run-off splashed against walls and swirled in tiny eddies in front of steel doors. Nate could have been behind any of them.

"Nate!" I grabbed the first knob and turned, the metal handle fighting back. "Nate!" I pounded a fist on the steel letting the echo bounce through walls and across the rising water. "Nate, it's Mal—"

Billy grabbed my arm and pointed back to the way we came in, to the steel stairs and the cascading waterfall running down them.

There were new voices, feet on steel, and the smell of guns.

Purple light from so many flashlights cast perverted shadows across the walls.

"They're coming," the kid said, his one working jaw unfolding as wide as it could.

"Shit. We've got to find Nate. I know he's here. I know he's—"

"Mallory!"

Even tired and ragged, my brother's voice rocked me to my very core. I wasn't sure I'd ever hear it in person again, my only brother saying my name, and now that I did, that was all I wanted to hear. I wanted to hear it again and again. I wanted to hear it amidst a backdrop of screams.

"Where is h—"

Billy never got to finish his words before I dragged him under the water. The teen panicked for a second, but a reassuring hand on his shoulder quelled the worst of it. This was our world. We could survive in the dark, without oxygen, without all of the things they needed.

They were weak.

We were strong.

Lights flashed overhead and purple rays bounced across the water's surface, but they didn't go deep enough to burn, at least not yet.

I dragged Billy against the raging current, finding the bottom of the steel stairs and swinging the two of us behind it. It was hard to make out the specific details of the men coming down the steps. Their bodies were like cheap watercolors, blending and blurring in the tumbling tide. They said things, their words muffled and without purpose. It didn't matter what they said, or how many of them came. Nate was here. My brother was close, behind one of these doors. It didn't matter which, because I would open them all, just like I would open these men. I would fill the water with their blood and swim in it like the monster I was.

Billy's stinger slipped out like an eel emerging from its

cavernous lair. Mine did too, the twin serpents gliding quietly in the churning water. He started to make a move and I pulled him back, then pointed a finger at their feet.

It was impossible to tell him exactly what I wanted, but Billy appeared to get it just the same. He sank deeper, sliding along the smooth floor like a hungry viper zeroing in on its prey. I followed him, my jaws rippling in the current while my eyes never left the prize. There was blood in those legs, and in the bodies sloshing through the water.

Their blood would be our blood, and the circle of life would continue unabated.

Billy looked back to confirm, and I nodded. It was time to show them who was boss. We sat on the top of the food chain, and it was high time they got that message.

Billy's stinger hit first, and mine came in second: two people, four legs, and so much blood. There were screams and then the wild rattle of bullets. I didn't focus on that. All I could do was turn my attention to the blood, and to the stinger that lapped at it. I knew the instant I pierced their skin that it was tainted, and that to drink it meant more danger. Billy pulled back first, breaking the surface to a hail of gunfire and killing light. Bullets tore flesh from bone and my single-wing son fell backward into the water, that one good jaw flapping like mad.

Billy!

I didn't think. In that moment, I wasn't capable of thinking.

I wasn't Mallory anymore.

I was wrath.

They were afraid of us, afraid of monsters, afraid of the things that bumped in the night. That fear gave me power and I took it.

My stinger wrapped the closest leg I could find and pulled. Whoever he was, he dipped forward, that gun barrel dropping below the water's surface just long enough for me to get a hand on it. I yanked it deeper, my fingers moving up the barrel and finding his. I wasn't sure exactly which leg I pointed it at, but squeezing the trigger filled the water with tainted blood and the air with his screams.

I didn't stop there. I climbed up his front, breaking free of the water's confines long enough to wrap my jaws around his neck and tear out the juicy parts underneath that sweaty flesh. I spit them out, then let him drop, another body left to rot.

How many more will it take?

How many more must I kill before I'll be free?

Bullets were my only answer. Fiery steel blasted my shoulder, splitting bone and tearing tendons. I knew I didn't have the blood to fix that, not now, but I also knew it didn't matter. All that mattered was Nate.

The only thing that mattered was my brother.

Everything else was secondary.

Everything else was death.

Killing purple light lit up the walls and bounced off the frothing water, but if they thought that was going to stop me, they were mistaken. I launched myself off the dying body, taking to the air and driving that broken shoulder into the closest shooter. He spun hard, slamming his face into the steel railing and splitting flesh from bone. The purple light fell, bouncing off the metal and casting its evil up the stairs. More were coming. More men and more lights.

I pulled his broken face back to stare into those eyes. I wanted him to see me, to see me as I was and to know fear.

My jaws swelled and the stinger beneath them quivered in anticipation of a meal it could not have.

"Where is he?"

The man's lips moved, but no words came out.

I pressed my stinger against a swollen eye. The snake-like thing circled that juicy orb, sliding it back and forth like my regular tongue would have enjoyed a nice candy.

"Where is my brother?"

Again his lips moved and almost nothing came out. "Fu..."

"I don't care. Do you understand me? I don't care how many of you I have to kill. How much of your blood has to run in the streets. Fill your body with all the poison you want. I will break you just the same. I won't stop until I have my brother. Do you hear me? I won't stop until I have Nate. I am inevitable. I am ruin. I am death and I have come for all of you. Give me what I want and I will make it fast. Deny me and I will give you pain like you've never known before."

More killing light flickered above as the water rose around us.

"Fuck yo—"

He never got to finish his words. My stinger sliced through that eyeball and deep into his brain. There was no poison there, but no blood either. I let his body drop, splashing into the blood-red water and roared.

I screamed for Billy, for Nate, and for me.

It was a primal scream, one born of so much pain and anger.

It was a scream that had an answer.

A distant door shook and with it came the word I'd longed to hear again. "Mallory."

"I'm here, Nate. I'm here." I grabbed Billy as he floated by, the kid struggling to stand, and turned all my attention on the door.

There was no steel in this world or the next that could hold me back from my brother. I hung Billy's arm around the rapidly vanishing stair rail, then threw everything I had against the muted metal.

I'm here, Nate. I'm here, and I'm never leaving you again.

CHAPTER 50
REUNIONS

I SLAMMED AGAINST THE METAL, an already ruined shoulder crying out in muted pain. It didn't matter. Nothing mattered except the door and the man on the other side. When we were kids he'd locked himself in the closet and like an idiot I'd torn the door down to get him out. Back then I could have just used a coat hanger. Dad had been nice enough to beat that lesson into me when he came home. There was no coat hanger now.

There was only me, and the door.

The water held me back, sloshing red with poisoned blood, it yanked at my waist and stole my momentum. It didn't want me to find him. It didn't want me to reach Nate.

None of them did.

They knew why.

They knew what he was capable of and they knew to fear me.

I threw myself against the metal again, dredging up memories of the locked closet and the little boy crying inside. I imagined that little Nate again, his bright eyes and cheerful grin. I imagined him and I hit the door. I hit the door like it was Dad, or Mom. I hit the door the way I wanted to hit them, to hit everyone that took something from me.

The heavy door's steel shuddered against its moorings, but didn't give way. I grabbed the handle and yanked, shearing metal off in a fit of frustration.

"Nate!" I screamed, banging on the door. "Nate, I'm here. It's Mallory. I'm going to find a way in. Just hang on. I'm going to find a way in."

I couldn't hear his words over the rising water. Bodies floated past, their usefulness long since expended. I pushed those poisoned things out of the way, but not before my foot caught on something.

I smiled, pulling it out of the water. I didn't know shit about guns, but I knew you just needed to point and pull the trigger. Nothing else mattered after that.

"Get away from the door!"

It was just like when we were little. I'd said the same thing then. Back in those days I didn't have a gun, or a second tongue. My face didn't unfold. I wasn't the monster, not yet.

Still, I cried back then, and I was crying now.

Blood-red tears stained my cheeks as I clutched the rifle. "I'm coming, Nate."

Bullets ripped through steel like my stinger tore through flesh and bone. I didn't stop. I didn't really know how. I was lost in the moment, more animal than person. Somewhere above us was purple light, more men with guns, and ruin, but right here was Nate.

Slugs kept coming with each squeeze of the trigger. The door shuddered. What remained of the sheared handle dropped off, splashing in the water as the whole door swung inward.

Water roared in behind it, crashing into the dark and taking me with it. I lost my grip on the gun, and my bearings in the swirling darkness.

"Nate! Nate, I'm—"

Weak hands found my broken shoulder and pulled me up.

For the first time in so long, I found my brother's face. "Mallory."

There were no words. There couldn't be words. Not for this. I threw my arms around him, squeezing the big man like had I let go I'd have been carried out with the tide.

"Mallory." His voice was hoarse and tired. It matched the weakness in his muscles. The folds of his face refused to close, they dropped like the wings of a butterfly caught in the rain.

"Nate. I found you. I told you I would find you. I told you, you moron." I pulled back and tried to push his jaws together with my hands. "Next time just wait in the car. Okay? The car."

He nodded softly, then brought up two bound hands from beneath the rising water.

I chuckled at the tiny cuffs, until I touched them, and found the angry red lines against his skin.

Silver.

"Okay." I put his hands back under the water. "It's okay. We'll find a way to get them off. We'll find a way to fix all of it. I promise. But first we have to get out of here. We have to find a way out of—"

"Did you find him?" Billy emerged from the door, his jaws mostly closed and a tired stinger drooping out beneath them. "You did. Wow, he's a lot bigger than I remember hi—"

Nate tossed me aside and threw himself at the kid. My brother might have been weak and broken, but Billy was bleeding. I could smell it, and I was sure Nate could too. How much had they denied him? How hungry was he?

"Stop, Nate! That's Billy. He helped me find you."

I might as well have been speaking Spanish for all the good it did. My brother drove the smaller kid beneath the water, his hungry stinger looking for one thing.

"Nate, no!" I dove after them, kicking against the swirling current. Clothes wiped and stingers churned up the water.

They were weak, both of them, but while Billy might have been more agile, Nate had size and strength.

Nate knew how to use both.

He wrapped his hands around Billy's neck, the silver biting into the kid's flesh. Billy's eyes bulged and he shouted something, but he lost his words to Nate's stinger. Nate knocked the kid's second tongue aside and rammed his home, past skin and under muscle, directly into the good stuff that lay underneath.

Damn it, Nate. Stop!

I wrapped my arms around his neck and pulled.

Nothing.

My brother would not be denied his meal.

No, Nate! No, no, no!

I let go and clawed my way in front, putting my face between his and Billy's. My brother's eyes shone dark red above the bloody water.

Nate, please. Billy is my son. He's one of us. He helped me save you.

There were no words beneath the water. There was nothing that could be said. All I could do was plead. Nate was my brother, but he was also a broken man. He didn't understand. He couldn't understand.

Because of how you made him.

Billy went limp beneath his hands, the kid's stinger drifting aimlessly in the rising water.

No!

My jaws snapped open and stinger emerged. It was hungry for a fight.

Without thinking, I was back on the apartment floor, my brother pinned beneath me. My stinger lined up at the soft spot beneath his skull.

Do it!

I didn't.

I couldn't.

Not even for Billy.

I let my stinger retract and grabbed Nate's face. I pushed those jaws together and pressed my forehead against his.

Nate's powerful arms let go, and his stinger retracted behind a face that had filled my every waking moment for too long.

You found him, and look what it brought you.

I looped a hand around Billy's shirt and pulled him up. Sightless eyes stared back at me, his lone jaw drifting gently in the water.

Billy.

I let my stinger go. I let it slip into his broken body and search for some sign of life, but there were none.

There was no more Billy, only Nate.

I hesitated, and that was when the pump kicked on.

The water pulled, yanking us away from the room and into the darkness. I remembered hitting a door, a lifeless Billy tight in my fingers. Nate came next, the big man smashing into me, and the three of us combining to throw the steel wide.

The roaring water carried us deep into the dark, away from the flashing lights and the sounds of men.

We tumbled end over end in the rushing water. It reminded me of the blood, and of the dark insides of a perfect stinger. My brother found me in that dark and hung on. The three of us banged against walls, then rigid metal. The water took on a slimy complexion, and before I knew it, we were ejected into the night, only to land in some algae-filled retention pond.

I dragged Billy to the shore, his body offering no resistance. Nate joined me on the soft sand and cattails, his face catching the moonlight as it reflected off the glossy water.

He didn't stick around long. My brother was up and moving before I could stop him. A distant house had caught his attention.

It came with the smell of blood and something else.

Cotton candy.

"Nate, stop! We can't—"

My brother didn't listen. His jaws open and his stinger out. This was the Nate I'd forgotten. The one that never stops being hungry. The one that eats whatever he wants.

The one that took my son.

I put a hand on Billy's cold chest and was surprised by the tears that followed. "I'm sorry, Billy. He's family. I… He's family. He's my family."

The young man didn't move. He didn't have a snarky response for me, and he didn't call me Mom.

Billy was no more, but I wouldn't have been there to hear it if he had.

I was already up and chasing Nate, and the smell of cotton candy.

CHAPTER 51
OF MICE AND MENUS

NATE MOVED FASTER than I remembered. My brother's looping gait took him over the tall grass with ease. He leapt the modest chain-link fence that surrounded the back of the property with ease, his body coming down light on the other side.

I did none of those things.

I chased him, but the tall grass hung me up. It clung to my legs and scraped at the skin beneath that soaking wet shirt. The fence wasn't something for me to leap over. It took time to climb, and even more to come down from it without landing in the bushes on the other side.

Thump.

I clamored to my feet, but Nate already had the back door open. The same cotton candy scent that had been so faint down by the retention pond was much stronger here. Sickly sweet, it came with its own memories, fresh ones.

I didn't dare go around the front, or look for a car, because I knew exactly what it would be. I'd sat in it. I'd sat in it and contemplated the unthinkable.

My stinger dropped out, forcing its way past jaws that weren't sure they wanted to open.

"Nate! Nate, get out of there," I hissed, my eyes on the piles of plastic toys lying in the grass.

Don't do it, Nate. Please…

Was there anything he wouldn't do?

No.

How long had I been building him up in my head?

He murdered Billy.

I pushed that thought down, stuffing it in some mental hole knowing it would only pop back up later. I packed it down and followed him into the dark, reliving the smells and the ghostly echo of hazy blood memories. The back door led into what looked like a utility room. A fancy looking washer and dryer consumed one wall, while a nicely folded stack of clothes lay beneath shelves on a nearby table.

This was someone's home.

This could have been my home.

I lost myself for a moment in that thought, and in the manufactured memories it created. I imagined myself folding that laundry, shouting at a husband I couldn't picture to pull something off the stove. Tiny hands tugged at my legs, their fingers coated in something unmentionable, but nevertheless driven out of a love I'd never know.

This isn't your life, Mal. It will never be your life.

I ripped the clothes off the shelf, letting them hit the ground and kick up even more of that sickly sweet smell. It was the same scent driving Nate, pushing him to feed. The smells drove us both. We weren't much more than animals, monsters that lived on pain and death, and on the blood.

Nate is an animal, or have you forgotten? Just ask Billy…

I pushed my way out of the utility room and through what looked like a tiny kitchen. Dishes sat stacked in the sink, clean dishes waiting to be put away. It wasn't much, but even those little white circles took me back. They dragged me kicking and screaming into the past and to a brother who never seemed to remember how to put them away.

"Damn it, Nate." I slammed a hand down on the counter. "Could you at least pretend to do something in the way of chores around this house? Something? Please?"

My brother wouldn't hear me. He never did. Even before I slipped my second tongue into his brain, Nate wasn't much for listening.

I was forever cleaning up after a kid that wasn't even mine.

I left the dishes and the domestic scene behind me, venturing out into a family room, terrified of what I might find.

There was no Nate, but there were all the signs of his passing. Muddy feet had left black spots in the carpet and glistening trails on the tile. I should have chased after them. I should have followed those feet up the stairs, but I didn't.

I lost myself in the family photos that lined a nearby table. For a second, it wasn't the husband and wife I'd seen in the car. Sure, he was still there, but she was gone and I was in her place. I was the one getting the hugs and the sloppy kisses. I was the one with the child hanging off her neck and smiling.

It was *my* life on display.

No, it's not.

My stinger reflected back at me in the hazy glass. I was a mother, but not like this.

I was a mother of monsters.

There was a scream and a thump, followed by the sound of a child crying.

Nate!

I hit the stairs two at a time, moving up as fast as my tired feet could take me. I reached the landing and found my brother just inside a bedroom door, his stinger out and jaws flapping. The blood came next, followed by some nonsensical stream of words.

Gun!

The sharp smell of gun oil made its presence known and

before I could reach Nate, the first bullet tore a hole in his chest.

That would have slowed me down, but it didn't do shit to my brother, if anything, it just made him more angry. He launched his body at the shooter, jaws wide and stinger only too happy to lead the charge.

I raced in behind to find Nate on top of the bed, his stinger impaling the husband and drinking deep. The wife, the same woman from the car, the same one I'd tasted once before, slipped a hand around the fallen firearm.

"Nate!"

My brother was too deep into his feast to notice her, or the weapon pointed at his skull, so I did the only thing I knew how to do.

I hit her.

I hit her hard.

Together we tumbled off the bed, the young mother and me. My jaws swelled, taking in the glorious smell of blood. She managed to get the gun up once, but pulling the trigger only left a grazing line in my arm.

I did much worse.

My stinger shattered her chest, splitting ribs and slicing through still breathing lungs. It was her eyes that fired back. They showed me the monster I was, the monster I would always be.

The stinger didn't care about those things. It only cared for the blood and the strength that it would bring.

It was the rest of me that took that winnowing blow. She wasn't just some mother, some young woman in the wrong place at the wrong time. She was me. She was everything I could have been, everything I *should* have been.

Blood memories roared over my second tongue, memories that weren't mine. There were passionate nights and exhausting mornings. There were days when I wanted to fall asleep and never wake up again. Then there were other days, ones I never wanted to end.

There was the joy on his little face, the smile that slipped into my head as sharp as any stinger. There was a string of broken and jagged words, the pattering of tiny feet on the tile, and being called mom.

Billy.

Billy had called me mom. He'd risked everything to help me, to get me to Nate, and what had it cost him?

I tried to pull my stinger free, but it wasn't interested in letting go. It wanted more blood. It wanted all of it. The memories kept coming, and I let them. I let the blood drown out everything else. I had become like the machine in that pump house Billy and I had hid from the sun in. It swallowed the canal just like I swallowed her.

Nate grunted and dropped his feast. The broken man from so many family photos hit the bloody carpet like a discarded pair of shoes. He wouldn't smile again. He wouldn't tell her how beautiful she was, or carry their child on his shoulders.

I tried to swim out of the blood's pull, but in the end, I was powerless to its embrace. It was all that mattered now. I'd found Nate. I'd found my brother and this would be our life.

It wouldn't stop.

Nate wouldn't stop.

This was who he was, who I'd made him to be. My brother was a broken thing and I loved him.

You love him enough for this?

I let my stinger retract. It pulled in like some languid serpent, warm and full and in much need of a nice rest.

It was a rest I didn't get.

The boy's crying raised me from that blood drunk stupor.

"Nate, no…"

My brother was already gone. He'd left the room and I knew exactly what he had in mind. I knew because I knew Nate.

I knew who he was, and who had made him that way.

CHAPTER 52
A MOTHER'S DAY

NATE HOVERED over the child's bed just like the monster he was. Dark like a malignant shadow against the muted walls. His jaws wide and stinger out, my brother was poised to gorge himself on a feast of living cotton candy.

"Nate!" I snapped at him, hoping my voice would do what it always did, break him out of his murderous haze. "No! Not kids. Never kids!"

He didn't listen. He wrapped his fingers around the rails gently, all of his attention on the little blonde haired boy screaming bloody murder in his crib. Nate's stinger slithered over that white wood and down into the bed itself. It was a cunning snake and very much interested in enjoying its prey up close and personal.

"Nate! I said no!"

My brother wasn't listening to me, not anymore.

Maybe he never had?

Maybe the man I remembered as my brother wasn't the one I'd saved?

His jaws snapped wide and hungry. I threw myself at him, coming around the crib only to take the big man's stinger to the chest. It sliced through flesh and bone with little effort.

Nate was so much bigger, so much stronger. It was nothing for him to slam me to the floor and bring his blood-soaked face close. Those jaws fluttered in and out, fanning my cheeks and taking me back to an earlier time, to a time before I'd ruined our lives.

"He's not gonna be coming around anymore." Nate leaned on the door frame, his strong muscles on display. He liked to do that, to flex a little for me. "I promise you."

"What did you do to him?" I pressed a wet dish towel against my face, the handful of ice cubes inside mostly melted by my tears and the red welt on my cheek.

"Nothing. We just had a nice talk and now he's not going to be coming back here. He's not going to be coming back here ever again."

"Nate." I shook my head, then immediately regretted that decision. "Damn it, Nate. It was an accident. He didn't mean it."

It was an accident.

Nate pushed off the door, shaking his own head and doing it without tears. "Nope. You don't hurt people like that by accident. You do that because there's something wrong with you. There's something wrong with him."

Something is wrong with him.

"He just doesn't want to be alone. He's terrified of it. He's—"

Nate raised a hand and cut me off. "It doesn't matter. You don't do that."

My brother's stinger drove deeper, twisting my gut and pulling at the blood that had pooled there.

You don't do that. You don't hurt people by accident.

The memory shifted, melting away like so much blood. I was back on the floor, pinning him down, and running my stinger deep into his skull.

It was an accident.

I may have said that. I may have convinced myself it was an accident, that I hadn't meant it, but that was a lie.

Nate had been right. There were no accidents when it came to hurting people like that.

Alone…

My brother's jaws flapped gently against the backdrop of the screaming child.

I was alone.

I would always be alone.

You can save him.

Nate pulled back, his stinger slipping free to find something far more delectable to enjoy. My brother was drawn to the cotton candy and the innocence of youth.

You've done it before. You can save him. You can keep him safe. You can…

Could I? Could I really?

Billy's dead body was a testament to my brother and to the power he wielded. Nate knew no boundaries, no control. He was a wild dog, a beast that was just as likely to bite me as some stranger.

No! You promised. You promised you would help him. You promised you would make this right.

I pushed myself up, weak from the loss of blood and from the slowly closing hole in my chest. As bad as those were, it was my heart that hurt more.

Too afraid to be alone.

Nate's jaws swelled wide, their fangs practically quivering with anticipation. His stinger coiled slowly, preparing to strike, to take that young life and make it his.

I knew then what I'd secretly known all along.

I was alone.

I was alone just like the child in that crib. I was alone and I would always be alone. Nate wasn't coming back. Whatever my brother had been, that person, he was dead. He was dead and buried and the thing that I'd created would never stop hurting.

I'm sorry, Nate.

My brother's stinger lashed out, cracking like a whip and ready to ruin that young life in its crosshairs. That evil second tongue never reached its target. I jumped on his back and pulled. Nate swung from side to side, his powerful body more than capable of holding me up, and also confused at exactly what had happened.

I wrapped my arms around his neck, both of our jaws flapping like mad. The kid kept screaming, but he wasn't the only one crying.

I cried too.

I cried for all the times we wouldn't have, for the families we wouldn't know, for the in-laws, the turkey dinners, the Christmases, and the children.

I cried because I'd killed my brother and now I had to finish it.

Nate slapped me against the wall, his stinger and his back fighting to scrape me off like gum on the bottom of a favorite shoe.

"I'm sorry, Nate. I'm sorry for doing this to you, for making you this thing. I'm sorry for taking your future. I'm sorry for so many things. I hope you forgive me."

My stinger dropped out, hungry for blood, but also leery of where I wanted to send it.

Nate crashed against a nearby rocker, shattering wood and costing me most of my grip. It was now or never. I'd already experienced never. Never was Billy. Never was this stupid life. Never was not seeing the sun. Never was blood on your hands with no way to wash it off.

Never had to end.

Never had to end now.

My stinger cut deep, racing beneath the soft spot at the base of his skull. It was just like before, just like on the floor of the apartment when he tried to leave. There was no leaving now. This time I would be alone.

I deserved it.

My second tongue sliced through tissue and past bone. It knew the final destination, the sweet meats deep inside.

"Mallory…"

Bloody tears raced down my cheeks, tears like the child crying in his bed for his mother. I hurt because I was dying too. Nate was like a child. He was the one person that mattered for so long, and now I was letting him go.

"Mal…"

The stinger sliced through gray matter, ripping it to pieces with each serrated pass. Memories came in that ruin, memories of a better time.

"Hush." I reached my arms around him, holding him close one last time. "It's going to be better now. You'll see. So much better. I promise."

"Ma…" His jaws folded and his stinger dropped. The monster that had been my brother slumped, his body dropping off the rocker and curling slowly on the floor.

"It's okay, Nate. It's okay." I wiped bloody tears from my eyes. "It's okay, I know you're going to be alright. You know how I know that? Because I'm right behind you. I'm going to see you soon. I'm going to see you and we'll have fun. Maybe we'll go out to dinner? Would you like that? We can get that girl you're seeing and we'll make it a date."

My brother twitched, his head turning slowly back as I removed my stinger from his brain. He opened his mouth to speak, but no words came out.

No words would ever come out again.

My brother was gone.

I laid down next to him, closing his jaws and pushing the hair out of those dark red eyes. I told him all the things I should have told him when he was alive. I told him how much he'd meant to me, and how much I'd always cared. I thanked him for beating the crap out of that guy that hit me and I teased him for his taste in women.

I laid there until the child stopped crying and the window took on a vaguely pinkish hue.

There was only one last thing to do.

CHAPTER 53
DAWN BREAKS

"911, WHAT IS YOUR EMERGENCY?"

"Everything." I dropped the receiver, letting it clatter on the countertop and start the child crying all over again.

Maybe the paramedics would show up in time for mom, but dad's body was cold.

Maybe she would be stronger?

I dragged Nate down the stairs and out into the yard, finding a decent spot in the back that should see full sun.

Full sun...

He looked so peaceful laying there, so much like the brother I remembered him being.

Stop, Mallory.

I wanted to stop, but the tears came just the same. They came when I rested his lifeless hands one over the other beneath the burning silver, and again when I gently pressed his jaws shut. They were there when I reached the water's edge and dragged a lifeless Billy up the shore.

"I promised you a last sunrise," I said, my hands under the kid's arms. "I keep my promises."

Do you now?

It took longer than I wanted to get him over the bent grass

and next to Nate, and even longer to stare into those sightless eyes.

"Don't look at me like that. I tried. Okay? I tried hard."

Did you?

Flashing lights in the distance told me it was time to go. I fished the stolen car keys out of my pocket and found the little sedan at the end of their driveway. I stopped only long enough to rip the car seat out and toss it on the sidewalk before hitting the gas. The first hints of smoke had already started to rise from my boys in the tall grass as I tore down the quiet street.

I had no interest in staying for the rest, or for the paramedics and cops that were sure to be here shortly.

I had my own place to be.

The car ran smooth, cool air blowing over my cheeks, and jaws that no longer held any desire to swell. My stinger remained mercifully hidden, that second tongue strangely quiet in the coming dawn. It didn't stir when the ambulance shot past, or the cop cars, and it didn't try to lure me down the street to Marie's house.

I did that all by myself.

I drove past the broken little bungalow with the piles of toys and now far more cars parked out front. Death was inside, a violent death had I elected to stop.

I didn't.

I kept driving. I gave the fallen water tower a wide berth and the service crews who were already working the scene. The little sedan was more than happy to take me past the little grocery store and the few motorcycles still parked out front. It was also more than happy to speed me along the main street, out of town, and into a sea of orange and green. Long rows of fruit trees caught the first few rays of a rising sun. I knew there was a pump house back there, and beyond them, a river soaked in blood and memory. I knew it was there and I drove past it just the same.

The highway's onramp was easy to find, and just as easy to slip onto in the wee hours of morning. A handful of semis shot past, their massive wheels rumbling the little family car. I didn't pay attention to them, or the well-lit Mecca that was the rest station. I wasn't sure, but there appeared to be plenty of police tape up and boards to cover the glass blocks we'd shattered.

You shattered.

I chuckled at the thought, but didn't argue with it.

I'd broken more than glass blocks.

Blondy and her family came to mind as the car raced down that blue-gray stretch of asphalt. Somewhere beyond those trees was a church, a dead church stained in red.

It doesn't matter now.

I flipped the visor down, staving off the sun fighting its way through the tall pines to introduce itself to me.

"I'll see you soon enough."

I switched lanes to get around a slow moving truck, the car almost pulling me off at the nearest exit. I knew what was down that exit. There was a little burned out bar, a place that no one would remember, but I'd never forget.

For a second I wondered about the empty freezer. Was it still there?

Did it matter?

No.

I drove on, letting that little family car eat pavement while the rest of my mind drifted. Visions of Nate and Billy played on repeat, so many scenes. I beat myself up over each one, over what I could have done, and what I did. I replayed all of it until there was no more pain left in the tank.

I was so deep in guilt that I almost missed the field, and the old twisted oak I always parked beneath.

This car was smaller, but just as happy to get off the road and cool her engine beneath the shade tree's branches.

I thought about taking the keys, but in the end just

dropped them at my feet. Maybe someone else would find the car and use it? Maybe someone better?

The sun cut over the tree line. It scorched my arms and burned my cheeks, but something was different this time.

This time there was no reason to keep going.

The squat and misshapen strawberry bushes long since left to rot were more than happy to let me pass. The tiny green things with their little red fruits would have been so welcome in the time before, but now they were nothing more than a reminder of the blood on my hands and on my soul.

I found the concrete cave exactly where I left it, thick with the scent of my brother.

I hesitated at the entrance. The dark of that empty building called to me, and to the stinger that had begun to stir in my throat.

"Mal?"

"Nate?" I looked down to find him on the front step, his butt resting on a broken patch of concrete. His face was no longer split, and no stinger threatened to drop out from beneath those human jaws.

It wasn't really him. The real Nate was long dead, but this one smiled and patted the ground lovingly with his hand. "Do you have any other brothers I don't know about?"

"Nate, I—"

The big man shook his head. "It doesn't matter anymore, Mallory. Would you like to watch the sunrise with me?"

Already the skin on my arms had started to peel, and my jaws had begun their flapping. Everything in my body cried out for the safety of darkness and the concrete cave, but my heart wanted to stay.

My heart wanted to sit with my brother.

"My last sunrise?"

Nate nodded, putting my hand in his. "Yes. How does that sound? One last sunrise, then we can go enjoy whatever comes next."

"I… I think I would like that."

My brother smiled. "Good." He turned to face the rising sun. "Look at it, Mal. It's beautiful. I guess I never realized how much I missed it until it was gone."

He was right. Even as my face peeled away and my eyes burned, I knew Nate was right.

You never realize how much you miss something until long after it's gone.

———

"Looks like we've got two dead. I'm guessing the parents." A skinny cop brushed his hands on his pants before rising up out of the tall grass.

"And the kid?" his partner asked.

"Fine. Amazing really. The kids are the first thing they go after." He kicked at the blackened bodies in the grass. "Well, the ones that are still moving."

"Did you find the girl?"

"No, but she's out there. We've got a BOLO on the car. We'll find it."

"Good. Alright, you wrap this up and I'll get back to the tower. This whole thing is a shit show."

"Amen."

Police cars rolled out, leaving the young cop and a handful of medical personnel to close up the scene. It would be easy. They had experience with this sort of thing. He'd wrap it up nice and clean and they'd get back to their lives. It might take a bit to find some next of kin for the kid, but the girls in the office would be on that right as rain, he was sure of it.

He made his way back into the house and up the stairs, pausing briefly at the kids room long enough to take in the signs of struggle. Maybe they'd fought over the child, the winner leaving the loser to burn in the sun?

But if that was true, why didn't they take the child?

He didn't want to think about it. He wanted to just be happy they hadn't, but it still bothered him.

It bothered him when he took a seat on the parents bed, and stared down at the partially zipped up body bags.

He had a kid of his own, well, almost. Sarah was due in June.

"Jesus. What a shit show." He turned to leave, but never reached the door.

An infantile stinger broke free from jaws that unfolded like a baby bird's wings.

She took him down hard, that second tongue's serrated tip driven by a hunger that she didn't yet understand.

Blood rolled over the glistening new appendage. It brought memories of a redhead, of death, and a child she *would* see again.

She drank deep, then let go, curling back into the shadows and waiting for more men to come. She needed her strength to find her baby and her revenge.

THANK YOU FOR READING

Thank you for reading. Books take time to write, but they also take time to read. Your time is valuable, and I very much appreciate you spending it with me.

If it's not too much to ask, we authors live on caffeine, panic, and reviews. If you'd be so kind as to leave one for this book, I'd be grateful.

SPREADING THE WORD

One of the biggest challenges I have is reaching new readers. The internet is saturated with creatives trying to share their creations, and for a person born long before the advent of social media, navigating those waters is terrifying at best.

How can you help? Simply put, tell a friend, make a post, share a link to this book:

martin-shannon.com/thelastsunrise

Tell people what you liked about it. It may sound small, but those connections matter.

They're genuine.

They're human.

They're powerful.

So, if it's not too much to ask, please share the link above with your friends or online and know that it means the world to me.

STAY IN THE KNOW

After a long deliberation, I've elected to forgo newsletters. Honestly, our inboxes are just too full as it is. Still, I want you to know when new books come out. So I'll make you a deal. If you provide your mobile number to this 3rd party service, I'll make sure they text you once (and only once) for each new book I release.

The service is private, GDPR approved, and allows you to STOP at any time. So, if you want to stay in the know, get a text from me when new books drop by signing up at https://martin-shannon.com/textme.

MORE BLOOD AND PULP BY MARTIN SHANNON

A Home for Darkness

The Last Sunrise

The Pearl

ABOUT BLOOD AND PULP

Blood and Pulp is a line of stories from Weird Florida LLC and a place for Martin Shannon's more experimental and non-conforming fiction.

You'll find numerous genres represented, along with strange worlds and even stranger characters. Through it all, Blood and Pulp retains its signature fast-paced, rapid-fire style. It harkens back to an earlier time when fiction filled magazine shelves and fun was the mission.

Enjoy a walk on the wild side of Martin's mind with a little "Blood and Pulp" for the soul.

ABOUT THE AUTHOR

Martin Shannon's been using his imagination to avoid weeding since he was in short pants. You can find out more at www.martin-shannon.com.